THE BROTHERS O'BRIEN
LAST MAN
STANDING

THE BROTHERS O'BRIEN
LAST MAN STANDING

WILLIAM W. JOHNSTONE

with J. A. Johnstone

PINNACLE BOOKS
Kensington Publishing Corp.

www.kensingtonbooks.com

PINNACLE BOOKS are published by

Kensington Publishing Corp.
119 West 40th Street
New York, NY 10018

PUBLISHER'S NOTE
Following the death of William W. Johnstone, the Johnstone family is working with a carefully selected writer to organize and complete Mr. Johnstone's outlines and many unfinished manuscripts to create additional novels in all of his series like The Last Gunfighter, Mountain Man, and Eagles, among others. This novel was inspired by Mr. Johnstone's superb storytelling.

All Kensington titles, imprints, and distributed lines are available at special quantity discounts for bulk purchases for sales promotions, premiums, fund-raising, educational, or institutional use. Special book excerpts or customized printings can also be created to fit specific needs. For details, write or phone the office of the Kensington special sales manager: Kensington Publishing Corp., 119 West 40th Street, New York, NY 10018, attn: Special Sales Department; phone 1-800-221-2647.

ISBN-13: 978-0-7860-2900-6
ISBN-10: 0-7860-2900-5

First printing: June 2012

10 9 8 7 6 5 4 3 2 1

Printed in the United States of America

Chapter One

"What the—" Luther Ironside exclaimed.

"I see it, but I don't believe it." Patrick O'Brien pushed his eyeglasses higher onto the bridge of his nose. "What is it?"

Ironside leaned forward in the saddle, his far-seeing eyes reaching out into the grassland where the buzzards glided. "It's just what it looks like, Pat."

"Smell it? I can smell it from here."

Ironside nodded. "A lot of dead folks down there, I reckon."

"I guess we should get closer and take a look." Patrick inched his horse forward.

Ironside turned and looked at the younger man, a frown on his weather-beaten face. "Pat, I think we're about to ride into big trouble."

"How so?"

"I can sense it. There's something bad coming down, and them wagons are a part of it."

The two Dromore riders sat their horses on a ridge a mile south of the San Pedro Mountains in

New Mexico Territory. Below, shimmering in the noonday heat, stretched a vast tableland of treed meadows and upthrust pinnacles of red rock. Farther to the east the land was scarred by dusty draws and shadowed, sullen canyons.

It was a hard, lonely wilderness offering nothing to pilgrims, yet there they were, six canvas-covered wagons of them.

What troubled Patrick and Ironside was that the wagons, drawn up in a rough circle, were completely enclosed by a three-strand barbed-wire fence.

Patrick kneed his horse into motion and Ironside followed. When he was alongside his companion, the older man said, "They got plows tied to the back of them wagons."

"Grangers?" Patrick wondered.

"Seems like."

"This is cattle country. Don't they know you can't plow two inches of dirt on top of bedrock?"

"Maybe just passing through." Ironside slid his Winchester from the boot under his knee. "I don't see anybody moving."

"Why the fence? To keep others out?"

"Or to keep the sodbusters in." Ironside grinned.

The meadow Patrick and Ironside rode across was surrounded by dense stands of spruce and mixed pine. Heat lay heavily on the land under a sky of polished brass and the prairie breeze from the east carried the stench of death. The circling buzzards took note of the humans and glided a distance away, biding their time. But as the riders drew closer a dozen more birds flapped upward from the circled wagons in ungainly panic heavy with . . . meat.

Twenty yards from the fence, Patrick and Ironside drew rein. The sickly sweet smell of decaying bodies and dead oxen was overwhelming and both riders pulled their bandannas up over their faces, only their horrified eyes showing.

Patrick's eyeglasses glinted in the sun as he turned to Ironside. "What happened here, Luther?"

"I have no idea." The older man's bandanna muffled his words. "I'm going to ride closer and take a look."

Patrick wanted no part of the stench. He was content to watch as Ironside got within five yards of the fence and then rode around the entire perimeter, the buttplate of his rifle resting on his thigh.

Riding back to Patrick, Ironside said nothing, but waved him away from the wagons. Patrick followed as the Dromore segundo led him to a stand of juniper a hundred yards from the wagons.

Taking his time, Ironside returned his rifle to the boot, lit a cigar, then said, "Everybody's dead in there, and all their oxen slaughtered."

"How many people?" Patrick asked.

"I'd say two score, men, women and young 'uns."

Patrick pulled his bandanna from his face, but the stench stayed in his nose. "What happened to them? And why the fence?"

"The answer to both your questions is, I don't

know. But there were four, maybe five, dead men on the ground who'd been shot." Ironside waited for Patrick to say something.

When he didn't Ironside continued. "I think it was punchers who put the fence up, Pat."

Patrick was horrified. "How do you reckon that?"

"After nearly thirty years of ramrodding at Dromore, I can always tell a puncher's fence work. It's never neat, nothing like how a sodbuster would do it."

"So the fence was erected to keep the people inside?"

"That's the way I see it."

"By cattlemen?" Patrick asked.

"Seems like."

"To keep the grangers off their land?"

"I can think of no other reason. Hey"—Ironside's voice was suddenly urgent—"look there." He pointed to the west where the Sandia Mountains stood purple against the sky.

Patrick peered in shortsighted earnestness in that direction, but saw only a shifting blur of land and sky. "What do you see, Luther?"

"Four riders coming in our direction and in an all-fired hurry." Ironside slid his rifle out of the boot again, levered a round into the chamber, and rested the butt on his thigh.

Patrick, being no great shakes with a long gun, adjusted the position of his holstered Colt. The riders could be friendly, but a man didn't take chances in wild country.

As it happened, the four men didn't greet Patrick and Ironside like visiting kinfolk.

"What the hell are you doing here?" Their leader was a huge, yellow-haired man who, despite the heat of the day, wore broadcloth and a soft white shirt with a black string tie. He had a wide, brutal face that was undeniably handsome, and a pencil-thin mustache guaranteed to make ladies' hearts flutter.

"Passing through." Ironside's instant dislike of the big man and his domineering attitude was obvious.

"From where, going where?" the man ground out.

"From Albuquerque to our home ranch," Patrick said. "Dromore, you may have heard of it."

The big man obviously had, and it set him back a step. "Are you one of the O'Brien boys?" he asked in a less aggressive tone.

"Yes, I am. My name is Patrick and this is the ranch segundo, Luther Ironside. We sold a Hereford bull in Albuquerque and were headed home when we found"—he jerked a thumb over his shoulder—"this."

"Cholera," the big man said. "We had to pen 'em up and shoot their animals or they would've spread disease all over the territory."

"A few of those men are carrying bullet wounds," Ironside said.

"They tried to cut the fence and escape." The man puffed up a little. "My name is Rafe Kingston, owner of the Rafter-K, or as it's sometimes called, the Fighting K. My land stretches from here to the Rio Grande in the west and south to Socorro."

"Mister," Ironside said, "don't claim range any farther east."

"Are you threatening me?" Kingston said, his face flushed.

"Yeah, I am," Ironside answered.

Patrick pushed his glasses higher on his nose. "Mr. Kingston, I'm very much afraid that I'll have to report the deaths of the people in the wagon train to the United States marshal."

"Why would you do that, O'Brien?"

"Because it was murder. Mass murder as it happens."

"All I did was pen 'em up," Kingston said. "It was the cholera that killed them."

"Apart from the men who were shot, you mean," Patrick pointed out.

Kingston smiled, showing white teeth. "Only to stop 'em from spreading their filthy disease. Try convincing a jury that it was murder."

One of Kingston's riders drew rein beside his boss. He was a small, slender man with the eyes of a carrion-eater. He wore two Colts butt forward in crossed cartridge belts, a seldom seen gun rig, but the small man looked as though he could make good use of it. "Trouble?"

"No trouble, Trace," Kingston said. "Unless O'Brien here chooses to make some."

"I'm better at making trouble than he is, Kingston." Ironside smiled, always an ominous sign. "Fact is, I enjoy putting bullets into pompous windbags and seeing them deflate."

In anybody's language that was fighting talk, and

Patrick moved to defuse the situation. "It would help your case, Mr. Kingston, if you and your men gave those people a decent burial."

Kingston laughed and his men laughed with him. "Mister, you know what those pilgrims were?"

"Farmers, I believe," Patrick said.

"Farmers, my ass," Kingston said. "They were sin-eaters who were tossed out of Nebraska and then Kansas. They planned to spread out over the territory and practice their trade. That was, until the cholera got 'em."

He leaned back in the saddle and spread his hands in what he obviously hoped was an *I'm a reasonable man* gesture. "Tell you what, O'Brien. I'll take down the fence and burn the wagons. How does that set with you?"

"You're still facing murder charges," Patrick said. "Two score of them, including women and children."

Suddenly Kingston's face was black with anger. "What are a bunch of crazy sin-eaters to you, O'Brien? Would your pa have done any different if they'd brought cholera to Dromore?"

"The colonel would not have penned them up and let children die of disease and starvation." Patrick's own anger flared.

Kingston turned his head. "Tom, come here."

A loose-geared puncher with a long solemn face, kneed his horse beside his boss.

"Go back to the ranch, bring as many men as you can round up," Kingston said. "I want the fence taken down and the wagons burned. Throw the corpses into the fires and burn them, too. Destroy every trace of what happened here. You got that?"

"Boss, the boys won't go near cholera wagons."

"A bonus of a month's wages to every man who volunteers. And a bullet in the belly from Trace Wilson's gun to those who don't."

After the puncher rode away, Kingston directed his attention to Patrick again. "O'Brien, if you can find the kin of any of these people, I'll send them fifty dollars. There, I can't say it any better than that."

"You're true blue, Kingston," Ironside said sarcastically. "I'm sure that'll make everybody happy."

The rancher's eyes iced. "If you weren't an old man I'd pull you off that horse and beat some respect into you."

Ironside swung out of the saddle and laid his rifle on the ground. "Care to give it a try, Kingston?"

Rafe Kingston looked stunned. He wasn't afraid, far from it, but it had been years since anyone had dared challenge him. He'd ridden roughshod over his part of the territory for years, crushing smaller ranchers and evicting sodbusters as he increased his herds and added to his range. He'd never lost a skull and knuckle fight and had mercilessly pounded men into the dirt, leaving a few crippled for life or wrong in the head. As he studied Ironside, older by a score of years, but standing tall, lean, mean, and ready, Kingston knew he'd be a handful. "I don't brawl with hired hands. Get back on your horse and behave yourself, old man."

"Your fifty dollars isn't going to cut it, Kingston," Patrick said. "You'll still face murder charges."

The gunman called Trace spoke up. "Boss, it seems like this O'Brien feller only knows how to sing one tune. You think I should change it?"

Kingston thought about that for a moment. He had no doubt a jury would fail to convict him of murdering a bunch of plague-ridden sin-eaters, but it might affect his courtship of Lucy Masters—muddy the waters so to speak. Her father did not approve of the match, and a murder charge could tip the scales against him even further.

Two men now stood in the way of what he wanted—Lucy and her father's shaggy acres. One of them was crusty old Hugh Masters. The other was an O'Brien, and that complicated matters, Kingston wasn't afraid of a war with the O'Brien clan, but he needed a little more time, time enough to wed and bed Lucy and claim her father's land as her birthright—once crusty old Hugh Masters was safely out of the picture, of course.

Rafe Kingston decided to roll the dice. "Make it look good, Trace. Burn their bodies with the rest so they'll never be found."

Chapter Two

Patrick O'Brien pushed his eyeglasses higher on his nose and looked at Luther Ironside. Their hurriedly exchanged glances confirmed what each of them knew . . . they were in for a gunfight.

Trace was joined by another man who wore a gun rig and fancy boots no cowpuncher could afford. The man's Texas roots and professional gunfighter status were as obvious as the broadcloth frock coat and flat-brimmed hat he wore.

"O'Brien," Trace said, "this here is Pleasant McLean out of the Fort Stockton country. A name to be reckoned with." The gunman waited until McLean smiled and touched his hat brim, then said, "I want you to know we got nothing personal agin' you. Understand?"

Patrick said nothing. His mouth was dry and sweat trickled between his shoulder blades.

"Well, I just wanted you to know," Trace said. "But business is business and we can't let you go carrying tall tales to the law, now can we?"

Patrick's tongue felt like it was too big for his mouth and he didn't trust himself to speak. He wasn't afraid, but he was mighty tense.

Trace looked at Ironside. "What I told him goes for you too, pops."

"What are you planning to do, you pile of dirt?" Ironside said. "Talk us to death? If you're gonna skin the iron do it now and get to your work."

Two thoughts flashed through Trace's brain. One, the tough-looking old-timer wasn't scared. Two, neither was O'Brien.

Then he had a third thought. Maybe he was making a big mistake.

Pleasant McLean had killed seven men in gunfights and, unlike Trace, he wasn't a talking man.

He drew.

And Patrick shot him.

In that one, awful instant, Trace knew he was a dead man. He'd forgotten something he should have remembered: the O'Briens, from mean old Shamus all the way down, were fighting men who'd been raised around weapons and taught the ways of the Colt. Patrick, slim and scholarly, was still an O'Brien and as fast and deadly as the rest.

As Pleasant McLean fell from his horse, Trace drew his weapon. He hurried his shot and missed. Patrick didn't. Hit hard, Trace swayed in the saddle. A second bullet, from Ironside, crashed into him, low in his left side.

Patrick was fighting his rearing horse. Trace fired at Ironside.

The old man staggered as the bullet hit, then he shot again. Blood, bone, and brain fanned above Trace's head and he fell, dead as stone when he hit the ground.

Patrick calmed his horse and swung out of the saddle. He looked over at Ironside who was lying flat on his back and saw blood soaking the older man's buckskin shirt just above his gun belt.

"I'm hurt bad, Pat. It's all up with me." He tried to lift his head to see, but let it sink to the ground again. "Did I get that dog turd?"

Patrick nodded. "He's dead and so is the other one."

Ironside smiled. "We teached you good, Pat, me and your pa. You're mighty slick on the draw, near as fast as your brother Jake."

"I've got to get you home, Luther. You need a doctor."

"I'm done for, boy," Ironside said. "Just leave me here."

"You're not done for, you tough old coot." Patrick grinned. "You'll still be above ground, raising hell, when the rest of us are under it. Come on now, I'll help you get on your horse before those Rafter-K riders get back."

Patrick helped Ironside, a tall heavy man, to his feet. Together they struggled over to Ironside's mount and Patrick helped him into the saddle.

Ironside looked down at his shirtfront. "Pat, I'm bleeding out."

"You've got enough to last you until we get to Dromore." Patrick swung into the saddle and rode beside Ironside. "Just hang on, Luther and don't pass out on me."

"I need a drink."

Patrick reached for his canteen.

"I mean a real drink." Ironside motioned with his head. "In my saddlebags."

After fumbling around for a few moments, Patrick found a bottle of Old Crow. He passed it to Ironside who took a couple of swigs, then wiped off the neck of the bottle with the palm of his hand and held it out to Patrick. "Want a belt?" There was blood on his lips.

"Damn right I do." Patrick drank, then handed the bottle back to Ironside. "Get some more of that down you, Luther. It will help with the pain."

"With pleasure." Ironside grinned.

As they took to the trail under a hammering sun, Ironside rode with his head bent, chin on chest. Patrick held the older man up in the saddle, and he was surprised when Ironside looked up at him. "That frock coat feller was mighty fast on the draw and shoot."

Patrick nodded. "Yeah, he was. He was real fast on the draw."

"Yet you beat him."

Patrick said nothing, but Ironside persisted. "I didn't know you were that fast, Pat. I mean, you being such a shortsighted, reading-books kind of ranny, and all."

"Save your strength, Luther. You'll wear yourself out talking." Patrick was silent for a few moments, then said, "I saw him just fine."

"You're not like Shawn; you never make a brag about being good with the iron."

"Maybe that's because I don't hold with violence, Luther. It's 1889, for God's sake. The time for all that is past."

"A man still has the right to defend himself, though, doesn't he?"

"Yes. I reckon he does."

"You're a lot more man than you look, Pat."

Patrick laughed. "Luther, you never were very good with compliments."

"What about Rafe Kingston?" Under his mahogany tan, the veneer of years, Ironside looked ashen.

"What about him?"

"I reckon we could have the makings of a range war on our hands."

"Kingston doesn't want Dromore range. He's got plenty of his own."

"But we can hang him, Pat, and he knows it. Don't forget that."

Pat nodded but said nothing. He realized if Luther Ironside died, the colonel would wage war on the Rafter-K until Rafe Kingston and all who were associated with him were dead.

And then he'd spit on their graves.

Chapter Three

"I've heard of him, Colonel," Samuel O'Brien said. "Rafe Kingston cuts a mighty wide path. He's grazes cattle on two hundred thousand acres, last I heard, and he's not a man to take a step back from anybody."

Shamus O'Brien slammed his hand on the arm of his wheelchair. "If Luther dies he'll step back from me because I aim to hang him."

"What about the dead pilgrims, Pa?" Patrick asked.

"I want to see that for myself," Shamus said. "If it's like you and Luther say, I'll call in the law and have him arrested for murder."

"Why not bring in a marshal now, Colonel?" Samuel said. "The evidence will still be there."

"You mean you don't know?" Shamus's eyes blazed. "Samuel, are you really telling me you don't know?"

Shawn, who'd been silent up until now, came to his brother's rescue. "Spread it around, Pa. I don't catch your drift either."

"Samuel?" Shamus asked.

Samuel waited until a maid had cleared the breakfast dishes. "If we bring in the law before Luther dies, we can't move against Kingston and his Rafter-K. A United States marshal would put a stop to that quick."

"Pretty darn quick," Shamus said.

"Colonel, we're talking about a war." Patrick's eyeglasses caught the morning sunlight. He looked like a man who should be teaching history at an ivy-covered university.

"I've never stepped back from war before, Patrick," Shamus said. "Do you think I should start now?"

Patrick shook his head. "No, Pa."

Shamus stared at his son from under shaggy eyebrows, like a mean old bull buffalo. "You did well yesterday, stood firm and killed your man."

Patrick said nothing, but he caught the colonel's drift. *You're Dromore, remember that. We fight for our own, no matter the cost, and we answer to no one but God.*

The dining room door opened and split apart the ensuing silence. Lorena O'Brien, Samuel's wife, stepped inside.

"How is he?" Shamus asked her.

"He's sleeping. I don't know if it's from his surgery or the bottle of Old Crow he drank yesterday."

Shamus continued with the questions. "Is the doctor sure he got all the lead out of him?"

"He's sure." Lorena smiled. "I think whiskey will kill Luther before a bullet does."

"Better for Rafe Kingston if that's the case. If it's not, he'll curse the day he was born and the mother that bore him." Shamus rolled his wheelchair away from the table to the window and stared outside at the new aborning day. "Samuel, you and Shawn ride down to the San Pedro mountain country and take three or four vaqueros with you. The more men who can testify to mass murder the better."

"What about me, Colonel?" Patrick looked at his pa.

"You stay here. You've done your share. Besides, Lorena will need help with Luther. He's a big man for a woman to handle alone." Without turning from the window, Shamus said, his voice tight, "I wonder where Jacob is."

"We all wonder that, Pa," Shawn said.

"It's been a year since he killed Luke Caldwell, then disappeared."

"I'm sure he's all right, Colonel," Samuel reassured. "Jacob has peculiar ways and he's a man given to dark moods."

Shamus nodded. "Many different parts make up the whole that is Jacob, not all of them admirable. He could be a famous concert pianist, yet he makes his living with a gun. He loves women, but never courts any." The colonel waved a hand. "That Sarah girl adores him, but I don't think he's ever given her the time of day."

No one said anything for a moment, then Patrick stepped into the silence. "I think Jacob is afraid of his own dark side. He plays Chopin well because he understands the composer's darkness and his almost constant depression."

Shawn said, "Are you talking about the consumptive little runt who shacked up with a cigar-smoking

French whore and hated everybody who wasn't rich or an aristocrat? If you are, Jacob is nothing like him."

"Jacob is like Jacob." Samuel tossed his napkin onto the table and rose to his feet. "Shawn, are you ready to ride? I'll go round up some vaqueros."

"Samuel, avoid gunplay if you can," Shamus said. "Just take a look at the wagon train and report back here. Make sure everybody sees it."

"I will, Colonel."

Shamus shook his head. "Luther shot to pieces. Sin-eaters. Cholera. What next?"

Chapter Four

With a pang of regret, Jacob O'Brien laid aside the robe of harsh brown wool and leather sandals he'd worn for the past year. The wood shutters of the unglazed window of his monk's cell were open and he saw the green apples ripening on the tree outside. He'd intended to stay long enough to pick them in the fall, but he knew his time at the mission was over.

As he dressed, his clothes felt all wrong. They fit tight to his body. His boots, pants, shotgun chaps, and washed-out blue shirt seemed alien to him, as though the monk's robe was the only garment he'd worn in his life.

Jacob had kept his gun clean and oiled and stood looking at it, the sheen of blue metal and yellowed ivory as beautiful as he remembered. He shook his head and shoved the Colt into the holster.

Behind him a voice said, "Brother Simon has prepared a special going-away breakfast for you, Jacob."

Jacob turned, surprised. "You knew I was leaving?"

"I knew." Brother Benedict smiled. "I've known for a week or more."

"I won't be here to pick the green apples."

"You'll be here in spirit, my son. Brother Simon and myself will gather the apples." Brother Benedict nodded, as though approving something. "You look much better, Jacob. Not so thin and drawn."

"And spiritually?" Jacob asked.

"Only you can answer that question."

"Then I'm better in all ways." Jacob held up the holstered Colt. "What do I do with this?"

"You do with it as you've always done. Or not. You must make that choice."

Jacob looked out the window. Jays quarreled in the green apple tree and above the high rim that surrounded the hanging valley, buzzards quartered the sky to the north. He turned to Brother Benedict and smiled. "Hard to believe that just a few months ago icicles hung from the inside of my window and touched the floor. They looked like rods of glass."

"And you lay on your cot in your robe and shivered." The monk matched Jacob's smile. "The past twelve months have not been easy for you."

"I didn't want them to be easy. They kept the black dog away."

"It's not gone, Jacob. It crouches in the dark corners and waits." The monk reached into a pocket of his robe and produced a folded, bright red bandanna. "Brother Simon made this for you. He hopes it will help keep the black moods away. He said a hundred and fifty paternosters over the cloth while he was cutting and sewing it, so it's a very holy bandanna." Brother Benedict smiled. "Or so Brother Simon says."

The monk loosely tied the bandanna around Jacob's throat and stepped back. "Ah, yes, very becoming."

"Thank Brother Simon for me," Jacob said.

"You can thank him yourself at breakfast. It's rumored that flapjacks and wild honey are on the menu."

"Then what are we waiting for?" Jacob shoved the cartridge belt and holstered Colt into his saddlebags.

Brother Benedict saw, but made no comment.

A year away from riding had cost Jacob O'Brien dearly. Even his horse showed no inclination to go any farther than Lobo Hill at the north of the Estancia Valley. Saddle sore and weary, he gratefully camped for the night in a stand of pine and wild oak. A plentiful supply of firewood was easily gathered and sweet water formed a shallow rock pool at the base of the peak.

Brother Simon had provided a meal of flapjacks and cold fried bacon, claiming to have said as many paternosters over the repast as he could manage while he packed it into a paper sack.

Jacob gathered wood and lit a fire. He boiled coffee in the pot Brother Simon had thoughtfully provided, and then reheated the bacon strips. These he wrapped in warmed over flapjacks, making a good meal for himself, surprised at how hungry he was.

As he drank coffee, wishing for tobacco but having none, the night crowded close, lanced through by blades of moonlight that made the shadows deeper. Coyotes left off their prowling along Big Draw and hunted close, attracted by the smell of food. From somewhere among the pines an owl asked his question of the night, and then waited patiently for an answer that never came.

A year of hard work at the mission had made him stronger. Best of all, the depression that haunted him constantly had skulked away, at least for the time being. For that he was grateful.

With a good meal in his belly and a beaming moon riding high, he felt relaxed, at peace with himself and the world. Except a sack of tobacco and—

A piñon rustled on a patch of sandy ground thirty or forty paces from Jacob's camp. He pulled his saddlebags closer and drew the Colt from the holster. Even as his eyes scanned the darkness, his action surprised him. He had a gun in his hand and it felt good. He'd drawn the revolver instinctively, without conscious thought. It had come as naturally to him as drawing a breath.

Refusing even a second to think about the implications of his act, Jacob rose to his feet and stepped out of the yellow dome of firelight. "Show yourself, or I'll drop you right where you stand."

That was a heap more menace than monk, Jacob thought, strangely disappointed. But he'd no time for a philosophical discussion with himself. It was a kill or be killed situation and under those circumstances a man doesn't ponder the right or the wrong of a thing.

More rustling . . . louder than before . . . then silence.

His Colt up and ready, Jacob stepped toward the piñons. His heart pounded in his ears and all his senses were alert, as tense and ready to pounce as a hunting animal. He saw nothing. Heard nothing, only the *crack crack* of his campfire behind him and the hungry yip of the coyotes.

For a few moments, Jacob stood perfectly still, hardly daring to breathe as he waited for a sight, a sound.

The night offered nothing.

He stood a little longer, then turned away. But as he did so, the moonlight revealed a footprint in the sandy hollow where he stood. He took a knee, thumbed a year-old match into flame, and studied the track. It was the print of a bare foot and so small and light it barely dented the sand. He reckoned it could only have been left by a very petite woman or a child.

"What the hell?" He scanned the darkness again. "Come out of the trees. I won't harm you."

He was answered by silence.

Jacob returned to the fire and picked up a flat slab of sandstone he'd seen when gathering wood. It was about the size of a family Bible and twice as heavy. He stepped back to the hollow and laid the stone near the footprint.

He later returned to the stone, carrying a flapjack rolled around bacon he'd warmed over the fire. "Suppertime," he called into the gloom. "Come and get it."

Then he went back to his blankets and slept.

When Jacob checked the stone in the early morning light the food was gone. There were more footprints in the sand, indicating a human had eaten it and that pleased him.

He drank coffee by the fire as the dawn brightened into day, once again pining for tobacco. It was a craving he thought he'd lost during his time at the mission, but it had only been lying low, returning to torment him.

He was drinking his second cup when the child emerged from the piñons, then stood looking at him.

She was small and thin, wearing a tattered calico dress, her long blond hair knotted and tangled with grass and twigs. The girl had huge blue eyes, smudged with dark shadows, and she was pale, as though she'd recently gone hungry.

Jacob guessed she was about eleven, but he'd never been much of a hand at guessing ages.

The child reminded him of the way his calico cat back at Dromore was with strangers. The girl held back, wary, wanting badly to come closer, but too afraid to take a step.

Jacob smiled, thinking the only thing his cat and

the girl in the calico dress didn't have in common was his cat's obligatory display of fine manners and good breeding. "Coffee's in the pot and there's still food left." He made no attempt to get to his feet. "Pity to let it go to waste."

The child took a hesitant step toward him, then another. Her eyes were as round as coins.

"Don't suppose you have the makings on you, huh?" He noted the girl's blank stare, and said, "No, I guess you don't." He smiled. "Just as well. Smoking stunts your growth. Just look at me. I should be twenty foot tall, but tobacco shrunk me to this size."

"Are you a giant?" The child stayed right where she was.

"Once upon a time. But now I'm just a little feller." He held his hand about three feet above the ground. "When I stand up, I'm only this tall."

To his joy the child smiled. It was slow in coming, reluctant and shy, but it was a smile nevertheless.

"Where are your ma and pa?" Jacob said. "No, first tell me your name."

"Alice. And my ma and pa are dead." She pointed behind her. "Far away to the mountains."

"Nice to meet you, Alice. I'm Jacob. How did you get here?"

"I walked." Alice lifted her foot and showed it to Jacob. It was cut and bruised, the skin raw and inflamed.

"My other one, too." She showed the other foot and it was more of the same, maybe even worse. "They hurt real bad because I've no shoes."

He was appalled but didn't let his alarm show. As casually as he could, he said, "Are you hungry, barefoot Alice?"

To his surprise, the little girl ran to him and threw herself into his arms, her head against his chest. Pretty soon he felt the warm stain of tears on his shirt and he patted her back. "There, there."

Apart from now and again holding his brother's son, baby Shamus, it was the first time Jacob had ever comforted a crying child.

And he realized he wasn't real good at it.

Chapter Five

"Nothing," Shawn O'Brien said in disgust. "Scorch marks where the wagons burned and then . . . nothing."

"I can see it," Samuel said. "It's what I don't see that's troubling me. Where is the fence? Where are the bodies?"

"Where is Rafe Kingston?"

"Worn out from taking down the fence and carrying away the burned wagons and the bodies, I reckon."

Shawn's Steel Dust tossed its head, the bit chiming, anxious to be going. "He's destroyed the evidence is what he's done. We've only got Patrick's and Luther's word for it that the fence and wagons were ever here."

Samuel nodded. "It will be tough to convince a jury to take in trust something they can't see for themselves, especially when it involves a rich and influential rancher like Kingston."

"Let's ride down there and take a look," Samuel said.

Shawn was horrified. "What about the cholera?"

"I reckon it burned away with the wagons. But just in case, stay mounted. Don't let your feet touch the ground." Samuel turned in the saddle and said to the four vaqueros, "That also goes for you men."

He saw the question on Shawn's face. "When a person has cholera stuff comes out both ends of the body and it's highly infectious. There might still be some of it on the ground."

Shawn sighed. "Boy, this is fun."

"Ain't it though."

"Like I said before, nothing." Shawn looked around him. "Even the holes for the fence posts have been filled in."

"You men scout around, see if there's anything that looks like a big grave," Samuel said to the vaqueros.

The Dromore riders didn't need any encouragement. There was nothing visible at the site, but a smell lingered . . . the rotten fish stench of cholera. They spread out to search the area.

Shawn and Patrick scanned the ground and surrounding hills before joining in the hunt.

There was no grave, no bodies. Around forty men, women, and children had disappeared off the face of the earth and only their death smell remained.

"We might as well head back to Dromore," Samuel said. "There's nothing more we can do here."

"Fine by me," Shawn agreed. "This place feels like it's got a gypsy curse on it."

"Cholera curse, you mean."

"Yeah, that too," Shawn's eyes moved beyond his brother to the grassland to the south. "Rider coming."

The vaqueros fanned out behind the O'Briens and slid rifles from the boots. Shawn did the same, then grinned. "It's a woman, and a right pretty one at that."

Samuel shook his head. "Shawn, you're a far-seeing man when there's a woman involved."

"You said that right, brother."

The woman who drew rein on her paint pony was pretty all right, but she was angry, mad clean through. "What are you doing here?" she demanded. "This is Rafter-K range and you are trespassing."

"Lady," Samuel said, "this is open range, last I heard."

"Then you heard wrong," the girl said.

Shawn decided she was even prettier than he'd first thought. She had a great, shining mass of chestnut hair that cascaded over her slender shoulders. Her eyes were green, shot through with gold, highlighting an oval face with high cheekbones and a wide, full mouth.

"My name is Shawn O'Brien of Dromore and this is my brother Samuel," Shawn said. "Who do I have the great pleasure of addressing?"

"That is none of your business."

"All right, then I'll call you Miss None-Of-Your-Business."

The girl's face reddened. "My name is Lucy Masters. My father has a ranch south of here, but this is my intended's range. And you're on it."

Samuel, less vulnerable to a beautiful woman than Shawn, got right to the point. "What did Kingston do with the bodies from the wagons?"

"If you're talking about Rafe, he burned them," Lucy said. "They were carrying the cholera."

"Yes, I'm taking about Rafe. He murdered some of the men. My brother Patrick saw the bodies and said they'd been shot."

"Of course they were shot," Lucy snappped. "They tried to escape and spread their contagion. When Rafe tried to stop them, they opened fire. It was a most singular occurrence and he was only defending himself."

"What about the fence?" Samuel asked.

"I know nothing about a fence," Lucy answered.

"Kingston strung a fence around the wagons and posted armed men around it. After that, the people inside had no chance of surviving. The men he shot were trying to escape from the fence. It was murder, pure and simple."

"Mr. O'Brien," Lucy said, "if I were you I'd be careful about leveling murder charges at anyone. A fact of the greatest moment is that your brother and another man shot down two of Rafe's cowboys in cold blood. If that wasn't murder, then tell me what is?"

"Did you know the dead men?" Samuel asked impatiently.

"What difference does that make?"

"One was Trace Wilson, the other Pleasant McLean. Neither had cowboyed in their lives, or ever done an honest day's work for that matter. They were hired guns, among the best of them. As to why Kingston felt he needed named gunfighters on his payroll, you'd better ask him."

Lucy went quiet, but a crease between her eyebrows revealed that she was thinking.

High in the sky, the sun was the color of washed-out denim and the heat was relentless, hammering the timbered high country. Only the San Pedro Mountains to the north looked cool. A man could close his eyes and imagine their shady, hanging valleys where apple-green frogs dived into ferny rock pools with a soft *plop!*

Shawn, ever the gallant one, parted the silence. "Miss Masters, you shouldn't be out riding alone. This country is no place for a lone woman."

"I can take care of myself," Lucy scoffed. "And Rafe has made all the land around here safe. The outlaws and rustlers are long gone." The thought of one occupation led to another. She looked at Samuel. "Did you know the people in the cholera train were sin-eaters?"

"So I heard."

"Do you know what sin-eaters do?"

"No. But I've a feeling you're about to tell me."

"At a funeral, a loaf of bread is handed to the sin-eater over the coffin of the departed. The sin-eater eats the bread and takes on all the sins of the dead person." Lucy pushed a strand of damp hair off her forehead. "Can you imagine how low you must be to do that for money?"

Samuel opened his mouth to speak, but the girl

cut him off. "Sin-eaters have been driven out of every state in the union, and that's why they chose to come into New Mexico. Not only were they about to spread their vile practice all over the territory, they were also carrying the cholera and would have spread that too."

Lucy's eyes met Samuel's like strikes of blue lightning. "Rafe saved us from them, and now men like you wish to persecute him. You should be ashamed of yourself."

The girl swung her paint away, but drew rein again. "One more thing, Mr. O'Brien. Take this message to the colonel: Rafe Kingston and the Rafter-K will not kowtow to Dromore. We will not permit Shamus O'Brien to level false charges against Rafe and plot to steal his range. We will fight him in the courts, and if it comes to a war, well, we're prepared for that, too."

"Ma'am," Samuel stated again, "Rafe Kingston is a murderer, and he'll be brought to justice."

"Give my message to the colonel," Lucy said. "Let him know who and what he's dealing with. Oh, and one thing more—tell him to read his land grant."

Shawn watched the girl gallop away to the south, then grinned. "She's a regular spitfire, isn't she?"

Samuel nodded. "Seems like."

"And pretty as a picture."

"Shawn, drag your mind higher than your belt buckle. We've bought ourselves a load of trouble."

Chapter Six

Jacob O'Brien watched Alice eat the last of the flapjacks and bacon, then lick grease from her fingers. "Lordy, child, are you finally full?"

"I was hungry," the girl said. "I ate berries, but they always gave me a tummy ache."

"How long have you been walking?"

Alice shrugged and spread her hands. "I don't know. A long . . . long . . . time."

"Where did you walk from?" Jacob asked.

"Back there." Alice waved behind her. "It was far."

"Weren't you afraid at night when it got dark?"

"Oh yes. I slept in trees because I was afraid of coyotes." Alice pointed to the Colt on the ground beside Jacob. "Is that yours?"

"Yes, it is."

"What do you shoot with it?"

"Oh, tigers mostly." Jacob held up his cup. "You want coffee?"

The child shook her head.

"Okay. So tell me about your ma and pa, Alice."

"I don't remember them. They died when I was little."

Jacob smiled. "Ah, a long time ago, huh?"

Alice nodded. "I got foster parents but they were mean to me and sometimes they punished me by not giving me any water to drink."

"And where are those parents?"

"Dead. They got very sick and so did everybody else in the other wagons."

"Wagons?"

"Uh-huh." Alice held up ten fingers. "Six wagons."

"So when your new parents died, you ran away?"

"Well, first men on horses came and they built a fence around the wagons because we were all sick. Then Mr. Johansen, my foster pa and other men tried to pull down the fence and the men on horses shot them." Alice looked at Jacob with a child's guileless eyes. "I wasn't sick and after my foster ma died I crawled under the fence in the dark and ran far, far away."

"Were the men on horses soldiers in blue coats?"

Alice shook her head. "No, they were dressed like you, but their clothes were nicer."

"You don't like my clothes?"

The child laughed. "Jacob, you're a raggedy man."

He smiled. "I guess I am."

"But you're nice."

"Ah, so speaks the woman-to-be."

"Why do you have that big scar on your face, Jacob?"

"Well, I cut myself shaving."

"You should grow a beard, but not a long one like my foster pa had."

"Well, I'll think about that."

As he finished his coffee, Jacob pieced together Alice's story. It seemed that the wagon train had a sickness that scared a bunch of punchers, probably cholera from bad drinking water, he guessed. They'd fenced the wagons and killed the men who tried to break out. It was mighty hardhanded. Alice, punished by not getting a water ration, had not gotten sick.

How she made it alive through the unforgiving country was a mystery. Brother Benedict would say it was a miracle, and maybe it was.

Jacob rose and undid the bandanna from around his neck. "Let me take a look at your feet, kid."

"No!" Alice said.

"Why not?"

"It will hurt."

"It won't hurt. This is a holy bandanna."

"It's got holes in it?"

Jacob tried again. "No, it's a magic bandanna, one that doesn't hurt."

The girl got to her feet and limped toward him. He didn't know if she was making a play for his sympathy or if she really hurt. Rather than take a chance, he picked her up and carried her to the rock pool.

Jacob bathed the child's feet and gently wiped away debris and the tips of cactus spines that had worked their way into the skin. "Hurt?"

"No. That water is real cold and it feels good."

Jacob picked a tiny rock fragment out of one foot

and Alice made a *shoo-shoo-shoo* noise, her mouth a little circle of pain.

"Sorry," Jacob mumbled.

"It's all right," the girl quipped. "It only hurts a little bit."

After he'd wiped the soles of Alice's feet clean, Jacob decided they looked a lot better, though there were blisters on the balls of her feet and heels that hadn't yet burst. "Now you wait right there until I saddle my horse. Don't move."

"Where are we going, Jacob?" Alice craned her head back as she looked up at his lanky height.

"We're going to Dromore. That's where my pa and my brothers live."

"Are there any little girls like me?"

"Oh sure, plenty of them, the daughters of our vaq—" he stopped himself—"of the men who work at my pa's ranch."

"Are they nice?"

"Sure they're nice."

"Will they play with me?"

Jacob sighed. "Child, you wear out a man with your questions. Yes, they'll play with you." Alice opened her mouth to speak, but he held up his hand. "Stay right there and don't move."

After he'd thrown the dregs of the coffee on the fire and saddled up, Jacob walked his horse to the rock pool. Alice had made boats from twigs and was sailing them on the water.

He picked her up and put her in front of the saddle, then mounted.

Once she was settled, Alice said, "Tell me about the little girls at Drum . . . Drim . . ."

"Dromore."

"Yes, that."

For the next half hour, Jacob made up lies about children he'd seldom met, then, totally bored, he spent the next thirty minutes adding lions, tigers, elephants, and the fairies that lived at the bottom of the kitchen garden.

Enthralled, Alice listened to every word, and when Jacob finally quit, she asked him to tell it all over again.

But suddenly his mind was on other things—the six riders who sat their horses on a rise directly ahead of him. Watching.

Jacob drew rein, studying the men on the ridge as they studied him.

The heat of noon lay heavily around him and there was not a breath of wind. A forest of ponderosa stood a hundred yards to his right and below them aspen rode a high rock ridge, scattered boulders at its base. If parlous times came down, he'd make his stand there.

"Alice, climb behind me."

"Are those bad men?"

"I don't know. Maybe."

"Will they put a fence around us, Jacob?"

"No. No, they won't."

Alice scrambled behind Jacob and he slid his Winchester from the boot, his eyes never ceasing to scan the rise. Two of the riders looked familiar.

He kneed his horse forward, and then angled toward the aspen ridge, moving unhurriedly at a walk.

Then came a shout from among the riders. "Jake, is that you?" It was Shawn's voice.

"Yeah, it's me."

"What the hell are you doing out here?"

Jacob yelled back. "I could ask the same thing about you."

"We're coming down."

The riders left the rise and rode toward him. He shoved the rifle back in the boot and waited.

When the men were closer, Shawn grinned. "I knew it was you. Nobody else I know sits a horse like a sack of grain."

"And has a nose that gets to where he's going an hour before the rest of him does," Samuel added.

Jacob nodded. "Uh-huh, I was waiting for that."

Shawn rode his horse forward and hugged his brother. "Dear God, Jake, where have you been for the past year?"

"It's a long story."

Shawn looked at Alice. "Is the kid yours?"

"Her name is Alice and she's got a story to tell."

"Howdy, Alice." Shawn wiggled his fingers at the girl.

Alice pushed her face into Jacob's back and said nothing.

"Shy, isn't she?" Shawn said.

"Some," Jacob replied, "when she isn't asking questions."

Samuel rode next to Jacob and hugged him. "The prodigal finally returns."

Behind them, the vaqueros grinned.

"How are things at Dromore?" Jacob asked. "How is the colonel?"

"He's doing fine, but Luther is right poorly."

"With what?" Jacob frowned, alarmed.

"Lead is with what."

"How did it happen?"

"That's another long story," Samuel said. "I'll tell you when we get back to Dromore."

"Hold on. Anybody got the makings?" Jacob desperately craved a cigarette.

A vaquero, like Texas punchers much given to the smoking habit, passed him a tobacco sack and papers.

Jacob quickly built and lit a cigarette, then inhaled deeply. "First smoke I've had in a year. My head is spinning."

"Jake, were you in jail?" Shawn frowned.

"Something like that," Jacob answered.

Samuel gave his brother a lingering, speculative look, but said nothing.

Chapter Seven

Despite the fussing of the female members of the Dromore household, Luther Ironside would not stay in bed. "It's bad enough that I've got to wear this pansy nightshirt, but I *won't* lie abed like an invalid. Get me my boots."

"Luther, you're shot through and through," Lorena said. "The doctor said you've got to lie down and stay quiet for at least another month."

"A month!" Ironside cried. "I'll be dead in a month. You pay heed to me, Lorena, them doctors have killed more white folks than the Apaches ever did, and that's a natural fact."

Luther looked around him and turned his wrath on Sarah, the former whore Jacob had helped find kitchen work at Dromore. "Bring me my boots, girl." He waved a hand at the steaming bowl on his bedside table. "And remove this vile swill from my sight."

"Mr. Ironside," Sarah said, "that's chicken broth. The doctor said it will do you good."

"Don't talk about doctors again! Am I to be forever plagued with doctors and . . . and chicken broth?"

Lorena sighed. "Give him his boots, Sarah. He won't be quiet until you do."

"And set one of the kitchen chairs outside the front door. Sunlight and whiskey is what I need, not"—Ironside spat out his next words like a man getting rid of a fly in his mouth—"chicken broth!"

Sarah looked helplessly at Lorena, but Samuel's wife nodded.

After he put on his hat and stomped into his boots, Ironside took his gun belt from the bedpost and strapped it around his waist.

Sarah, inclined to giggle, bent her head and slapped her hand over her mouth. The sight of a man in a long white nightshirt wearing hat, boots, and a gun, tickled her funny bone.

Lorena, made of sterner stuff, eyed Ironside with disapproval. "Luther, you're disobeying doctor's orders, and mine, so be it on your own head if you catch your death of cold outside."

"Woman, it's a hundred degrees in the shade."

"Then you'll burn up with fever."

"Sarah," Ironside said, "help me get outside, away from fussing females."

"I will, but I'm telling the colonel," Sarah said.

"Hell, the colonel wouldn't lie in bed either," Ironside growled.

* * *

Luther Ironside, a glass of whiskey in his hand, a hound dog at his feet, and his eyes on the distance, watched the shimmering Dromore riders emerge through the heat haze.

It took awhile before he made out Jacob, who still rode like a sodbuster on a plow horse. "Ranger, that's Jacob all right," he said to the dog. "I thought he was dead fer sure." He pointed to the oncoming riders. "Go get them, boy."

Ranger, never partial to running under a full sun, gave Ironside that *What, are you nuts?* look that dogs do so well. But he did raise his head and prick his ears. When he recognized the riders, he went back to dozing and the interrupted flies went back to buzzing around his head.

As the riders got closer, Ironside, not wishing to greet them seated like an invalid, rose to his feet—a move that saved his life.

The bullet that would have crashed into Ironside's chest, slammed into the CS buckle of his gun belt. The impact of the .44-40 rifle round winded him and sent him to his knees.

His world cartwheeling around him, he heard shots and the thud of hooves.

Suddenly Jacob was at his side, lifting him to his feet. "Luther, are you hit?"

Ironside looked at Jacob's face, but it was a blur. "I don't think so"—he struggled for breath—"unless I've got another belly wound."

Jacob sat the older man on the chair, and then looked him over. He smiled. "Hell, you're so bandaged up, I don't think a bullet could get through to your belly."

"That's them females," Luther complained.

Jacob undid Ironside's gun belt and held it up so he could see. "The lead's embedded in the buckle, Luther. That old chunk of Reb brass saved your life."

"Damn right it did. If it'd been a Yankee buckle I'd be gut shot and vomiting black blood right now."

Samuel swung out of the saddle. "How is he?"

"Ask me, sonny," Ironside said. "I'm the one that keeps getting shot to pieces."

Jacob smiled and passed the gun belt to his brother. There was no need for words.

Samuel examined the belt. "You should've been in bed, Luther, not stopping bullets."

"What happened here?" Shamus O'Brien shouted, Patrick pushing his wheelchair. He glared at Ironside. "Why are you out of bed?"

"To get away from fussin' women, that's why."

"And you're drinking whiskey," Shamus said. "And probably teaching the dog to drink whiskey like you taught my sons."

"Well, I don't have any whiskey now, Colonel. The dog spilled it when he ran away from the shooting."

"Proves that he's a hell of a lot smarter than you." Shamus suddenly realized his youngest son stood next to Ironside. "Hello, Jacob."

"Pa."

"Where have you been this twelve-month?"

"Away, Colonel."

"We'll talk about that later. You look like death itself." Shamus watched the vaqueros climb to the rim of the mesa. "How many do you reckon?" he asked Samuel.

"One shot, one bushwhacker." Samuel scanned the mesa summit. "He's probably long gone by now."

"Let the men search," Shamus said. "They might find something."

The colonel's eyes drifted to Alice who was standing beside Jacob's horse, looking wide-eyed and uncertain. "And who are you?"

The girl shook her head and said nothing.

"Her name is Alice and she wandered into my camp at Lobo Hill," Jacob explained again. "She has a story to tell."

Shamus looked at Ironside. "What do we do with her, Luther?"

"Why ask me, Colonel, a man with a bellyache? Let them fussin' women take care of her and give her a bath. Her face is dirty."

"Why is her face dirty, Jacob?" Shamus asked.

"I don't know, Colonel. She came to me that way."

"Cleanliness is next to godliness, Jacob." Shamus looked at his son, from the scuffed toes of his boots to his battered, sweat-stained hat. "Perhaps there's a lesson in that for you." He shook his head. "You really do look like hell."

"Pa, I suggest we take Luther inside and I'll ask Lorena to take care of the kid," Samuel said, saving his brother from further scorn. "I reckon we've got some storytelling to do, all of us."

Shawn told of the wagon train and Patrick gave an account of his and Ironside's shoot-out with Rafe Kingston's gunmen. Jacob then told Alice's story about her escape from the fence under the cover of darkness.

"So the child is the only one who can give an eye-witness account of Kingston and his murderers," Shamus said.

Jacob nodded. "Seems like."

"We can hang him with this . . . and today's attack on Luther was Kingston's doing, I've no doubt of that." After a silence, Shamus said, "Jacob, does the girl have the sand to testify in court?"

"She's got sand aplenty. She proved that by walk-ing all the way from the San Pedro Mountains to Lobo Hill. That's rough country and a lot of from-here-to-there, even for a grown man. I reckon she'll speak up in court, especially if I'm there."

Ironside, who had insisted on being at the meet-ing, sat in an easy chair in boots and a nightshirt. "If Kingston finds out that the girl is a survivor he'll try to kill her, as sure as there's dung in a donkey."

"Then we must protect her until the U.S. marshal arrives," Shamus said. "In the meantime, we'll get Sheriff Moore over here from Georgetown to talk with the girl."

"Pa," Shawn reminded, "Moore is a bull moose, He'll scare the poor kid to death."

"Exactly, and we'll see how she stands up to him. Trust me, Rafe Kingston's lawyers will be a lot scarier."

There was a lull in the talk, and Jacob looked over at Patrick. "Pleasant McLean was a man to be reckoned with, a cool head and fast on the draw."

Patrick nodded. "He was all of that."

"Pat beat him fair and square, Jake," Ironside said. "You've no call to think anything different."

"It never crossed my mind to think otherwise," Jacob acknowledged. "I was just saying that Pleasant was good with the iron."

"All my sons are good with the iron, Jacob," Shamus stated. "It's something Luther taught each of you, for good or bad I've never quite decided."

"A man's got to take care of himself, Colonel," Ironside gibed.

"You could start taking care of yourself by getting back to bed," Shamus said. As Ironside muttered under his breath about fussin' women and frettin' females, Shamus turned his attention to Jacob. "Tell me."

"Do you really want to know?" Jacob asked.

"You're my son. Of course I want to know."

"I spent the past year at a mission," Jacob said.

"Where?"

"South of here. I don't know if I could find it again, or if it's still there."

"A strange thing to say, Jacob."

"I know. But then, it was a strange year."

Shamus thought for a while. "To be a monk requires

a vocation inspired by the Holy Spirit. In the eyes of God, it is a holy and wholesome thing."

Jacob smiled. "I wasn't a monk, holy or otherwise, Pa. I helped pick green apples from the trees behind the mission. I gathered wood for the winter fires and did anything else Brother Benedict ordered me to do. I wore a brown robe and attended prayers with the monks. Last winter, in the middle of the night when I rose to attend compline, there were icicles in my cell two feet long."

The others in the study sat in profound silence and stared at Jacob. They would have been less startled if he'd flown around the house and came in through a window.

Shamus spoke for all of them when he said, "Why did you do this thing?"

"I wanted a year of peace to find myself, discover who I am."

"And did you?"

"I don't know, Colonel. I think maybe the black dog still stalks me."

"Now you're talking in riddles, Jacob. What black dog?"

Ironside said, "Hell, Jake, just shoot the son of the devil."

"It's not a real dog, Luther," Jacob explained quietly. "It's depression I'm talking about, moods as dark as night. They come on sudden, those mornings when I don't want to get out of bed because what's the point? I'd only have to get through another empty, endless day."

"I feel like that after too much whiskey," Ironside said. "Lay off the busthead for a few days, find yourself a willin' woman, and you'll feel right as rain, cheerful as one-eyed dog locked in a smokehouse." He looked around him. "Ain't that right, everybody?"

"No, Luther, it's not right," Shamus said. "Whiskey and fancy women are your cures for everything. But they won't cure Jacob."

"Then what will, Colonel?" Ironside asked, irritated that his advice had been dismissed.

"Jacob must stay here and take his rightful place at Dromore." Shamus laid it on the line. "Honest toil and good grub will soon make him whole again, mentally and physically."

"Hear, hear," Shawn said.

"What do you say, Jake?" Samuel asked.

After a silence, Jacob answered. "I'll take it under consideration."

"That's all I ask, Jacob," Shamus said.

"You came at a bad time, Jake," Ironside said. "I mean, with a war brewing an' all."

"You mean Rafe Kingston?" Shamus waved a hand in the air. "Bah, I'll crush him under my boot like a bug."

Chapter Eight

The twelve hundred ton trading bark *Eliza,*
Captain Ezekiel Sherrod commanding, tied up in
the port of Galveston after a twelve-month voyage
during which she'd crossed the Atlantic twice and
sailed as far south as German West Africa.

Outward bound, *Eliza* had carried a cargo of fine
Virginia cotton and two-dozen Henry repeating
rifles. When she returned her hold was crammed
with Spanish brandy in barrels, aniseed in demi-
johns, ale and olive oil in bottles, vinegar in casks,
wine in casks and cases, Spanish almonds, filberts in
bags, salted beef (a superior quality in cases), Biscay
iron, Milan steel, cheap tin trays, Havana cigars, qui-
nine, window glass, hollow glassware, printed books,
shoes, vicuña hats, ribbons, sewing silk, English steel
needles, reams of letter paper, Irish linen, ostrich
feathers, assorted spices, and a supply of men's colored shirts to be sold on the dock by the ship owner
at cost.

Supervising the unloading of the cargo was the

ship's third mate, a tall, lean, young man with a shock of auburn hair and steady gray eyes.

Captain Sherrod joined his officer on the quarter-deck. "A hot day for it, Mr. Lazarus."

"It's all of that, sir." Miles Lazarus kept his eyes on the longshoremen working in the hold and on the dock.

"Still, we obtained a fine anchorage and the unloading will be completed well before dusk," Sherrod said.

"That is my opinion," Lazarus agreed.

Suddenly the captain leaned over the rail and yelled, "Easy with them wine casks, you swabs. Handsomely, now, handsomely." He turned to Lazarus again. "Danged lubbers, not a seaman in the bunch."

Sherrod was a small, quick man with smiling brown eyes, his red, swollen nose betraying his lifetime love affair with rum punch. "Have you considered my offer, Mr. Lazarus?"

"Indeed I have, sir," the younger man said. "And the answer is still no. I needed a year at sea to clear my mind and give me time to think about my future. The year is over and now I have to be moving on."

"A first mate's berth and a share of the cargo. It's no small thing I offer."

"I know that, Captain, and I appreciate it," Lazarus replied. "But it's not for me."

"Miles"—Sherrod called Lazarus by his given name for the first time ever—"you've done well. From ordinary seaman to third mate in a year is a remarkable achievement and you deserved it. Will you throw it all away and go back to the life you had before you joined the *Eliza*?"

"Captain, I don't know the answer to that question. At least, I don't know it yet."

Sherrod broke off to again turn the air blue as he cursed out the longshoremen. When he turned to Lazarus, he said, "I knew who you were when I signed you on. Galveston is a busy international port and men of all stripes talk in the taverns. The name Miles Lazarus was well known to them, the famous gunfighter with ten notches on his gun."

"I never notched my guns. That's a tinhorn's trick."

As the captain had done earlier, he stepped quickly to the rail and ordered the bundle of shirts to be left on the dock.

"Those Limey shirts will be the death of me." Sherrod shook his head. "I bet the owner doesn't sell a one and he'll blame me, of course."

"Jonathan Powell could sell moonshine at a Baptist prayer meeting. If he doesn't get rid of them here, he will in San Francisco, and make a profit."

"I sure hope so." The captain looked into the younger man's eyes as gulls yodeled above the ship's masts. "Don't go back to what you were, Miles. If you do, your future will be written out for you and the last sentence in the book will read, 'He died with a bullet in him and his face in the sawdust.'"

"I'll take that into consideration," Lazarus said.

"If you change your mind, you can come back and take your rightful place as first mate of the *Eliza*."

* * *

Dark was crowding close and a sea breeze carried the smell of shoaling fish in the bay as Miles Lazarus walked along the Strand toward his hotel.

The Strand, called by many "the Wall Street of the southwest," was a bustling thoroughfare filled with wholesalers, cotton agents, paint, drug, grocery, hardware, and dry goods stores, and ships' insurance companies. Well-dressed merchants in broadcloth, their wives in rustling silk on their arms rubbed shoulders with whores, pimps, bronzed seamen from a dozen countries, wharf rats with quick, calculating eyes, and cutthroats and robbers of all kinds. Here and there slack-jawed rubes counted the coins in their pockets and sidestepped pale-faced preachers, Bibles clutched to their breasts, who warned all within earshot that hell was yawning open to receive every last one of them.

The crowds drifted, thinning out then swelling again, but the sea was the one constant, always there, making its presence known by sight, sound, and smell.

After months at sea, Lazarus found the steadiness of the land unsettling, and his rolling gait was that of a sailor washed up on shore. But he loved every moment of his walk. He felt as though he was coming home. He smiled.

The prodigal returns.

* * *

The clerk at the Tremont Hotel didn't raise an eyebrow when Lazarus stepped to the desk in his seaman's slops and battered, peaked cap, a ditty bag slung over his shoulder. "I'm happy to see you again, Mr. Lazarus."

"It's good to be back."

"Your room is just as you left it." The clerk handed him the key. "When we heard the *Eliza* was arriving in port, the bed linen was changed and the bar stocked. There is also a box of fine Havana cigars, some sacks of smoking tobacco, and a box of Belgian chocolate."

His smile was mechanical, but tinged with envy. Lazarus was a handsome man to be sure, and much admired by the ladies. He could cut a dash, a thing the clerk had never even attempted. And he was a famous gunman, but that was never mentioned at the Tremont, at least out loud.

Lazarus nodded. "Thank you, I appreciate it."

"Will there be anything else?" the clerk asked.

"If there is, I'll be sure to let you know."

Miles Lazarus emptied his ditty bag onto the bed and a spare shirt, shaving gear, and an Ancient Egyptian Shabti figure tumbled onto the patchwork quilt. The Shabti, of faience painted the color of a green apple, portrayed a young slave girl, the inscription on her long skirt reading VERILY, I AM HERE WHEN THOU CALLEST. He had paid ten dollars for the little figure during a visit to Germany's west African colony, and he considered the money well spent. Only four inches tall, it pleased him for reasons he couldn't quite fathom.

Reaching into the bottom of the bag, he removed a revolver wrapped in an oily rag, a beautifully tooled holster, and a cartridge belt of mahogany leather. He lifted the cloth and stared for a long time at the blue, short-barreled Colt with its worn, stag horn handle.

He thumbed back the hammer, opened the loading gate, and spun the empty cylinder. It rolled slick, and when he squeezed the trigger it felt as finely tuned as ever, breaking like a glass rod. The shortened, four-inch barrel and honed action was the work of a Jewish gunsmith in San Francisco, and it hadn't come cheap. Neither had the .44-40 Henry he'd bought from Abraham Levy, but, like the Shabti, it had been worth every penny.

After he'd considered the Colt and recalled its ways, Lazarus wrapped the revolver in the cloth and laid it in the drawer of his wardrobe, where the Henry already lay, wrapped in its own protective cloth. He put the gun belt with the revolver and closed the drawer.

He'd just straightened up when a knock came to the door.

For a moment, he thought about retrieving the Colt. A man in his line of work had many enemies. But he settled for, "Who is it?"

"Who the hell do you think it is? Open up."

Lazarus smiled and stepped to the door. Before he

opened it, he called out, "I should keep you standing out there, Dolly, for cussin'."

"That ain't cussin', big boy. This is cussin'." Diamond Dolly Edmond opened up her lungs and turned the air around her blue.

"Enough." He opened the door. "You'll get us both thrown out of here. This is a high-class joint."

"So what? I'm a high-class whore." She stepped inside and threw her arms around Lazarus's neck. She kissed him, and then stepped back. "What the hell are you? John Paul Jones?"

The tall man grinned. "How did you know I was back?"

"Everybody knows the *Eliza* tied up last night," Dolly said. "I saw you walk to the hotel while I was standing at the parlor window, getting pawed by Sam Wallace. He's a toad, but he owns half of Galveston."

Dolly Edmond was a tall, red-haired girl with beautiful green eyes and the kind of body that keeps a man awake of nights. As befitted her nickname, she wore diamond earrings, a diamond necklace, and a glittering rock on her finger the size of a river pebble. Too hard in the face to be called pretty, she was nonetheless a handsome woman and the arcs at the corners of her mouth betrayed a wicked sense of humor. Dressed in fine yellow silk, she was not a poor man's whore.

She looked around her. "You've been visiting foreign ports for a year. Did you bring me something?"

"Only me," Lazarus said.

"You know better than that." Dolly frowned.

"Oh, I forgot." Lazarus dug into the pocket of his white seaman's pants and produced a diamond bracelet that he dropped into Dolly's open palm. "South African diamonds. I won it in a poker game. The German gentleman I was playing with ripped it off his wife's wrist before he called me. A man holding treys and knaves should've known better."

If Dolly heard the story she didn't respond. "Oh, Miles, it's beautiful." Avarice, more than affection filled her eyes. "The prettiest bracelet a man's ever given me."

"Dolly, you've probably got a dozen just like it." Lazarus grinned.

The woman smiled right back. "Well, I'll add it to my collection."

Someone scratched on the door, and Lazarus turned. The hotel clerk stood there.

"Come in." Lazarus waved the man inside.

He bowed his way inside. "I forgot to give you this telegram, Mr. Lazarus. It came for you yesterday."

"Just drop it on the desk there," Lazarus said.

The clerk did as he was told, took one lingering look at Dolly's dazzling voluptuousness, then backed his way out, like a Chinese peasant taking leave of his emperor.

"Wake up, Miles, for God's sakes."

"Huh? Huh?" Lazarus surfaced from a dream.

"You were tossing and turning and talking in your

sleep." Dolly lay naked beside him, her eyes amused. "Did you have a bad dream?"

"How long have I been asleep?" Lazarus noticed that blades of sunlight still shone though the gaps in the window shade.

"At least an hour, maybe longer."

"I was dreaming."

"I know that. What would you call it? Having a daymare, I guess."

Lazarus reached for the makings on the table by the bed. His hands trembled as he built a cigarette.

Dolly smiled. "You need a drink, big boy." She got up from the bed and fixed two glasses of bourbon. Handing one to him, she carefully climbed back in bed.

Lazarus drank and smoked for a while, then said, "It was just a dream."

"Tell me about it."

After a few moments of silence, he began. "I was riding in the mountains and I came on this hanging valley, and there was a monastery of some kind there."

"Monastery? A bit out of your line, huh, Miles?"

He ignored her comment. "Anyway, I was hungry and at the back of the monastery there was a green apple tree. So I rode my horse in there and ate an apple."

"Ah, and got a bellyache," Dolly said. "That's why you were tossing and turning."

"No, nothing like that. But a most singular event happened next. A monk in a brown robe saw me and demanded to know what I was doing there. I told

him I was hungry and that I'd eaten a green apple."
Lazarus took a drink of whiskey. "That's when it got
strange."

"Do tell." Dolly yawned, showing white teeth in a
pink mouth.

"Well, the monk said, 'Do not come back here
again, Miles Lazarus, or the green apples will mean
your death.'"

"Well, I should think they would, if you ate too
many of them."

Lazarus shook his head, then spoke aloud, but
more to himself than to Dolly. "What did he mean
by that?"

Dolly flopped onto her back, took the cigarette
from Lazarus's mouth, and inhaled deeply. As blue
smoke curled over her, she said, "It was only a dream.
It means nothing."

Lazarus nodded. "You're right. It was only a
dream."

Dolly crushed out the cigarette in the ashtray next
to her, then propped herself on one elbow. "Miles"—
she smiled—"why have you put up with me all these
years?"

Lazarus returned the smile. "Because, my dear, I
don't need to love a whore."

The day was shading into night when Dolly left.
After she was gone, Lazarus lit a lamp and opened
the wire the clerk had brought. It was short and to
the point.

LAZARUS I NEED YOU STOP
$10,000 WHEN THE JOB IS DONE STOP
COME QUICK STOP

The sender was a man named Rafe Kingston. And the wire had been sent from Albuquerque in the New Mexico Territory.

Lazarus smiled. Word sure traveled fast that he was back in Galveston. That's what a gun rep did for a man.

He sat on the tumbled bed, deep in thought, the wire in his hands. His year at sea had not paid him much, and although he had money in the bank it wasn't enough. Bonded whiskey, glossy whores, and fine horses didn't come cheap. He needed Kingston's $10,000. The man was probably an arrogant braggart and bully, like all the clients who hired him, but he was paying well for a kill and it would be cash on the barrelhead.

This last job, Lazarus decided. *Then no more.* When it was done he could prosper in dry goods or the shipping business. Odder things had happened.

He rose, tossed the wire on the bed, and stepped to the wardrobe. He picked up the Colt and loaded five chambers from the cartridge belt, the hammer on the empty sixth. He holstered the revolver, a sign of commitment. *What did a year at sea teach me in the end?*

The answer was simple. It had shown him the way to a better life. He would do this last, final job, then hang up his guns forever. It was a valuable lesson, and one he'd learned well.

A scratch at the door, and the clerk stepped inside. "The manager thought you might like these, Mr. Lazarus. Fresh in this morning."

In his hand he held a bowl of green apples.

Chapter Nine

"Look at me, child," Sheriff John Moore said. "Are you afeard?"

Alice held onto Lorena O'Brien's skirt and stared at the lawman with huge eyes.

"I will call you Alice. And you will call me Sheriff John C. Moore. But be warned, I take no sass or back-talk from young 'uns."

"Oh for heaven's sake, Sheriff," Lorena exclaimed. "You're scaring the wits out of the poor child."

"Yeah, ease up a shade, John," Jacob agreed. "She's not one of your prisoners."

"The truth, Jake. A lawman must dig out the truth while the wound is still raw and bleeding, like a doctor digs a bullet out of a man's belly." The sheriff swung on Alice again. "And you have been wounded, child, or so you say. Now, speak up and mind your manners."

Alice stared big-eyed at Moore and said nothing.

"The child is simpleminded" Moore threw up in his hands in a grand gesture. He looked around the room, taking in the O'Brien brothers, Shamus, and Ironside. Sarah stood in a corner, but she had eyes only for Jacob. "I put it to you," the sheriff said, "that this girl is slow. In short . . . she's a dunce."

Confident that he'd clearly stated his case and established Alice's lack of mental prowess, he looked at Samuel. "Now, Sam, I'll take that drink you offered. If you please."

"Alice," Jacob said, "come over here to me."

"She's really frightened." Lorena slanted her gaze to Moore. "I don't think she's used to being bullied."

The lawman snorted, but not wishing to take on Lorena, who could have an acid tongue, he accepted his drink from Samuel and kept quiet.

The girl crossed the floor and stepped between Jacob's open knees.

Jacob put his hands on her shoulders. "Tell me what happened to your foster ma and pa. Say it loud enough so the big bad man can hear."

Moore harrumphed and looked annoyed, but he kept his mouth shut. He didn't want to antagonize Jacob either.

"Jacob, will he beat me for running away?" Alice asked in a low voice.

"He won't beat you, I promise. Now speak only to me and tell how everybody in the wagons got sick and what happened next."

Moore listened intently while Alice recounted her tale, leaving nothing out and making no changes to the events. When she finished speaking, he said,

"Children have active imaginations, you know. She could've dreamed the whole thing."

"Did she dream a thirty mile walk from the San Pedro Mountains to Lobo Hill?" Jacob frowned. "Look at her feet, for God's sake."

Moore laid his drink aside. "Look at me child, are you telling me the truth?"

Alice used Jacob's leg as a barricade and did not answer.

Moore tried again. "Tell me my name, Alice."

Silence.

"It's Sheriff John C. Moore. I already told you that." He shook his head. "Colonel O'Brien, do you recollect the sodbuster that lived up on the Sapello River yon time? Had two simple sons, Jesse an' Jeptha?"

Shamus looked irritated. "I don't."

"Well, I used to ride up that way once or twice a year, on account of their ma made the best bear sign in the territory. She baked a fine apple pie, too, but it was her bear sign that took the blue ribbon. Why, I mind the time—"

"John, get to the point," Shamus said, letting his annoyance show.

"The point is, Colonel, I'm used to simple. Simple is as simple does, I always say, and the girl there does it. Her silence won't turn a jury against a respected man like Rafe Kingston."

Moore held out his glass toward Samuel and coughed. "My pipe's dry."

Shawn grinned. "Why don't we just give you the key to the wine cellar, John?"

"Shawn, John is our guest." Shamus drew down his shaggy eyebrows like a mad old buffalo bull. "I thought I told you and Patrick to get out on the range and check the bottoms for grass. We need to start stacking winter hay real soon."

Shawn rose to his feet, as did Patrick. "We're on our way, Pa."

"And while you're at it, make sure the water holes haven't slacked off too much. Forget the one over to White Bluffs, the vaqueros say it's been dry for a week."

"It was never dry when I was on my feet," Ironside growled.

"Luther, if you were on your feet it wouldn't dare," Shawn answered.

"Damn right." Luther smiled, pleased.

After Shawn and Patrick left, Moore said, "Colonel, I could ride over to the Rafter-K and speak with Kingston, get his side of the story. Mind you, I've got no jurisdiction there, but sometimes the star on my vest is enough."

"You do what you think is best, John," Shamus said.

"Anything you want me to discuss with him?"

"No, no discussions. Tell him two things, John, from me. Tell him to ride to Dromore and surrender himself into my custody until the United States marshal gets here."

"On what charge, Colonel?" Moore said, horrified.

"Murder. Multiple counts of murder."

"Colonel . . . he won't do that."

Shamus ignored the lawman's protest. "Secondly, tell him to bring the man who took a pot at Luther two days ago. He will also face a charge of attempted murder."

"Damn right he will," Ironside said. "My belly still hurts."

"Colonel"—Moore struggled to find words—"what if he says no?"

"Then tell him Dromore is coming after him."

Chapter Ten

Miles Lazarus couldn't sleep. His wide-open eyes stared at the shadowed ceiling of his hotel room. He missed the creak of the ship, the wind in the rigging, and the soft surge of the surfing sea over the bow, the lullaby the good ship *Eliza* sang to her drowsy mariners.

Finally, he rolled out of bed and his feet met solid ground, still a surprise for a man used to the constantly pitching deck of a square-rigged bark. He slipped on a robe of scarlet silk, poured himself two fingers of bourbon, and lit a cigar. Stepping to the window, he pulled aside the curtain.

Galveston was the first city in the state to install electric streetlights, but they hadn't yet reached the area around the Tremont. Gas lamps still cast a blue glow on the damp cobbles and gathered shadows in the gloom beyond their reach. A mist, as gray as a ghost, had drifted in from the bay. It haloed the line of gas lamps stretching from the hotel to the Strand and transformed them into a procession of emaciated Gothic saints. A hansom cab clattered along the street, the horse's hooves clanging loud in the midnight quiet.

Lazarus watched for a while and was about to turn away when a movement in the street caught his attention. He thought he saw the glint of a revolver barrel. Three men stood in the shadowed doorway of an apartment building, one of them craning his head around a corner to watch the Strand.

Robberies were not uncommon in Galveston where rich merchants often carried large sums of money, to say nothing of expensive watches and diamond stickpins. Strictly an interested observer, Lazarus waited to see how the play went down. The footpads were merely practicing their profession and it was no business of his.

Then suddenly it was.

In the distance, weaving in and out of gaslight, came a short, stout man with the rolling gait of a sailor, made more pronounced, Lazarus guessed, by the libation of a good many glasses of rum punch.

Captain Ezekiel Sherrod, a fair wind at his back, was homeward bound, stepping carefully among the hazardous cobbles with that dignified demeanor only the very drunk can muster. He owned a house and kept a woman near the Tremont. Lazarus remembered it as a cozy enough berth for a seafaring man.

His eyes on the mist-shrouded road outside, Lazarus waited just a few seconds longer. Then he saw how it was going to be.

The three men stepped out of the darkened doorway and hurriedly arranged themselves into the tableau Lazarus had seen so many times in the past—two friends carrying home their paralytically drunk companion.

The three men, the one in the middle dragging his toes along the cobbles, staggered in the direction of Captain Sherrod who seemed blissfully unaware of the danger he faced.

Lazarus wore only a silk robe, but he skinned his Colt from the leather as he dashed for the door. He ran past the startled desk clerk who yelled something after him that he didn't hear, and pounded into the street. The stone cobbles were cold and damp under his bare feet.

Ahead of him, in the blue haze under a streetlamp, Sherrod struggled with the three men. One of them knocked him to the ground and the captain roared, "Damn your eyes, you thieving lubbers."

Then their boots thudded into his body.

"Leave him be!" Lazarus yelled.

One of the men turned, the British bulldog revolver in his hand coming up fast.

When Lazarus thought back on it, the sight of a man in a scarlet robe with a Colt in his hand should have given all three robbers pause. But the man with the bulldog chose to make it his fight.

It was a mistake.

Lazarus triggered a shot and the bullet hit Bulldog's front collar stud, tearing through the man's throat and exiting the back of his neck. Blood and bone fanned over his body. The robber collapsed, dead when he hit the cobblestones.

The dead man's companions stared at the still body in disbelief. One of them, his face gray with shock, held out his hands in supplication. "Don't shoot, mister. I was only trying to feed my family."

"Jim is speaking the truth, sir, as ever was," the other man said. "Our young 'uns are hungry and Ned"—he pointed at the dead man—"said he'd show us a way to get money. I swear, we didn't even know he was carrying a gun."

Lazarus nodded. "Sounds plausible." In the distance he heard police whistles. "Why did you go in with the boot?"

"Miles, I'm not hurt," Sherrod said. "I guess you can hold these two until the law gets here."

Lazarus shook his head. "It's too late for that, Captain. When they used their boots on you, they stepped it up too high."

He fired twice. And two robbers lay dead on the ground.

Sherrod was stunned. "Miles, why?"

The echoes of the shots rang like iron along the street.

"Why?" he said again.

Lazarus turned eyes on the captain that were cold and gray as a sword blade. "Why? Because I haven't changed as I thought. I'm still me."

Everyone in Galveston knew that Captain Ezekiel Sherrod's word was as binding as a hangman's knot. When he said Lazarus had shot all three men in self-defense, the police accepted his statement without question. That Miles Lazarus was a famous gunfighter and mankiller didn't enter into their thinking. If Ezekiel said it was a fair fight, then by God, it was so.

The police identified the dead men as James Wainright, Edward Brown, and Peter Broughton or Brownlee. They weren't sure which. All three were married and residents of Galveston.

After the police questioned him, Lazarus had no further interest in the proceedings and went back to the hotel.

But as the bodies were loaded into a police hearse, Captain Sherrod, who had sobered rapidly, took a young lieutenant aside. "I'd like to make some small provision for the families of the deceased."

An earnest young man with brown eyes and a somber, spade-shaped beard, the lieutenant proclaimed, "That's a capital plan of a most singular nature. Your generosity will do much to allay the tears of the grieving widows and their starving broods."

"It is the least I can do." Sherrod meant every word.

Captain Sherrod sat at the corner of Lazarus's bed and lit a strong Indian cigar. After a few moments of quiet contemplation, he said, "What are you, Miles?"

"I am what I am," Lazarus answered.

"How can a man who knows more about the ancient dynasties of Egypt and can regale people for hours on the vagaries and peccadilloes of pharaohs, princesses, and potentates, gun three men in cold blood?"

"Only two. One was armed with a bulldog revolver in .44 caliber. It was hardly a toy."

"Two, three, we're splitting hairs, Miles."

"But all three of them would've killed you, Captain. The boots were going in. If I hadn't stopped them they'd have kicked you to death."

"Two of them tried to surrender," Sherrod pointed out.

"It was too late for that." Lazarus poured himself a drink. "A man takes his chances."

"What do you feel, Miles?" Sherrod asked.

"Feel?"

"Yes, right now, this very minute, what do you feel?"

"Nothing."

"No remorse?"

"Why should I feel remorse?"

"Pour me one of those, Miles." Sherrod waited until Lazarus handed him the drink, then said, "Why should you feel remorse? Because you killed three men."

"I've killed a lot of men."

"Never regretted a one?"

"Not a one."

Sherrod tossed off his bourbon, then rose to his feet. "I'm tired and I hurt all over. This old man's going home to bed."

"Can a man's soul die, Captain?" Lazarus asked. "Can it shrivel away and lie inside him dry and rotten like an Egyptian mummy in a coffin?"

"We have immortal souls, Miles," Sherrod responded. "And immortal souls don't die. That's what the Bible tells us."

"Do you believe it?"

"I don't know what to believe any longer." Sherrod stepped to the door, put his hand on the handle, then stopped and pressed his forehead against the varnished oak. "Miles, you can't go back to sea. I was wrong about that. You are what you are, and there's no changing a man like you. I can't change it. Nobody can change it."

"So my year at sea made no difference?"

Sherrod turned. "No, not a single bit. My heart breaks to tell you that, Miles."

Lazarus lay on the bed. Beside him the Shabti figure seemed to burn with green fire. He closed his eyes, his lips moving as he said words from the *Soldier's Song,* a poem of ancient Egypt's New Kingdom he'd committed to memory.

I saw a bright star fall near the walls of the
    mud fort where I stood lonely guard.
I hurried to the place where the burning orb
    fell but found only a smoking cinder.
"Take it back, warrior," a voice said. "The great
    god Amun-Ra has returned thy lifeless soul."

"Then so be it." Lazarus closed his eyes and slept without dreams

Chapter Eleven

Sheriff John Moore was so apologetic he stumbled over his rush of words, then fell silent, his tongue locked.

"Take it again, Sheriff. More slowly this time." Rafe Kingston waved one of his men forward. "Get the sheriff a drink."

"Me pipe is dry," Moore managed.

Kingston nodded. "It's a fair piece from George-town to here."

"Ah, well, that's what I was trying to say, Mr. Kingston. I've not come from town, I've come from Dromore."

"How interesting." Kingston wore riding breeches, English boots, and a frilled white shirt unbuttoned to the middle of his chest, revealing the flat planes of his pectoral muscles and the tanned column of his throat.

A young puncher with insolent eyes handed the sheriff bourbon in a cut crystal glass.

"But I'm not here in an official capacity, you understand," Moore explained. "I have no jurisdiction outside the town limits of Georgetown."

"No, you don't," Kingston agreed. "So what brings you here, Sheriff? How is Colonel O'Brien?"

"As to the colonel, he's just fine, but still confined to a wheelchair, poor soul. As to why I'm here"— Moore hurriedly downed a gulp of whiskey—"I'm afraid there's been talk."

"What kind of talk?" Kingston's eyes blazed, unfriendly as a forest fire.

Moore recognized the warning signs, but the lawman had sand and didn't shy away from what he'd come to say. "Well, talk about a wagon train an' cholera an' folks being shot down an' murdered an' sich."

"Are you talking about the sin-eaters?" Kingston asked.

"Those would be the ones." Moore didn't like the looks of the kid with the bold eyes and crossdraw Colt.

"I didn't murder anybody," Kingston said. "Those pilgrims died of cholera. End of story."

"There was talk of a fence," Moore said.

"Yeah, I fenced them up. They were planning to head north and spread their contagion everywhere. The fence stopped them."

"And the bodies and the wagons?" Moore's arid glass warmed in his hands, but no invitation to partake of another bourbon was forthcoming.

"I burned them," Kingston said. "You can't take chances with cholera."

"Ah, then that explains why I could find no trace of them when I swung down that way."

Kingston nodded. "That would explain it, all right. Well, Sheriff, I'm glad we cleared that up." The rancher made to get to his feet, but Moore's voice stopped him.

"There's one more thing, Mr. Kingston. A mere formality, you understand."

"Now what?" Kingston's smile was wearing thin as his patience.

"It's of no consequence, really," the sheriff said.

"Then why are you wasting my time with it?"

"It's a message for you from the colonel."

Now Kingston was listening. "What kind of message?"

"Oh, nothing really, just one old friend extending an invite to another old friend."

"O'Brien and me are not friends, old or otherwise. What does he want?"

Moore sighed and placed his glass on the small table beside him.

Kingston didn't bite.

The sheriff faced reality. Unlike Dromore, old Southern hospitality was sadly lacking at the Rafter-K. "As I said earlier, a mere formality. The colonel wants you to surrender to him at Dromore on multiple murder charges and wait there for the arrival of the United States marshal."

Kingston's face was black with anger and he opened his mouth to speak, but the sheriff talked right over him. "Furthermore, he wants you to bring the man who took a pot at Luther Ironside a few days ago. The colonel says he'll face a charge of attempted murder."

Then he added a little payback for Kingston's stinginess with his bourbon. "I should mention there's been talk of judicial hangings."

Moore expected Kingston to explode in rage, but the man did nothing of the kind. "Walk with me," he said.

Rafe Kingston's ranch house had none of the pillared, plantation splendor of Dromore, but it was a pleasing, single story dwelling in the British colonial style, designed by an architect who knew his business. The Manzano Mountains provided a dramatic backdrop to the east, the Rio Grande to the west.

"Look around you, Sheriff." Kingston raised his hand, pointing in each direction. "As far as the eye can see you're looking at the Rafter-K, all the way to the Malpais in the west and east to the Estancia."

Impressed despite himself, Moore nodded. "That covers a lot of range, Mr. Kingston."

"You're darn right it does, and I employ two dozen top hands to run it. Now, does a man like me go crawling to Colonel O'Brien and say, 'Please arrest me, Shamus, I've been a bad boy'?"

Moore looked around him at the white-painted fences surrounding the house, the corrals, barns, bunkhouses, and scattered outbuildings, all in a perfect state of repair. "No, I guess not."

"Don't guess, Sheriff, know for sure that I won't surrender myself to O'Brien or anybody else for that matter. I've done nothing wrong, nothing that O'Brien wouldn't have done himself."

"What do I tell him? Just that?"

"No, you tell him to go to the devil. And one more thing, tell the mick that none of my men took a pot at Ironside. If I wanted Ironside dead, I'd come straight at him with a gun in my hand."

It seemed to Moore that the talking was done and it was time for him to move on, but Kingston still had something to say.

"Dromore riders murdered two of my men, and that's a thing I haven't forgotten. To protect myself and my punchers, I'm calling in a gunfighter by the name of Miles Lazarus. Now you tell the colonel that."

The sheriff smiled. "You're joshing me, right?"

"Do I look like I'm the mood for joshing?"

"Mr. Kingston, you know and I know that Miles Lazarus doesn't exist. He's just a big story that the Texicans made up to scare folks."

"No, he's real, and he's coming here, to my ranch."

John Moore was not a quick-thinking man and he had to corral his thoughts before he spoke again. "You're hiring an . . . imposter who calls himself Miles Lazarus, maybe so."

"No, he's the real article, Miles Lazarus out of Galveston. Spent years in Egypt before he became a hired gun, digging up . . . well, whatever he dug up."

"You real sure it's him, Mr. Kingston?"

"Would I pay ten thousand dollars to an imposter?"

Moore slowed down and thought again. Finally he said, "If he is Lazarus, a gunman who's killed men on every continent on earth, what are you going to do with him?"

"Use him to destroy Dromore if necessary."

"Jacob O'Brien might have something to say about that." The sheriff's face was mild.

"Lazarus will swat Jacob O'Brien like a fly and not give it another thought," Kingston said.

Moore stepped to his horse. "Well, you do what you think is right."

After the lawman swung into the saddle, Kingston grabbed the reins and looked up at him. "Tell Shamus O'Brien one more thing—his old Spanish land grant for Dromore is worthless. A few weeks ago the Surveyor General in Washington declared the Spanish grants null and void and sold the Dromore grant to me. So, in effect, I now own Dromore and all the lands pertaining thereto."

Moore shook his head. "Mr. Kingston, the colonel won't like this."

"Well, he'll just have to live with it, won't he?" Kingston let go of the sheriff's reins and smiled. "Tell the colonel my lawyer will be in touch."

Darkness caught up with Sheriff John Moore and he made camp in a treed draw twenty miles southwest of Dromore. He built a small fire and made a supper of jerky and the pint of rye whiskey he kept in his saddlebags.

The silence of night gives a man peace and quiet to think and Moore took advantage of it. Like a seer trying to divine the future in the flames, he stared into the fire, a thing he would never have done in the old Apache days. He let loose a great, shuddering sigh, a man who felt suddenly out of his depth.

The news of Miles Lazarus coming to the territory badly upset the sheriff. He liked the people at Dromore, even dour old Luther Ironside, but they could not stand against Lazarus, a man more legend than flesh and blood. The flames spoke to Moore. Soon would come the end of everything and it would be a step into nowhere.

Chapter Twelve

"I just thought you should know, Colonel," John Moore said.

Shamus nodded. "I thank you for that, John." He studied the sheriff.

Moore's duds were covered in dust and his face was gray, like a man who hadn't slept much and had missed his last six meals.

"Patrick, get the sheriff a drink."

Moore said, "Where are Samuel and Shawn?"

"Out on the range, getting the winter hay cut." Shamus looked at Jacob. "Have you heard of this man, this Miles Lazarus?"

"I have Pa. Some say he's the fastest man with a gun who ever lived or will live."

"Do you believe it?"

Jacob nodded. "Yes. I do."

Shamus sighed. "Well, that's reassuring."

"He doesn't scare me none," Luther Ironside chimed in. "Some fool Texan is always claiming to be the fastest gun alive. A bullet in the belly will slow his draw right quick."

Jacob smiled. "You stay away from him, Luther. He's faster than you can imagine."

"You think so, Jake? Well listen to me, I haven't met the Texan yet that can corral Luther. Why, I'll—"

"Luther, be quiet," Shamus interrupted. "An old man in a nightgown isn't going up against Lazarus or anybody else for that matter."

Patrick rose to his feet. "Excuse me, Colonel. I'll be right back."

Ignoring Ironside's outraged muttering, Shamus turned to the sheriff. "How is your brandy, John?"

"It's just fine, Colonel. I sure needed it."

"You looked used up. A good meal is what you need. Later talk to Sarah in the kitchen and she'll fix you up with a steak and some eggs."

"I'll do that." Moore nodded.

After a pause, Shamus said to Jacob, "Kingston refused my offer, so where do we go from here?"

"We can ride to the Rafter-K and arrest him," Jacob said. "And the bushwhacker who took the pot at Luther."

Ironside uttered a cuss, glad someone would listen to it.

"Luther, Kingston says it wasn't one of his men who took the shot," Moore declared.

"And you believe him?" Shamus asked.

"Strangely enough, I do, Colonel. Kingston says if he wanted Luther dead he'd come right at him with a gun in his hand."

"That's the last thing he'd ever do," Ironside said. "Why, I'd skin my old Colt and—"

"Luther, be quiet." Shamus interrupted him again, then turned to Moore. "If it wasn't one of Kingston's men, then who was it?"

"I don't know," the sheriff said. "Luther, anybody from your past hate you enough to kill you?"

"How many fingers and toes do you have?" Ironside said sarcastically. "And that's only men. If you want to add women, count them over again."

"Be on guard, Luther," Moore said. "It's clear someone wants you dead."

The study door opened and Patrick stepped inside, holding two books in his hands. "I thought I'd heard the name Miles Lazarus before." He held up one of the books and read the spine. "*A Concise History of Ancient Egypt*, by Dr. Miles Lazarus." He read the second. "*Three Years in the Valley of the Kings*, by Dr. Miles Lazarus." Patrick passed the books to Jacob. "Could it be the same man?"

"It's not a common name, so it could be," Jacob reckoned.

"Wait," Moore said, "Kingston said Lazarus had spent years in Egypt, digging stuff up."

"Then it is the same man," Patrick reasoned.

Ironside smiled. "Since he's a sawbones, maybe I could get him to take a look at my belly."

"He's not a physician, Luther." Patrick explained. "He's got a doctorate in archeology."

"Arky—what?" Ironside spit out.

Patrick smiled. "He digs for ancient artifacts, like pottery and bones."

"A man don't need to be a doctor to dig holes in the ground. All he needs is a shovel and a strong back," Luther sputtered.

"What do you make of it, Jacob?" Shamus continued to ignore Luther.

"All kinds of men with all kinds of backgrounds in the West, Colonel. Remember Jerome Spooner who ranched over Largo Canyon way? He killed Mexican Bob Castillo in a fair fight in the Lone Star saloon in Santa Fe, and nobody considered Bob a bargain."

"Spooner was an Englishman, wasn't he?" Shamus questioned Jacob.

"Yes, he was. He went back to England, took a seat in the House of Lords, and wrote a book about his western adventures."

"Spooner was a gunfighter and then found respectability. It seems Lazarus did the opposite." Shamus shook his shaggy gray head in puzzlement. "What demons drive a man like that?"

Patrick, aware that he might give offense, stared at the floor. "Perhaps Jacob can answer that question."

The awkward moment hung in the air like a mangled iron beam. Even Ironside, a man given to ill-considered statements, suddenly spotted something of vital interest on the ceiling.

Jacob took it in stride. "I'd say there's a darkness in Lazarus that he discovered only recently. Instead of remaining in the light, he chose another path, a walk into night. It can happen to any man."

"He was brilliant," said Patrick. "A first-rate scholar and a creative writer."

"Depression and darkness is the opposite side of the creative coin," Jacob said.

Ironside spoke up. "Jake, all this highfalutin talk about another Texas gunhawk is giving me the croup. Bang a bullet into his guts and he'll die like any other man."

"That's true, Luther," Jacob said. "But who is going to draw down on him?"

"You can take him, Jake," Ironside insisted. "You're the fastest man with a gun I ever seen."

Jacob said nothing, but his face was closed, like a man looking ahead to an uncertain future.

The Dromore butler tapped on the door and stepped inside. "A gentleman wishes to see you, Colonel."

"His name?"

"Mr. Barnabas McCrae. He says he's a lawyer."

Shamus turned his wheelchair so he was facing the door. "Show him in."

Barnabas McCrae was a small, thin, goblin of a man with a pale, pinched face and searching black eyes lost in deep sockets. He wore frayed broadcloth, yellowed linen, and a habitual scowl. He walked directly to Shamus and said in a broad Scottish accent, "Colonel O'Brien, I presume."

Shamus nodded. "As ever was."

"I will not beat about the bush, sir. Directness has always been my way, though it does not please some."

"Very commendable, I'm sure." Shamus already did not like the man.

"I represent Mr. Rafe Kingston in all legal and business matters. Come, sir, do you understand?"

"I guess I do." Shamus hesitated purposely.

"Then I will come to the point," McCrae said.

"A brandy with you?"

The lawyer scowled. "I will come to the point, sir."

"What does Kingston want?"

"Want? What every man wants, peace, prosperity, and the leisure to enjoy it. The very rights embodied in our Constitution."

Shamus said nothing.

McCrae opened his briefcase and removed a file. He made a show of fitting a pair of pince-nez spectacles to the end of his pen-sharp nose before leafing through papers. "Ah, yes, it seems you have leveled unwarranted allegations of murder against my client and slandered his name to members of the constabulary." The lawyer peered over the top of his glasses at Shamus. "Do I speak the truth, sir? Come now, lets us not be elusive. Just answer my question."

"Rafe Kingston will face charges of murdering at least forty men, women, and children. It is possible that several of those were killed by his own hand."

"Harsh, Colonel O'Brien. Very harsh and cruel."

"I speak the truth in my own house," Shamus said. "He built a fence around those poor people and let them die of disease and thirst, apart from those he shot."

"Supposition, conjecture, postulation, fantasy," the lawyer answered back. "You have no proof to support such a vile accusation."

"Mister, I saw the fence and the dead bodies," Ironside said. "And so did Pat over there and four of our vaqueros. That ain't accusin'. It's sayin'."

McCrae looked as though he'd just smelled something bad. "Who, pray tell, is the person who just addressed me, Colonel?"

"Luther Ironside, my segundo."

"I didn't come here to talk with the hired help." The lawyer shuddered.

"Then say your piece and get out of here." Shamus's anger flared.

"Very well, then back to the point." McCrae continued. "Mr. Kingston also saw the wagons, and so did a dozen of his men. Yes, he built a fence around them, but only to stop the spread of contagion. Despite his help, clean water, and food, all the people died. Only then did Mr. Kingston, out of sense of civic duty give them a decent burial."

"McCrae, that's bullcrap and you know it." Shamus's anger flared again.

"I would tell a court of law, Mr. Kingston's men were set upon by ruffians from the Dromore ranch and two of their number were viciously slain. Why? the jury might ask, and who can blame them? Because, I would say, Colonel Shamus O'Brien has cast avaricious eyes on the lands and cattle of the Rafter-K and he intends to frame an innocent and God-fearing man for murder to further his diabolical scheme."

"All right, McCrae, you've said enough." Shamus roared, "Get out of my house."

"I will, but not without saying one thing more." The lawyer's eyes were mean. "This is no longer your house. All the land of Dromore and buildings pertaining thereto now belong to Mr. Kingston."

"Jacob"—Shamus's eyes locked on McCrae, his voice ominously quiet—"give me your Colt."

"No, wait, Colonel," Patrick said, "let's hear him out."

"You're on thin ice, McCrae." Shamus's gaze was fierce. "I strongly advise you to step carefully."

"The federal government recently declared most of the old Mexican land grants in the New Mexico Territory null and void. The Court of Private Land Claims considered two hundred and eighty-two Mexican grants and confirmed only eighty-two of them. Dromore was not among those confirmed. Mr. Kingston contacted me in Washington by wire and ordered me to immediately purchase the vacant Dromore grant, which I did." McCrae spread his white, blue-veined hands. "You are now, Colonel, to put it bluntly, squatting on Mr. Kingston's property."

Shamus turned in his chair. "Patrick?"

"I'll check on it, Pa."

"McCrae, you tell Kingston to prepare for a court battle that will cost him so much it will break him."

Shamus wheeled closer to the lawyer. "That is, after his trial for murder."

"Come now, sir, there is no need for such unpleasantness. Mr. Kingston has enough land and cattle of his own. He has no desire to exercise his right to Dromore. That is, if you and he can reach an agreement."

"What kind of agreement?" Shamus frowned. He didn't trust a word the lawyer said.

"You will cancel your request for a United States marshal, and give me your sworn affidavit that the people behind the fence died of cholera, despite my client's heroic efforts to save them."

"Simple as that, huh?"

"Yes, it is that simple."

"Well, Mr. McCrae, you and your client can go to hell." Shamus's face was beet red.

"Is that your last word?" The lawyer didn't budge.

"That's all the words you're going to get from me, McCrae."

"Then I must ask, nay command you, to vacate this property within a fortnight from this date."

"Patrick, show Mr. McCrae the door." Shamus pointed to the entryway.

Jacob, who had been silent until now, stood. "McCrae, give Rafe Kingston a message from me. Tell him that if he makes any moves against Dromore, I'll be calling on him."

"Just that?"

"Yes, just that. He'll know what I mean.

Chapter Thirteen

The train was an hour out of Austin, butting through the thick air of west Texas, when Miles Lazarus felt the engineer apply the brakes. Reluctant to leave the comfort of his brass and red velvet private compartment, he opened a window and looked outside. The guard passed at that moment and Lazarus said, "What's the holdup?"

"I don't know, Mr. Lazarus, but I'm about to find out."

"Let me know, huh?"

"Yes sir, as soon as I'm told what's happening my ownself."

Five minutes later the guard tapped on the door and stepped inside. "Seems like they're making repairs to a trestle bridge over a dry wash five miles ahead. We'll be held up for a couple of hours."

Lazarus poured himself a bourbon. "Then all I can do is wait."

"There's a spur a mile ahead and the engineer wants to load up on wood and water. There's a town there by the name of Comanche Falls. It has a saloon and a couple of whores, if you're so inclined."

"Where are the falls?" Lazarus asked.

"There ain't any. Call it wishful thinking."

The guard opened the door to leave, then said, "If you need anything, Mr.—"

"I'll let you know."

The train's two carriages, boxcar, and caboose clanked as the locomotive belched steam and lurched forward. A few minutes later it stopped at the spur beside a water tower and a pyramid of firewood.

Lazarus stepped to the window and looked outside. Beyond the spur lay a small cow town. Its shacks, located by chance, wandered onto flat brush country as though they'd lost their way. The main street, if that's what the natives considered it, consisted of a single row of buildings, a couple of false-fronted stores, a warehouse of some kind, and the saloon. Cattle pens were boxed close to the spur, but judging by the lack of smell, he figured they hadn't held cows in a long time.

Unwilling to stay cooped up for hours, he removed his frockcoat and decided against buckling on his heavy gun belt. But as was his habit, he slipped a Sharps .32 caliber revolver into his waistband at the small of his back. Lazarus had killed men with the stingy gun and had faith in it.

The heat of a rainless land hit him like a fist when he stepped off the train and made his way past the water tower. Around him brush flats stretched all the way to the horizon. The sun-hammered distances bent and stretched and shimmered. The cattle and branding pens glittered with yellow dust. Many of the boards had rotted free of their iron nails and slanted to the ground, forming triangles of shadow. The quiet, as oppressive as the heat, was broken only by the *chuff-chuff-chuff* of the steaming locomotive, but as Lazarus walked closer to the town he heard insects make their small music in the bunch grass.

A single road, no bigger than a weedy, buggy trail, led out of town and arrowed straight across the flat for the horizon.

He stopped and stared at the gray-haired woman who sat in a wooden chair in the middle of the street. The woman looked neither left nor right, but kept her gaze glued to the road, now and then shading her eyes when she saw a dust devil do its dervish dance in the distance.

Waiting for somebody, Lazarus decided, then put the woman out of his mind.

The Texas Belle Saloon boasted a lofty false front of sawn timber that promised a grand interior. But when Lazarus stepped inside he found himself in a narrow structure with board walls and a V-shaped canvas roof that was rotted enough to leak rain . . . if it ever rained. The air was thick and close and smelled of smoke, spilled beer, ancient sweat, and of the outhouse at the back.

The bar was respectable enough, about ten paces long of planed wild oak. Behind it was a large mirror, and above that was a sign that read HAVE YOU WRITTEN TO MOTHER?

A pillar of respectability, the bartender was a magnificent creature with pomaded hair parted in the middle, a brocaded vest, and a diamond stickpin in his cravat. "What can I do for you, stranger?"

"Any cold beer?"

"Warm beer."

"Then what do you have that passes for whiskey?"

The bartender looked over Lazarus, noted his expensive frilled shirt, a vest even better than his own, and long-fingered hands that had never done a lick of manual labor. He reached under the bar and came up with a dusty bottle. "Old Grand Dad suit your taste?"

"It'll do."

After blowing dust off the bottle, the bartender poured a generous shot. "Have one yourself," Lazarus said.

"Don't mind if I do." The bartender beamed. "I can't afford the best whiskey, not in this job."

Lazarus sipped his drink. "You should move to a city. Fine-looking, well set-up fellow like you should be able to find bartending work real easy."

The man shook his sleek head. "Just between you and me, mister, I'm on the scout, ever since I killed a man down Laredo way a few years back."

"In a fair fight?"

"No. I killed him with an axe while he was sleeping beside my wife. I chopped her, too."

"Nobody going to blame you for killing a cheating wife and her lover," Lazarus said.

"Yeah, well the Texas Rangers have a different

opinion on that. They took a set against me so I made a run for it. That was back in the spring of '84 and I've been here ever since." The bartender leaned forward. "Be careful, stranger, you're being watched."

"I know." Lazarus smiled. "Bad moves coming down."

"The tall kid with the yellow hair is Dan Storm," the bartender said. "He's fast with the iron and he don't take a step back from anybody."

"Good to know."

Looking in the mirror behind the bartender, Lazarus scanned the saloon. An old-timer sat at a table nursing a beer and a saloon girl played unenthusiastic poker with a man who looked like a drummer. The gunman stopped his gaze at the two young men standing at the far end of the bar. He had seen their kind before, wild, reckless kids dressed in shabby range clothes, sweat-stained Stetsons, and down at the heel boots with big-roweled Mexican spurs.

They'd worked cattle at one time, but not anymore. Likely they were running stolen cows into Old Mexico. A double-eagle lay on the bar in front of the towhead, more money than an honest puncher would have on a Monday afternoon.

Lazarus kept his eyes on the two snake-eyed kids in the mirror, especially Storm who had the reputation as a gun hand.

"You haven't come far," the bartender said.

"Off the train on the spur yonder."

"Maybe you should get back on it real quick. I'm not pushing you, mind, just saying."

Before Lazarus could answer, the kid called Storm turned his head. "Hey fancy pants, you keepin' that good drinkin' likker to yourself?"

Lazarus smiled and spoke to the man's reflection in the mirror. "No, I guess not. Bring your glass."

"That's not what I had in mind," Storm said. "See, me and my amigo here want all of it."

"Ah, sorry." Lazarus pulled his watch from his vest pocket and thumbed it open. "I have another hour and a half before my train leaves, so this bottle is both wife and child to me. I can't part with it."

He pushed himself away from the bar and faced Storm. "Especially to a piece of white trash like you. Boy, you wouldn't know good whiskey from five cents a shot rotgut."

Storm was mad clean through. He stepped away from the bar, clearing his gun arm. He wore his rig high on the waist, horsemen style, unhandy, but Lazarus had seen it work.

"Mister, get out of here and leave the bottle." Aware the eyes of the other patrons were on him, Storm grinned. "You ain't even heeled. That's why you talk so loud. Now scat, afore I lower your britches and take a switch to you."

The saloon girl giggled nervously and the drummer looked worried.

"You shouldn't talk to your elders like that, boy," Lazarus said calmly.

"If you ain't through that door in one minute, I'll let my gun do the talking," Storm bragged.

The game had gone on long enough and Lazarus was done with it. "Skin that Colt, boy."

"You ain't heeled," Storm said.

"Maybe I am, maybe I'm not. Draw and we'll see what happens."

Storm looked into Lazarus's eyes and couldn't read them. They were empty, emotionless. Gray as death. The kid felt a sudden pang of regret over starting this and was visibly relieved when his companion said, "Ah, let him go, Danny. He's scared to death."

Storm nodded. "Maybe he was gonna spit on me."

He and his amigo laughed.

Miles Lazarus poured another drink for himself and the bartender.

"Sure is hot today, isn't it?"

Storm snorted and lifted a glass to his sneering lips with his right hand.

It was the moment Lazarus had been waiting for. He drew from the waistband and fired. The .32 bullet shattered Storm's thumb with the glass. Blood, whiskey, and glass shards splattered over his face. The kid screamed and clutched his right wrist, staring in horrified fixation at the bleeding stump where his thumb used to be.

Lazarus held the smoking revolver on Storm's companion. "Are you making a play or not?"

The man's answer was to make a dash for the door. He stumbled over a chair, fell on his face, and then scrambled to his feet again. Frantic with fear, he bolted through the door and hit the street running.

"You SOB," Storm screamed at Lazarus, "you shot my thumb off."

"Seems like. Now get out of here unless you want to go for two."

Storm read the writing on the wall. This man, whoever he was, was not to be trifled with. He staggered to the door, still holding his wrist, and stumbled outside. Behind him he left a trail of scarlet splotches on the saloon's timber floor.

"Now he better learn to shoot with his left hand," Lazarus said to the bartender.

The man shook his head. "Mister, when you get mad at a person, you stay mad, huh?"

"Yeah, I guess I do. It's a character fault." Lazarus lifted the bottle. "Drink?"

The clanging locomotive bell summoned wayward passengers back to the train. Lazarus drained his glass before asking the bartender, "Why does the old lady sit out there in the middle of the street?"

"Her son went off to the war down that road and she sits there every day from sunup to sundown waiting for him to come back."

"You mean she's been doing that every day for what—nearly thirty years?"

"I do. Maisie Lawton says her boy will come home down the road, wearing the gray like he did when he left. Of course, everybody's tried to tell her that her son isn't coming back, but she refuses to believe it."

"It must be hot out there, day after day," Lazarus said.

"Maisie doesn't mind."

"I have to be going. Stay away from the Rangers."

The bartender nodded. "If I feel their cold breath on my neck, I'll get the hell out of Texas."

"And don't go taking an axe to anybody else, you hear?

"Wish I could bring 'em back, both of them."

"Well, like the old lady's son, they're not ever coming back." Lazarus tipped his hat and walked out of the bar. Despite the incessant bell, he walked to the mercantile two doors down from the saloon and stepped inside.

The proprietor, a tall, thin man with a red beard down to his waist, smiled. "Three customers before two o'clock. Things are looking up."

"Folks from the train?" Lazarus asked.

"Yeah, two ladies buying soda pop and stick candy. What can I do you for?"

"I need a parasol."

The bearded man was taken aback. "For your ownself?"

"No, I just need a parasol."

"I think I have one in the back." The proprietor disappeared into the back and returned with a cream-colored parasol. He opened it up with all the panache of a magician pulling a rabbit from a hat. "Pure China silk, guaranteed to last a lifetime and to give satisfaction in every way. Other retailers sell this little beauty for two dollars, but I'll let it go at cost for only a dollar ninety-six."

"I'll take it." Lazarus plopped a coin on the counter.

"An excellent choice, sir." The proprietor scooped up the coin.

Lazarus left the shop and walked down the street, stopping beside Maisie Lawton.

The woman looked up at him with faded eyes.

"Any sign of him?" he asked.

"Not yet," the woman said, "but Tom be home directly, you'll see."

Lazarus opened the parasol and handed it to Maisie. "This will keep the sun off you." It was apparent to Lazarus that the woman never had much and didn't expect much.

Her eyes widened. "This beautiful thing for me?"

"All for you." Lazarus stepped away. "I hope your son comes home soon."

"Bless you, mister," Maisie said. Then, "Wait, take this."

She reached inside the pocket of her threadbare dress and dropped a bright green apple into Lazarus's hand.

Chapter Fourteen

"Colonel, them sin-eaters don't mean a thing to us. I say we forget the whole business and pretend we never heard of Rafe Kingston." Luther Ironside shifted in his chair.

"Forget his men shot you?" Shamus O'Brien looked at Ironside in consternation.

"I got bullets into two of his. I reckon we came out even."

"Luther, directly or indirectly, Kingston murdered men, women, and children. If I let it go now, I couldn't live with myself."

"Then round up the vaqueros and let's go gun the guy."

"And make ourselves as bad as he is? I can't do that either." Shamus studied the ash at the tip of his morning cigar, and it seemed that he spoke to the ash, not Ironside.

"If you'd died, Luther, I would have done just that, rode to the Rafter-K and killed Kingston and whoever else had a hand in your death. It would've been a reckoning, but who's to say it would've been right or just."

"Then what do we do, Colonel?" The stiff set of Ironside's shoulders revealed his exasperation.

"We need proof of Kingston's guilt." Shamus was adamant.

"We have the girl."

"You saw what happened when John Moore questioned her. Alice fell apart. We can't depend on her as a witness."

"Where are we going to get proof?"

"Where the people died," Shamus said. "I'm going there myself."

"Then I'm riding with you," Ironside insisted.

"No, you're not. You're still too weak from your wounds."

"Colonel, I can ride."

"Yes, and I'd bring you back hanging over your saddle."

Ironside's eyes were bleak. "Maybe you're right, Colonel."

"I know I'm right."

"Then for God's sake take Jacob with you."

"I was planning on it. I'm not that brave, or foolish."

"We must be getting close, Jacob." Shamus was roped to a quiet bay mare and he had his old army field glasses around his neck. "We've got to be two miles south of the San Pedro."

Jacob studied a ridge to the west that sloped gently

down to a grassy meadow bright with wildflowers. "Patrick and Luther were on that ridge to your right, Colonel. This has to be the place."

Shamus scanned the meadow with his field glasses. "I don't see any burned areas."

"Probably grass has already grown over them. Let's go take a look." Jacob turned to his father. "How are you holding up, Pa?"

Shamus's face stiffened. "I'm just fine, no need to ask."

Jacob had touched a nerve and a slight smile played on his lips. He'd forgotten that the quick Irish pride of the O'Brien patriarch was a mighty sensitive thing. The blade of the old Apache war lance wedged against his spine pained him more than he cared to admit.

Storm clouds bruised the sky above as Shamus and Jacob began their search.

Fifteen minutes later, they found faded scorch marks on the ground where the wagons had burned. Scouting farther into the surrounding pines, Jacob rode into a clearing with visible signs of disturbed ground.

He dismounted and led his horse forward, walking through knee-high grass and wildflowers. After only a few steps the black balked and reared, arcs of white showing in its eyes. Jacob fought to calm his mount, but the big horse jerked the reins from his hand and cantered away in the direction of the meadow.

Then Jacob smelled what the horse had smelled and he saw white bones scattered across the grass like drifts of snow. He shook his head, his face grim. *You SOB, Kingston. You didn't even bury them deep.*

The mass grave had been torn open in several places and ravenous coyotes had dragged out bodies and torn them apart. The stench of rotting flesh hung over the clearing coupled with a solemn silence. Even the birds had deserted the place.

The colonel had hoped the United States marshal could exhume the corpses and find gunshot wounds. But Jacob realized it was impossible. The bodies were already in an advanced state of decomposition and would reveal nothing . . . even if the marshal felt inclined to dig them up in the first place, and that was highly unlikely.

Jacob was glad to leave that clearing of death and walked back to the meadow. Shamus held the reins of his horse and, judging by the expression on his father's face, he also held a lecture in check until Jacob got closer.

"Do you know what can happen to a man in this country if he lets his horse get away from him, leaving him afoot?"

"There's a mass grave in the clearing," Jacob said. "He shied away from the smell of rotting bodies."

Shamus was visibly shocked by that information, but he was not about to let Jacob off the hook. "I blame Luther Ironside. The old reprobate taught my sons plenty about whiskey and whoring and shooting revolvers. It would've been better for all concerned if he'd spent a little more time on the basics of horsemanship."

The last thing Jacob wanted was yet another argument with his father, but the sudden flat statement of a rifle and a groan from the colonel froze any retort he might have made.

He ran to Shamus, who was holding the side of his head, blood trickling through his fingers. "Pa, are you hurt bad?"

"I'm fine," Shamus said, gasping a little.

A drift of gray gunsmoke clung to the pines off to Jacob's right. After one final look at his father, he swung into the shadow and galloped in that direction. He skinned his Winchester and dusted three shots into the smoke haze. There was no return fire.

Jacob struck a dim game trail leading into the pines. He charged headlong into the trees, fully aware of the risk he was taking. If the dry gulcher had nerve, he could hole up somewhere and cut loose at a range where he'd be unlikely to miss.

But no one took a pot at Jacob as he pounded along the trail through the trees, and then splashed into a stream that skirted the base of a high cliff. After half a mile the stream angled away from the cliff that had become much lower with a wall of aspen growing on a ledge halfway up the slope.

Jacob drew rein and listened. Ahead of him he heard a distant hammer of hooves and he kicked the black into another distance-eating gallop. He rode into a dust cloud kicked up by the fleeing rider and figured he was only about a hundred yards behind him.

Ahead, a narrow wagon road curved from Jacob's

right, then ran straight toward what looked like an old stage station, burned almost to the ground with a few charred beams sticking out of the ashes like skeletal arms. He saw no sign of a dust cloud beyond the ruin and figured the rider had holed up somewhere.

Alarms bells clamoring in his head, Jacob swung out of the saddle and dived for the ground, expecting a bullet at any time.

It never came.

The burned station lay dead and silent in the afternoon heat. Bees buzzed in the bushes close to where he lay and a hawk quartered the sky, gliding below low blue-black clouds.

Where is the bushwhacker?

Jacob rose to his feet, his rifle at the port, and stepped closer to the cabin. Then he cursed himself for being a complete fool. The wagon road ran in front of the cabin, but to the right where it ended, the ground was carpeted with grass. The fleeing rider had swung off the road and took to the grass, knowing he'd kick up less dust.

Jacob shaded his eyes and scanned the shimmering distance. After a hundred yards there was a stand of pine, among them some ancient junipers, and the rider had probably headed straight for them. Swinging into the saddle again, he approached the trees at a walk. He saw nothing and heard nothing but the restless rustle of the rising wind in the trees.

His face was grim. He'd been outsmarted by the bushwhacker, who had left him to kick his heels and cuss into emptiness.

Thunder crashed and fat raindrops ticked around him as Jacob mounted, then rode back to the meadow.

Shamus, tied to his horse, did not have the option of dismounting. He'd sought shelter among the trees and called out when Jacob rode in sight.

As rain lashed across the meadow and the wind made the wildflowers dance, Jacob joined the colonel in the trees. He looked at his father's wound and the fingers of blood already crusting on his left cheek. "That looks nasty. I'd better get you back to Dromore."

"It's a scratch. But it will give me a headache for a week." Shamus looked out at the rain. "We're not going anywhere until this passes."

As thunder rolled and lightning flashed dazzling white above the meadow, Jacob built a cigarette.

"Missed him, huh?" Shamus said, watching his son thumbnail a match into flame and light his smoke.

"He outfoxed me, Colonel . . . and that's a natural fact."

"You tried, Jacob. Some men are better riders than others, that's all."

Jacob let that go. "You were the target, Colonel. There's no doubt about it."

"Since I'm the one that got shot, I'd say it's likely." Shamus's anger flared. "It seems that since I put the crawl on his lawyer, Rafe Kingston wants me dead. But, damn his eyes, he'll rue this day, I assure you."

His gaze angled to Jacob. "You don't share my anger?"

Jacob thought a while before he spoke. "Colonel, I believe the bullet that hit Luther's belt buckle was meant for you. Whoever the bushwhacker was, he mistook Luther for you."

Shamus also took time before he spoke. After a loud roar of thunder directly overhead that made the horses prance in fear, he said, "That's possible. We're both gray and I often sit outside in the fresh air." He quieted his mount. "Then this was Kingston's second attempt on my life, the hound."

Jacob rubbed his cigarette out on the heel of his boot, and then flicked the butt into the wet grass. "I don't think it was Kingston."

"Who else could it be?"

"I don't know. An old enemy, maybe?"

"All my old enemies are dead. And most of my new ones. No, this was Kingston's work all right and he'll pay."

"What do you have in mind, Colonel?" Jacob asked, a strange fear in him, as though he didn't want to hear the answer.

Shamus answered the question with one of his own. "You say the bodies have decayed, is that right?" He blessed himself. "God rest their poor souls."

"The marshal, when he comes, won't dig up anything but bones," Jacob said.

Shamus nodded. "Then I plan to crawl Kingston's hump. What I have in mind is war, Jacob. War to the finish."

Chapter Fifteen

Samuel waited until the galloping vaquero was within shouting distance and yelled, "Pedro, don't run your horse like that!"

The vaquero drew rein and his mount skidded to a dirt-flying halt. "Sorry, *patrón*, but there's trouble on the north range."

"What kind of trouble?" Samuel had been cutting hay since first light and wasn't in the best frame of mind.

"A herd pushed onto our grass early this morning, *patrón*, maybe a hundred head of longhorns, no more."

"How many punchers?" This came from Shawn.

"Ten. Maybe twelve," Pedro said.

"See the brand?"

"No, *señor*, and I didn't wait around to find out."

"You don't need a dozen men to drive a hundred head," Samuel shook his head.

"Not unless it's Rafe Kingston opening the ball, firing longhorns at Fort Sumter," Shawn said.

Samuel looked at the three vaqueros stacking hay onto the wagon. "You men arm yourselves and mount up. Pedro, get yourself a fresh horse and come with us."

"*Sí, patrón.*"

Shawn drew his Colt and spun the cylinder, checking the loads. He thumbed a round into the empty chamber under the hammer, and smiled at his brother. "I want to be ready."

Samuel frowned. "Let's do this without shooting."

"If we can."

"Yeah, Shawn, if we can." Samuel's face clouded with concern.

The longhorns had been driven into a shallow, tree-lined valley a mile north of Glorieta Mesa and grazed among the placid Dromore Herefords. The Rafter-K punchers, a hard bunch, were dismounted and drinking coffee near a smoking fire.

When Samuel O'Brien and the others came in sight, a few men stood and adjusted the hang of their gun belts. The rest sat where they were, but their eyes were wary and missed nothing.

Samuel and Shawn drew rein. The vaqueros, outnumbered and outgunned, spread out behind them.

"Howdy, boys," Samuel said, "it seems like you've lost your way. This here is Dromore range."

The rest of the Rafter-K punchers stood. A lantern-jawed man in a black and white cowhide vest took the lead. "That's not how Mr. Kingston tells it."

"Are you the boss of this outfit?" Samuel said.

"Name's Josh Sanders. I'm the segundo."

"Well, Mr. Sanders, round up your herd and get them off Dromore range." Samuel smiled his growing anger. "I don't mean tomorrow or the next day, I mean now."

"Mr. Kingston won't like this," Sanders replied.

"I don't care what Mr. Kingston likes or dislikes," Samuel said. "His cattle are on my range and I want them gone."

Shawn watched a man on his right who stood apart from the others. He was young and had arrogant eyes. His yellow hair cascaded over his shoulders and he wore an unusual two-gun rig. A downy mustache adorned the man's top lip that seemed to be fixed in a permanent sneer. Shawn guessed that whatever the man's name was it ended in Kid—Billy the Kid, the Apache Kid, the Topeka Kid. There were plenty of Kids around and all of them were dangerous.

As Shawn watched, the Kid cocked the Colt in his right hand holster, trying to shave a fraction of a second off the draw and shoot. He'd be fast.

Shawn wondered how fast.

Josh Sanders chewed on his mustache and said to Samuel, "What O'Brien are you?"

Samuel gave his name, then added, "This is my brother Shawn."

"Shawn O'Brien." Sanders pondered over the name. "I've heard tell you're a gun hand."

"Nah," Shawn said, "I'm a lover, not a gunfighter."

The Kid's eyes moved to Shawn and stayed there. "That wasn't funny."

Shawn's stare slid over the Rafter-K riders. "Any of you men think it was funny, what I just said about being a lover?"

He was met with a sullen silence, and Shawn turned his attention to the Kid and sighed. "I guess you're right, longhair. It wasn't funny."

The Kid nodded and fixed his sneer in place. "I'll tell you something funny, O'Brien. Want to hear it?"

"Sure," Shawn said. "I like a good joke, but only if I can tell it at prayer meeting."

"Well, then here it is. If you and your brother don't cut a path off Mr. Kingston's range, I'll shoot you right off'n that pony." The Kid turned to the other riders. "What do you think, boys? Was that funny?"

The Kid was rewarded by bellows of laughter. A man said, "That's tellin' him, Dixie."

Shawn smiled. "Boy, for sure you spin better jokes than me."

"That wasn't a joke, mister."

Sanders rounded on Dixie. "Rimes, you keep your mouth shut. I'll do the talking here." He turned his attention to Samuel again. "So what if I say the herd stays right where it's at?"

Samuel didn't hesitate for a moment. "Then there will be dead men on the ground. You, me, and a heap of others."

Sanders had been around hard, violent men for most of his life and read Samuel's eyes, not liking what he saw. "Mount up, boys, we're moving the herd back to Rafter-K range. We'll let Mr. Kingston make the next move."

Sorely disappointed that Dixie Rimes was not a Kid, Shawn's voice was edged when he spoke to Sanders. "That's the wisest decision you'll make today, maybe all year."

Begrudging every word, Sanders responded. "I reckon I bit off more than I care to chaw. For now."

But Rimes wouldn't let it go. "Sanders, are we just gonna cut and run and leave the O'Briens to strut around as bulls o' the wood?"

"You heard me, Rimes. Only for now."

"You're yellow, Sanders. Yellow clean through."

It was in Shawn's mind that he would have to kill Rimes, that day or some other day, but Samuel took the play out of his hands and surprised him.

Coldly furious, he stepped out of the saddle, and advanced on Rimes, his mouth set in a hard, determined line. "Boy, I've heard enough from you."

Taken aback for a moment, Rimes's hand streaked for the cocked Colt in his holster. But Samuel's fist shot out like a striking rattlesnake and slammed into the man's chin. Rimes dropped like a polaxed steer and the revolver fell from his suddenly relaxed hand.

A tall puncher strode toward Samuel, his fists bunched, but Shawn's voice stopped him. "I wouldn't, Lofty."

The man looked at the gun in Shawn's hand and backed away.

"Good man," Shawn said. "This is a friendly fight."

Rimes got to his feet, swinging. But his efforts were clumsy and ill timed. Samuel knocked the man's flailing arms aside, then landed a left hook into Rimes's

belly. The breath knocked out of him, he made a
gasping O of his mouth and Samuel landed a straight
right to his slack chin. Rimes staggered back a step,
but Samuel stepped after him and pounded punch
after punch into the man's body and face. Rimes,
blood from his broken nose pouring over his mouth,
fell on Samuel who pushed him away and let him fall.

Shawn was impressed. Samuel had been taught
skull and knuckle fighting by Luther Ironside and
he'd been an apt student. He'd honed his skills on
dozens of rough and tumble fights with the sons of
vaqueros, losing only a few.

"Sanders," Shawn said, as Samuel, his fists still
clenched, stood over Rimes's twitching body. "You
better pick up what's left of Mr. Rimes before my
brother lays a real hurtin' on him." He turned to
Samuel. "He's had enough, Sam. I swear, sometimes
you remind me of Jacob."

Sanders turned to the tall puncher. "Long Henry,
get Dixie on his hoss."

"Wait." Samuel stripped Rimes of his Colts and
gun belts, and looked at Long Henry. "Dixie would
want me to have them, if he was conscious."

Long Henry's face was sour as curdled milk.
"O'Brien, you've played hob. Mr. Kingston won't let
this pass."

Samuel looked him in the eye. "And I don't give
a hoot."

* * *

After the Rafter-K punchers pushed the longhorn herd west and disappeared into the distance, Samuel sat his saddle in silence, his face set and grim.

"You ever going to talk again, Sam? Huh?" Shawn smiled at he brother..

Samuel stared at Shawn. "I think we just started a shooting war."

"No, Rafe Kingston started it when he pushed a herd onto Dromore range."

Samuel was a worrier and it showed in his eyes. "Do we have a legal leg to stand on?"

"I guess we'll know soon enough. Patrick is working on it."

"Going back all the way to the 1848 Treaty of Guadalupe-Hidalgo, the federal government has never been keen on the old Mexican land grants."

Shawn frowned. "But the colonel bought his grant from the army. Patrick seems to think that will make a difference. And besides, Pa has friends in Washington."

"I hope they're good friends."

"So do I, Sam, so do I."

Chapter Sixteen

Miles Lazarus was on the last leg of his journey from Galveston, his destination Albuquerque. From there he'd ride to the Rafter-K and meet with Rafe Kingston. As a gun for hire, it was not in Lazarus's nature to speculate on what manner of man his employer was. Kingston paid top wages and that was all he cared to know.

The train hammered though darkness, its dim kerosene headlight barely piercing the night. Rain rattled against Lazarus's window and ran across the pane in thin rivulets. He lay on his bunk, a glass of whiskey close, and studied the green Shabti figurine on his chest.

VERILY, I AM HERE WHEN THOU CALLEST. He read the inscription and ran his thumb over the figure, enjoying the feel of three thousand years of history. He wondered who had held the Shabti before him. Egyptian priests probably, or perhaps a queen or a doe-eyed concubine grieving for a dead pharaoh.

He closed his eyes. *My God, has it been eight years*

since the Valley of the Kings? Eight years since Lady Victoria Lytton, my beloved Vicky, died?

Miles Lazarus had made a vow to himself that he'd never look back to what had been. That knife was already buried in his heart and he'd no desire to twist it and relive the pain. But the rainy night, the close confines of the train compartment, and too much bourbon made him melancholy. Melancholy led to brooding and brooding made his mind drift back to what was. He remembered a smile, golden hair, and the musky scent of a woman in the desert heat.

Lazarus let himself journey back through the years to the summer of 1880 . . . another place and time.

The tomb lay in the east valley, a short distance off the main wadi on the west bank of the Nile at Thebes. Around the tomb entrance stretched a sun-hammered wilderness of sand and raw limestone cliffs where no breeze ever sent a shaft of coolness through the day's intolerable heat.

Sir Richard Lytton, elderly, scholarly, and dignified, was convinced that an intact burial chamber lay behind the rubble that blocked the entrance. "Miles, if I'm correct, and I believe I am, the tomb of Rameses the Fifth lies within the cliff. All we have to do is dig deep, my boy, and we'll find it." He smiled his quick, shy smile. "By Jove, Miles, we'll be famous and Vicky will be able to finally return to the green fields of her beloved Somerset."

Lazarus returned the smile, but had trouble meeting Sir Richard's eyes. The old man treated him like a son, loved him like a son probably, but he was hugging a viper to his bosom. Lazarus loved Vicky with an all-consuming passion that she returned in full. Their lovemaking burned with a devouring, white-hot heat, but afterwards and always when the fire cooled and they lay beside each other exhausted, the dry ashes of guilt sifted over them.

Vicky, a beautiful woman with huge brown eyes and corn silk hair, said it a dozen times. "Miles, we must stop this. Richard is a fine man, a kind man, and I don't want to hurt him."

She'd sit in her tent for a day, sometimes two, feigning a female problem, but always rushed back to Lazarus's arms and the flames rekindled and burned even brighter than before.

Lazarus opened drowsy eyes, memories fleeing from him, as the train *clank-clanked* to a halt, the locomotive venting steam like an iron dragon. For a while he stared at the ceiling of his compartment and listened to the sounds outside as the locomotive took on wood and water. The rain relentlessly drummed on the carriage roof and from somewhere a man yelled . . .

"Miles, we're almost there," Sir Richard yelled. He did a strange little jig. "A couple more days and we'll break through."

Lazarus stood near Vicky, but an arm's length away, so not to even hint at intimacy. "We could use some more men, Sir Richard. Where is that scoundrel Ahmed with the diggers he promised us?"

Sir Richard smiled. "He'll be here soon, I'm sure. A chap can get lost in the desert through no fault of his own."

A chiffon veil fell over Vicky's face from the brim of her pith helmet to protect her from the sun, but beads of sweat covered her forehead and across her nose. "I'm so happy for you, Richard." She smiled. "You've waited years for something like this."

"Be happy for both of us, my dear. Once the tomb is opened and the artifacts cataloged we can return to England." He smiled at her, then turned to Lazarus. "And you must come with us, Miles. Unless you're dead set on going home to America."

"It's something to think about, Sir Richard."

"Richard, I'm sure Miles wishes to remain in Egypt," Vicky said. "I don't think there's much in Somerset to interest an Egyptologist. As I recall, when we first met Miles in London he told us he absolutely loathed wet, cold, and rainy Britain."

Lazarus knew then that Vicky wanted to end it. She wanted out of a destructive, runaway relationship that could wreck three lives. He couldn't blame her, but her rejection hurt.

"Well, think about it, my boy," Sir Richard said. "I'm sure I could find you a spot in the British Museum where your talents would be put to good use."

Vicky stared straight ahead, not looking at Lazarus, as though it was a stranger who stood beside her. It was a small thing, but it was a twist of the knife.

As was his custom, Lazarus woke at dawn the following

morning and left his tent in search of ahwa, the fragrant, spiced coffee the Egyptian laborers brewed so well.

But the men were gone.

Picks and shovels lay scatted in front of the tomb entrance as though the men had left in a hurry, and their fires had burned down to ashes.

Lazarus shook Sir Richard awake and spoke softly to avoid wakening Vicky. "The laborers are gone. Every last one of them."

"Confound them, I'll bring the rascals back." Sir Richard swung his legs over the side of his bunk, pulled a pair of khaki pants over his long johns, then reached for his boots and shirt.

Once outside, Sir Richard looked around him. "Miles, whatever got into those lads? Did something scare them?"

Lazarus smiled. "Maybe the pharaoh's mummy left the tomb and chased them."

"Stranger things have happened in Egypt," the older man said. He sat on the sand, laced up his boots, and then got to his feet, pulling on his shirt. "Right, Miles, let's find those ruffians."

Those were the last words Sir Richard Lytton, soldier, scholar, and explorer, ever said. A .45 caliber bullet fired from a Martini-Henry rifle crashed into his forehead, ending his life instantly. Lazarus, standing next to him, was splattered with blood, brain, and bone.

Unarmed, Lazarus turned to face the threat. Desert raiders, five Tuaregs riding small Arab horses, charged toward him at a gallop. A huge man with a terrible scar across his face came directly at Lazarus, the curved saber in his upraised fist ready to administer a killing, downward blow.

Instinctively, Lazarus stepped back, but reached up to grab the Tuareg's billowing, blue and white robe. Trained since childhood to fight with the sword, the raider shifted his point of aim and his flickering blade slammed into the side of Lazarus's head. As the Tuareg galloped past, Lazarus fell. He saw the sand rush up to meet him, then open wide to receive his body, and he plummeted headlong into a bottomless black pit streaked with lightning bolts of searing scarlet.

He woke to pain.

His head pounded and he tasted blood in his mouth. When he reached up to touch where the sword had cut him, his fingers came away bloody. Thinking back on it later, Lazarus realized that stepping away from the Tuareg at the last second had lessened the impact of the saber and saved his life.

*But right then, a more urgent thought occupied his reeling mind—*where is Vicky?

The sun was high in the sky and Lazarus reckoned only a couple hours had passed since the attack. Vultures had already gathered, drifting like pieces of charred paper against the sky.

He rose to his feet, staggered a few steps, then immediately dropped to his knees again, the valley cartwheeling around him. He fell on his front and pressed his face into the hot sand. He couldn't get up. It was impossible.

He lay there and remembered. He'd caught a glimpse of Ahmed, the former work gang foreman, with the Tuaregs. The man was a traitor and he'd led the raiders to the camp. Lazarus rose to his hands and knees, blood from his head dropping crimson beads onto the sand. He planned to kill Ahmed. He planned to kill them all.

My God! Where is Vicky?

Again Lazarus struggled to his feet and his world continued to spin around him. He staggered to the tent where he'd left her sleeping—and found it empty.

Supporting himself with the tent pole, he stepped outside and scanned the land around the camp. He saw the distant shimmer of heat over the desert brush flats, rocks and dunes . . . a vast . . . nothingness.

Turning in the opposite direction he saw tracks leading into the desert. In the breezeless environment they would scar the sand for days, if not months. He would follow them—and find Vicky. Then take her home to England, away from this land of the dead.

He ducked back into the tent again, his head clearing, and took Sir Richard's British Army service revolvers from under his cot. The two Beaumont-Adams .442 caliber revolvers in their walnut case were complete with percussion caps, balls, wads, and a flask of powder. The beautiful revolvers were oiled and gleamed with blue light, mighty steel weapons forged in white fire hotter than the molten lakes of hell.

And Miles Lazarus's anger was no less hot and his urge to kill Ahmed and his Tuaregs consumed him like a disease.

Lazarus was not asleep, though the rocking carriage tried its best to lure him into slumber. The son of a Boston college professor and a cello-playing mother, educated at Harvard as an archeologist, he had been unfamiliar with arms and their use. As the train pulled away from the water station he closed his eyes and remembered studying the big Beaumont-Adams revolvers until he understood their ways . . .

Lazarus loaded all five chambers of each weapon with powder and ball. There were no holsters, but coiled inside the gun case were a couple of white lanyards. He clipped the lanyards to the revolvers then looped the cords around his neck. He shoved the two and a half pound weapons into the pockets of his canvas pants and stepped out of the tent.

Rounding up three canteens, he filled them from the water wagon and settled a wide-brimmed hat with a zebra skin band on his head. The international set in New York, Paris, and London called the new headgear safari hats and considered them shadier and more secure than pith helmets . . . which they were.

But Miles Lazarus paid that no mind. His entire focus was on the men who'd killed Sir Richard and taken Vicky. That the Tuareg were born to war and the most feared fighting men on the African continent did not enter into his thinking.

But it should have.

The train racketed through alternating bands of rain and no rain. Lazarus's holstered Colt hanging from a hook above his head thumped gently to the rhythm of the rails against the compartment's mahogany paneling. He took down the cartridge belt and holster and pulled his revolver, enjoying its feel, balance, and the play of lamplight on its engraving and ivory handle.

Lazarus remembered other revolvers, the pair of Beaumont-Adams .442s. Fine firearms they were, powerful and deadly . . .

Miles Lazarus followed the tracks across the desert for three days, walking even through the fierce heat of the day. He sustained himself on brackish water from the canteens and a few dried dates.

Since horses are not as enduring as men, the Tuaregs favored their mounts and stopped often to rest them. On the late morning of the third day, he found horse dung that was still moist and the tracks of men and animals much less eroded. He was close.

Two hours later, staggering forward under a sun that burned like a white-hot coin, Lazarus found Vicky.

The woman lay naked, sprawled in a rocky wadi at the base of a high, rippled sand dune. A despairing cry escaped his throat and he launched himself down the slope, tumbling head over heels the last half of the way. He rose to his feet and took a knee beside her body.

She had a single bullet wound to her right temple and in death her face was in repose, as though she was asleep. Lazarus had often propped himself on an elbow and watched her sleep, enjoying her serene, high-cheekboned beauty, the gentle rise and fall of her breasts under the sheet. But now the life in her had fled and all that remained was a pale corpse, as still and white as an alabaster statue of an Egyptian queen.

At first light Lazarus laid Vicky on the ground and covered her partially with sand. If others passed by they would not see her nakedness. He stood beside her for several minutes, piecing things together in his mind. That she had been raped was obvious. That she'd taken her own life was more obvious still. He recalled a preacher saying that a suicide could not enter heaven, but surely in Vicky's case God would make an exception.

A man not given to prayer, that last thought was all he had. He hoped it was enough.

Miles Lazarus climbed the dune and followed the tracks. The blazing anger in him had cooled to a dull black rage that lay in his belly like lead.

He found the Tuaregs at the start of the short desert twilight marking the divide between dusk and dark. They sat huddled close to a fire, brewing tea. Around them lay a small oasis consisting of a few date palms and a pond of brackish water. The Tuaregs, not expecting enemies, had stacked their British rifles and were armed only with the Haussa, a straight-bladed knife, strapped to their upper arms.

They looked up, their black eyes glittering, when Lazarus stepped among them and inflicted a terrible slaughter. The Beaumont-Adams revolvers bucking in his fists, he gunned down all five Tuaregs in the space of a few heartbeats.

Then Lazarus saw Ahmed. He had been tending the horses when the shooting began.

He ran to Lazarus and went down on his knees, his

joined hands raised in supplication. "Mercy, effendi," *he* *shrieked.* "I am but a poor man with many mouths to feed."

"You're a traitorous dog, Ahmed," *Lazarus said.*

"Indeed I am, effendi," *Ahmed wailed.* "I am dirt under *your feet, but spare me for my wife and children's sake."*

Lazarus shoved the muzzle of a revolver between Ahmed's *eyes and pulled the trigger.*

After contemplating the destruction he'd wrought, *Lazarus looked down at the smoking revolvers in his* *hands. He'd discovered a gift he'd no idea he possessed, a* *skill with arms that is bestowed on one man in ten thou-* *sand, perhaps in a hundred thousand.*

It was a skill he would use.

The train hurtled through the leaking tunnel of the night and Miles Lazarus stared open-eyed into darkness. His memories fading away like fairy gifts in the dawn light, he could barely recall the sandstorm that had swept away all traces of Vicky. He'd never found her body again. She was still in the Sahara, mummified, dry dust that had once been a beautiful, vibrant woman.Closing his eyes, willing himself to sleep, Lazarus knew that he had the capacity to love only one woman. He'd used up all the love he had. It was gone, drained, like the last grains of sand through an hourglass.

Perhaps it was for the best. A man who killed for a living needed no love in his soul.

Chapter Seventeen

Jacob O'Brien waited until breakfast was eaten
and only he and Patrick remained at the table before
mentioning his dream.

Samuel and Shawn had left early and were already
out on the range. The colonel had retired to his
study where he was intent on spoiling his grandson.

"Want to hear about it, Pat?" Jacob asked.

Patrick dabbed his mouth and mustache with his
napkin and smiled. "I have an appointment in Santa
Fe with an army major about this land grant business.
But I guess I can spare you a few minutes."

"Maybe some other time."

"No, tell me, Jake. I always like to hear about your
dreams. They're always kind of bizarre."

"This one was."

"Then shoot."

Jacob lit a cigarette, tested the temperature of the
dregs of his coffee, and made a face. Finally he said,
"I was in a desert."

"Good place to start."

"But it wasn't here. I mean, it was in a foreign country."

"How did you know that?"

"I don't know how I knew it. I just knew."

"Ah, now it's getting bizarre." Patrick grinned. "Go on."

"Well, I was on top of a sand dune and I saw this tall man walking toward me. He had a revolver in each hand and he planned to kill me."

"Did he tell you that he was aiming to puncture you with bullets?"

Jacob shook his head. "No, again I just knew that was his plan. He was walking fast, kicking up a cloud of sand with every step."

"So you drew down on him, huh?"

"No, I didn't. I just stood there and let the man get closer."

"Then what happened?"

"I don't know. I woke up."

Patrick laughed. "Jake, that's a boring dream. There wasn't even a woman in it."

"But what did it mean, Pat?"

"It means the summer heat is getting to you. That's why you dreamed you were in a desert."

"And the man with the revolvers?"

"That was the colonel."

Jacob laughed. "I guess it's always the colonel in my nightmares."

"And mine, too, if I don't saddle up and get out of here."

After Patrick left Jacob poured himself more

coffee and lit another cigarette. He was finishing both when the door opened and Luther Ironside stepped inside.

Ironside was healing well from his wounds, but he'd lost weight and was weaker than he made out to be. He'd refused to stay in bed and was dressed in range clothes and a pair of fringed shotgun chaps. "Jake, you got something planned for today?"

"Sam wants me to stay around the house. I guess he's afraid Rafe Kingston might show up."

Ironside took the makings from Jacob's shirt pocket. "That Hereford bull we just bought has wandered away again. And this time he took a couple of heifers with him." He lit his cigarette and dropped tobacco and papers back into Jacob's pocket. "You mind rounding him up? I'll stay on guard here."

"What direction was he headed?"

"South. He always heads south. I guess he wants to go back to Texas."

Jacob rose to his feet. "I'll bring him back."

"I appreciate it, Jake. I'd go myself, but I just ain't up for it yet."

"Keep your eyes skinned for Kingston's boys," Jacob said. "He might try to put the sneak on you."

"If he tries that, it'll be his first time an' last time." Ironside tested the coffeepot, then poured an inch into a cup and drank it, giving him time to gather his thoughts before speaking again. "I spoke to the colonel last night. Talked him into waiting a week to see if the marshal gets here before he moves against Rafe Kingston."

"Pa's taken a set against Kingston and he won't rest until the man is behind bars on a charge of murder," Jacob pointed out.

Ironside nodded. "It's all about the rule of law and the American way, and the colonel stands by both those things. Them sin-eaters were murdered near enough on his own doorstep and he won't let that go."

"He could lose Dromore."

"If that's the price he has to pay to see Kingston hang, then he'll pay it."

"Maybe the marshal will get here and we can avoid a war."

"Amen to that, Jake. We've been in a range war afore, down there on the Estancia, and it ain't a thing I'd care to repeat anytime soon."

"Me neither. But the colonel's a man of principle and a war could be forced on him." Jacob stepped to the door.

Ironside's voice stopped him. "Jake, this Miles Lazarus feller . . . how good is he?"

"I guess he's as good as he needs to be, Luther. From what I've heard, it seems a lot of folks set store by him." Jake smiled. "And he walks on sand."

"Hell, Jake, what does that mean?"

"I don't know, Luther. I just don't know."

It was almost noon when Jacob picked up the tracks of the Herefords in timbered, broken country a couple of miles north of Mesa de la Mula. As Ironside had predicted, the cattle were aimlessly moving south. Jacob followed the tracks, riding up on several places where they'd stopped to graze, and then saw that the bull had led the way east along a dry wash, in the direction of the Simpson's Nugget ghost town.

He had often seen the town at a distance but had never stopped there. The rumor was that old Jed Simpson himself haunted the place, forever grieving for the Spanish gold mine he'd found, then lost again. A lot of prospectors had offered to help Jed find the mine and within a couple years the town boasted a population of several hundred. But by 1867 disillusionment, coupled with Apache attacks, forced the abandonment of the place and it was slowly fading away like a Civil War tintype.

Jacob cursed the Hereford. The animal didn't have a lick of sense. If the bull holed up in the ghost town he'd have a devil of a time rousting him and the two heifers out of there.

The dry wash led straight toward Simpson's Nugget, then curved around the east side of town. Juniper, piñon, and mesquite had invaded the place and spread branches inside a couple of buildings. Bunch grass and sagebrush grew in the single street, but when Jacob rode in, he saw tracks in the dust, some barefoot, others made by boots.

It seemed Simpson's Nugget had not given up the ghost just yet.

He dropped his hand to his gun as he looked around. The town consisted of a cluster of shacks, sod shanties, and several more substantial timber buildings—a saloon, general store, and what looked like a bank. The rough-sawn boards had turned silver with time and many had warped, yanking rusty nails from their frames. A smell of decay and an echoing silence hung over the town as though the buildings were quietly pining for the sound of human voices once again.

The saloon door swung open and a gray-haired woman stepped into the street, carrying a water bucket.

Jacob lifted his hand to touch his hat brim. "Howdy, ma'am. I'm looking for a Hereford bull and a couple cows. Have you seen sich?"

The woman stared at him, through him, then turned and walked to the town well. She tied a rope to the bucket and dropped it into the water. Following the splash she waited, hands on hips, for the bucket to fill.

Jacob took the woman for a squatter on land Dromore claimed as its south range. But that was Samuel's concern, not his.

Without sparing Jacob a glance, she lopsidedly carried the bucket to the saloon and disappeared inside.

A moment later a man wearing a gun stepped out and stared at Jacob, his scarred face scowling. "What are you doing here, cowboy?"

The man's tone was belligerent, but Jacob let it pass. "I'm looking for cattle that strayed off their home range."

"A Hereford bull and a couple of cows?"

"Yeah, that's them."

"They're penned up out back."

Jacob smiled, deciding to be sociable. "It's real white of you to keep them for me. I'll mosey around there and get them."

"The hell you will," the man growled. "Them cows belong to me."

"They belong to the Dromore Ranch."

"Finders keepers. My gain, your loss, my friend."

"That's a seven hundred dollar bull, mister," Jacob explained.

"Good, then he'll bring an even thousand in Old Mexico."

The door opened and two other men stepped into the street. Like the first one, they were dressed in whatever shirts and pants they could buy or steal, but their boots and gun belts were of good quality and their Colts were low and handy.

The last thing Jacob wanted was a fight, but he would not return to Dromore without the Herefords. That was not the O'Brien way.

His eyes moved beyond the three gunmen to the saloon window, only one pane of glass remaining from its original four. There were a couple of faces peering at him from behind the glass, children about seven or eight years old by the look of them.

Jacob silently cursed. If he drew and cut loose, his bullets could hit the kids and there was no Hereford bull on earth worth the lives of two children.

Besides that, odds of three to one were not to be taken lightly.

Playing the part of an aggrieved puncher, Jacob said, "Colonel O'Brien won't like this."

"I don't care what he likes or dislikes," the man said. "From what I hear, he can afford to lose a few cattle."

"I'll tell him that." Jacob nodded.

"Yeah, you do that, and be grateful you're getting out of here alive."

One of the other men, a thickset Mexican with a blue chin and a carrion-eater's eyes, grinned, showing a mouthful of gold teeth. "Want me to gun him, Link?"

"Nah, let him go." The man's eyebrows shot up, as though a sudden inspiration had just hit him. "Hey, Tin Cup, how much you figure that there hoss is worth."

The man called Tin Cup ran his eyes over Jacob's mount. "Hoss, saddle, and bridle, his guns, way more than the bull is worth. He ain't no thirty-a-month puncher, Newt, an' that's a natural fact."

"Looks like you're walking, my friend, whoever you are." Newt's gun flashed into his hand. "Now climb down."

"I'm no gunfighter, so I guess I'm facing a stacked deck." Jacob allowed his voice to quiver a little.

"I'd say that, but if your boots ain't on the dirt real quick you'll be dead and all your worries will be all over."

"Don't shoot." Jacob swung out of the saddle and as his right leg came down he jabbed a spur into his mount's hock. Startled, the big black jerked into a canter as Jacob held on to the horn. He let himself drag for a few yards, then let go of the horn, rolled, and came up with a gun in his hand.

Jacob ignored Newt and shot at the Mexican, figuring he was the fastest gun of the three. His bullet hit the man in the belly and he shrieked and staggered back. Dirt kicked up close to Jacob as Newt fired. Jacob fired back, missed, and fired again. Hit hard, Newt rose up on his toes and fell on his face.

Alarm bells rang in Jacob's head. *Where is the third gunman?* He swung his gun to cover the saloon.

A moment later, a shotgun blasted from inside. His arms cartwheeling, Tin Cup crashed backward through the door and splintered it off its hinges. His back hit the ground and raised a cloud of dust. He groaned once and lay still.

Still wary, his ears ringing from the roar of the guns, Jacob saw that Newt and Tin Cup were dead. Only the Mexican showed signs of life. The man's scarlet hands clutched at his belly, teeth clenched against pain that was beyond pain. Gray death filmed his eyes. "Who . . . are you?" There was blood on his lips.

"Name's Jacob O'Brien."

"Why didn't you tell us that?"

"There wasn't time for proper introductions."

"I'm . . . I'm . . ." the man fought against the stunning agony in his belly. "It doesn't matter who I am. Do it, O'Brien."

"*Vaya con Dios, mi amigo.*" Jacob shot the Mexican between the eyes and put an end to his pain.

The gray-haired woman stepped through the shattered doorway, a smoking scattergun in the crook of her arm. "Are they all dead?"

Jacob glanced at the Mexican. "They are now."

"They planned to take me and my children to Mexico and sell us. Then you came along."

"All I wanted was the bull back." Jacob shook his head.

"He's behind the saloon."

"Yes. I know."

The woman looked at Tin Cup's body sprawled in the street. "Now I've killed two men."

Jacob was surprised. "There was a fourth bandit?"

"No. It was a while ago, after a rancher fenced in our wagons." She turned bleak eyes to Jacob. "We had the cholera among the wagons, you see. It killed some and spared others for reasons I don't understand."

"What's your name, ma'am?" Jacob said, his interest in the woman quickening.

"Constance Baker." Then, for no apparent no reason, she said, "I'm twenty-seven years old."

Jacob thought maybe the woman was excusing her gray hair.

That was the case, because she added, "I had jet black hair until recently. Strange, isn't it?"

"My name is Jacob O'Brien and I know about the wagons. You've been through it."

Constance said nothing. Her children, as timid as deer, stepped through the door and clung to her skirt. The skirt was bright red, a color Jacob had seen worn by saloon girls, but never by respectable women. A cast-off, he decided. Constance Baker had the drawn look of someone who'd gone hungry too many times.

"What about them?" She pointed at the dead men.

"I'll find a place for them." Jacob stripped the dead men's guns and belts and gave them to the woman. "You can sell these."

"I don't want them." Constance propped the shotgun against the saloon wall. "I don't want that either. It belonged to them."

Jacob dragged the bodies behind his horse until he was half a mile from the ghost town and left them in an arroyo. Returning to the saloon, he remembered the gray faces of the dead men turned to a sky they could no longer see.

A strong wind had picked up and Simpson's Nugget banged and creaked and groaned, a gaunt ghost bewailing its fate.

Jacob rode to the back of the saloon where the renegades had made sloppy and makeshift repairs to a pole corral. Their horses were there and the Herefords. The saloon sheltered the corral from the worst of the wind and the black entered without a fuss.

Ignoring the back door to the saloon, he walked head bent against the brawling wind to the front and called out the woman's name before he stepped inside.

Constance sat at a table with her children, sharing

a meal of bacon fried with pounded hardtack. "Would you care for some?"

Jacob heard the hesitancy in her voice, as though she feared an affirmative answer, for, in truth, the meal was barely enough for her and the kids. "No, thank you. But I smell coffee."

"On the stove." Constance nodded her head in that direction. "Newt Dunn and his men had coffee with them. There's sugar, too, if you like it sweet."

"It's just fine as it comes, ma'am." Jacob strode to the stove and poured coffee from a rusty pot into a rusty cup. Drawing a rickety chair to the table he sat down and took out the makings. Observing proprieties even in a ghost town, he asked, "May I crave your indulgence, ma'am?"

"Please do," Constance said. The kids had finished eating and the boy, still hungry, licked the plate.

Jacob lit his cigarette. "How did you escape the fence?"

"When the shooting started."

Constance saw the question on Jacob's face. "Some of the men who could still stand tried to break out, my husband among them. The cowboys started firing on them and I saw my husband fall. He was dead when I reached him. I picked up his revolver and turned and ran to get the children."

"And then what happened? I imagine there was a lot of shooting and confusion."

"No, by the time I got the children the shooting was over. All the men who tried to break out were dead. But all the cowboys were together, firing into the bodies, and that's when I tried the fence."

"And you made it."

"Yes, we crawled under the bottom strand of wire." She turned and showed her back. The white shirt she wore was slashed with cuts and streaked with dried blood. "I was bigger than the children and the wire was low and cut me up badly."

"But you got away." Despite the depression that weighed on him, Jacob managed a smile. "Obviously."

Constance took the plate from her son. "It's all gone. You've licked it clean." Then to Jacob, "We almost didn't get away. A cowboy saw us and galloped at us as though he was going to ride us down. But he had a gun in his hand."

The woman closed her eyes for a few moments, and then opened them again. "I shot him."

Jacob didn't push it, but Constance wanted to give voice to what she'd relived when her eyes were closed. "He galloped past us then fell off his horse. I grabbed the children and we ran into the trees."

"And then you came here?"

"There were mountains to the west, so we went the other way. Then Newt Dunn found us and brought us here. He said he was a desperate man who was on the scout and if we gave him any trouble he'd kill all three of us. He said he'd take us to Old Mexico and sell us to a good home." Constance shook her head. "It was as though we were just animals to him."

"Ma'am, did they . . . I mean . . ." Jacob didn't finish his sentence.

"No, they didn't. Mr. O'Brien, Newt told me I was a dried up old crone and that no man would want me and that's why he'd sell me cheap." She stared at Jacob, her eyes pleading. "Do I really look like that? Like an old crone?"

"No, of course you don't." Talking pretties didn't come easily to him, but he reached deep. "You're a little tired, is all."

"My hair is gray."

"It will come back."

Constance studied Jacob's face. "The light's gone out in your eyes. Why is that?"

"I get this way sometimes." He saw the woman wait for an explanation, and said, "Depression is rage spread mighty thin. I guess I'm angry that those men made me kill them. I'm angry that your husband was killed and your kids are hungry." Again he managed a slight smile. "I'm just angry, I suppose."

"I am a sin-eater. Does that make you angry?"

"No, that doesn't make me angry."

"It seems sin-eaters spend all our lives in a wagon, hounded out of one town, trying our luck in the next."

"Is what you do so evil?"

"No, we take on the sins of the deceased. Is that evil?"

"Depends on the sins, I guess," Jacob said.

"Big sins, little sins, we take them all." Constance smiled. "We live in hell so the dead loved one can live in heaven."

"And what happens when you go to meet your Maker, weighed down by other people's sins?"

"God will understand. He knows we only strive to do good and how persecuted we are. He'll forgive us. I believe that."

The blustering wind drove sand through the saloon windows and door and threatened to lift the roof off the building. The warped false front rattled like a snare drum and Jacob figured the whole place could come down around their ears. Blowing sand obscured the sun and shadows gathered in the webbed corners where the spiders lived.

"Ma'am," Jacob began.

"Please, Constance."

"Constance, the man who built the fence and murdered your husband and the others is a rancher by the name of Rafe Kingston. My father and brothers plan to bring him to justice for his crimes, and we've already sent for a United States marshal." His hands busy building another cigarette, Jacob said, "There was another survivor, a girl. Her name is Alice and—"

"Why that's Alice Brownlee," Constance said. "She was a little orphan girl. She managed to escape?"

"Yes, she did, and we want her to testify in court against Kingston, but she's too young. A defense lawyer would eat her alive."

"So you want me to testify?"

"Yes, I do."

"Then I will. If this Kingston man is the one behind the fence he should answer for it."

Jacob felt a surge of relief. "Constance, I want you and the kids to come with me to my family's ranch. It's called Dromore and it lies just to the north of here."

"I'm not leaving here, Mr. O'Brien."

"But . . . Constance! You're down to the blanket. You'll starve to death in this place."

"The Lord will provide, Mr. O'Brien."

"Why do you want to live in a ghost town? There's nothing here but . . . ghosts."

"I told you it seems I've spent all my life moving from town to town, a few times chased by a tar and feather mob. Both my children were born in the back of a wagon and now, for them and me, I want a house that doesn't move."

"Not here," Jacob said. "Not in a tumbledown saloon in the middle of nowhere."

The wind shrieked a war song as it pounded Simpson's Nugget. Sand rattled like buckshot against the tottering buildings and the sky had turned the color of rusted iron.

"For the moment at least, I have everything I need, Mr. O'Brien," Constance said. "There's a heating stove over there and plenty of firewood. I can cook on that stove."

"But you've nothing to cook," Jacob said, his frustration growing as his black mood grew darker.

The woman nodded and smiled. "I admit that's a problem I haven't solved yet."

"You'll never solve it here. You and the kids can't eat grass."

"I know that, Mr. O'Brien."

The boy took mention of food as his cue. "Ma, I'm still hungry."

"Me too, Ma." The girl looked to be about five, her brother maybe a year older.

Jacob looked at the pale, pinched faces of the children and suddenly remembered the lunch Sarah had packed for him. There was probably enough in his saddlebags to feed three strong men, let alone a woman and two little kids. He rose to his feet. "I'll be right back."

Chapter Eighteen

Constance Baker waited fifteen minutes but Jacob had not returned. She sat at the table with the kids for a while longer then, worried, got to her feet. "Adam, Martha, stay here. I'll be right back."

She realized she had just echoed Mr. O'Brien's words before he left. *Where is he?*

The woman retraced Jacob's steps to the back door of the saloon and stepped outside. The horses and cattle stood with their butts to the wind, but sheltered by the building, they didn't seem to be in any distress.

Jacob's big black was still there and the horses of Newt Dunn and his men. A pair of saddlebags lay on the ground and Constance picked them up. One bag was open and inside was a brown paper package loosely tied with string.

Is this why Mr. O'Brien left? To bring his saddlebags inside?

The wind tugged at her skirt, lifted strands of her hair and tossed it across her face. The driving sand stung and when she glanced at the tan colored sky the sun had disappeared.

Constance put her hand to her mouth and yelled, "Mr. O'Brien, are you there?"

Her words were flung back at her by the wind and her open mouth was gritty with sand. There was a space of about ten feet between the saloon door and the corral and Constance walked to the corner of the building.

She called out for Jacob again, but again there was no answer.

Constance stepped into the alley between the saloon and the adjoining building, but the tunneling wind and hurling sand drove her back to shelter.

A door slammed somewhere off to her left and she walked to the opposite corner of the saloon. The door banged again, with more force.

"Mr. O'Brien!" Constance shouted. Then, realizing such formality in the middle of a raging sandstorm was ridiculous, called out, "Jacob!"

She heard nothing but the *bang bang bang* of the door, a muffled drum adding to the doom of the dreary, wind-torn day.

Ten yards of open ground separated the saloon from the building next door. The former hardware store was set back from the street, in front of it was the carcass of a broken-backed freight wagon. Wary of leaving her children alone any longer, Constance still worried that Jacob could be hurt and had slammed the door to attract her attention.

Or was it just the wind?

The woman made up her mind and made a dash for it. Stung by hurling sand that stung like a swarm of hornets, she ran to the front of the store and bolted inside. Opposite her, where once the entrance to the back of the shop had been, a door hung askew on one hinge and slammed back and forth in the wind.

There was no sign of Jacob O'Brien.

Suddenly Constance was afraid. If someone, or something, had taken a full-grown, armed man, what might it do to her and her children?

Her eyes burning red with grit, she returned to the saloon and stepped inside.

Into a scene of horror.

Jacob O'Brien, bloody and stripped to the waist, sprawled across a table on his back, his eyes closed. Around him stood three men, all of them rank, giving off a feral, wild animal smell. They wore greasy, beaded buckskins, their necks adorned with bear claw necklaces and their chests with scalp locks.

Constance had seen their kind before. They were the worst of the frontier riffraff, killers who made a living scalping Apaches to sell to the Mexican government. If there were not enough Apaches available, they substituted the scalps of Mexican peons and no one knew the difference, or cared. But the scalp trade had dried up with the end of the Apache wars, and men like these were looking for a new line of work, so long as it was dishonest and easy.

One of the men stepped forward, grinning, showing teeth that looked like green slime on beach rocks. "Well, well, well, what do we have here?"

"Who are you men?" Constance asked, pretending a confidence she didn't feel. Her children ran to her and buried their faces in her skirt.

"You gonna do her, Eli?" Dirty yellow hair fell in tangles over the man's shoulders to his waist.

"Well, Ezra, she ain't much, but she's better than nothing," Eli said.

Knowing her fear showed, Constance asked again, "Who are you?" Her voice rose. "And what have you done with Mr. O'Brien?"

Eli glanced at Jacob. "Nothing, yet. He's got a bump on his head, is all." He looked at the saddlebags Constance still held in her hand. "What you got in your poke, little lady?"

"I don't know. The saddlebags belong to Mr. O'Brien."

Eli grabbed them. "Let's take a look." He removed the brown paper package and undid the string. "It's grub, boys."

Sarah had packed two thick roast beef sandwiches and a golden wedge of sponge cake, a red line of strawberry jam in its middle.

Eli picked up the cake in his dirty paw. "Ezra, Enoch, grab a sandwich."

"Mr. O'Brien intended that for my children," Constance informed them.

Ignoring her, Ezra said, "Hey, Eli, a feller read to me from a newspaper one time and it said that old

Queen Vic likes that kind of cake. I mean, the kind with jam in it."

Eli grinned. "Then I'm eating like royalty."

"How can you eat that when my children are hungry?" Constance fisted her hands and stomped her foot.

"That's their hard luck, ain't it?" Eli forced the last of the cake into his mouth with the palm of his hand. "Enoch, go see if Newt's hosses are out back."

"They're out back," Constance said.

"Enoch, go see," Eli said again.

The man returned quickly. "The hosses are there. I recognized Newt's dun."

"So where is Newt?" Eli looked at Constance. "I'm talking to you."

"I don't know."

"He said he'd meet us here," Eli said. "We got a job planned, a bank up Santa Fe way. So where is he?"

"I don't know," Constance repeated.

Eli's backhand was sudden and hard enough to knock the woman off her feet. The two children went down with her.

"Where is Newt?" Eli grabbed Constance's arm and hauled her to her feet. "You got ten seconds or I'll shoot the girl. Another ten and I'll gun the boy."

"I killed them." Jacob raised himself on the table to a sitting position.

"You're a liar," Eli said. "Maybe you could've taken Newt, but you sure didn't draw faster then the Mexican."

"None of them were worth a dime." Jacob said.

Eli pointed at him. "You shut up. I'm thinking." After a few moments he looked at his brother. "Ezra, can we take that bank alone?"

"It was Newt's play, Eli. He had it down, did Newt. He wasn't a man to throw a rope without building a loop first."

"He didn't know nothin' we don't know," Eli said. "We'll take it ourselves."

"Brother Eli, what about them?" Enoch pointed at Constance and the children.

Eli was quiet for a moment, thinking. "We'll enjoy the woman for a spell, then kill them all."

"The brats as well?" Enoch asked.

"Well, we sure ain't takin' them with us."

"And him?" Enoch nodded at Jacob.

"I'll kill him my ownself. I figure he shot ol' Newt an' them in the back." Eli grabbed Constance's arm. "You come with me, girlie."

"Eli, you're an idiot. But I reckon you know that already." Jacob stared at him.

Eli drew his gun, the triple click of the hammer being drawn back loud in the room. "Right, cowboy, you get it first." He raised the Colt. "Here it comes, smack between the eyes."

Chapter Nineteen

"I'm worth a fortune to you alive," Jacob O'Brien said quickly. "And so is the woman."

Eli hesitated. "If you're telling me a windy you get it in the belly first."

"Pull in your horns, Eli," Jacob said. "How much is the bank job worth to you? If you can even take it, that is. Looking at you three I don't have much confidence in that."

"Newt said five thousand."

"Each?"

"No. It's a hick bank in a hick town."

"The woman is worth twice that and maybe more." Jacob grinned. "And I'm worth twice what the woman is."

"You on the scout?" Eli's eyes glittered. "Got a dead or alive reward on your back-shootin' hide, maybe?"

"Nope, nothing like that."

Eli waited, expecting more, but Jacob only sat there, his fingers probing the bloody gash on his head.

Frustrated, Eli let out a swoosh of breath. "Mister, say it plain. An' remember, any more high-talkin' an' you get leaded."

"Feed the kids," Jacob said pointedly.

Eli was too taken aback to be angry. "What are you talking about?"

"Before I tell you how you can make enough money to keep you all in whiskey and whores for the rest of your life, feed the kids. You must have brought grub with you."

Eli turned to his brothers. "Do you believe this?"

Ezra shook his head. "I hear it, but I ain't believing it."

"Mister," Eli said, "you're a toothless dog and a toothless dog chews careful. You catching my drift?"

Jacob shrugged. "Then let a fortune slip through your fingers, Eli. See if I give a damn."

A silence stretched, taut as a fiddle string.

Eli frowned. "Ezra, bring in the grub."

"You doin' what he tells you?" Ezra looked at Eli in surprise.

"Bring the grub!" Eli shouted. "Now you git or I'll take a whip to you!"

Muttering to himself, Ezra stepped outside into the raging wind. Eli watched him go, then turned to Jacob. "Mister, my patience is wearing mighty thin. Are you gonna make war talk or do I gun you? Make your choice."

Jacob sighed as though he was about to disclose a secret he'd rather keep to himself. "The woman's name is Constance Baker. She belongs to a rancher named Rafe Kingston over to the Rio Grande country. But she ran away from home and took their two kids with her. Kingston offered me ten thousand to bring her back and offered to up the fee if she's in good shape and hasn't been messed with, if you catch my meaning."

Eli's slow mind sifted through Jacob's words, then he looked at Constance. "Is this true, what he's saying?"

The woman's eyes met Jacob's for an instant, read their message. "I don't want to go back. He . . . he beats me."

"I don't care about that," Eli said. "Is he offering a ten thousand dollar reward for you?"

"Rafe is a rich man," Constance said. "He must be offering a big reward because Jacob O'Brien is a bounty hunter and he doesn't come cheap."

Eli turned his attention back to Jacob. "Is that your name, mister? O'Brien?"

"Yeah, that's my handle."

"From up in the Glorieta Mesa country?"

"Right again, Eli. And my pa will pay plenty to get me back alive."

"I heard he's a Mick and a heller. They say he's hung more men than old Judge Parker."

"That's not true," Jacob said. "My daddy is a kindly, white-haired gentleman and his old heart will break if anything happens to me."

"Is he thirty thousand, kindly?" Eli asked.

"Yes. That and more."

Greed makes a man gullible, and Eli fell head over

heels for Jacob's story. "I knew the Cotton brothers were destined for great things. This clinches it as a copper-bottomed certainty."

"Seems like," Jacob agreed.

Ezra came back inside and made a show of slapping sand from his buckskins. "Here's the grub, Eli." He held up a burlap sack.

"What have we got?"

"Same as we always got, salt pork an' tortillas."

"You, woman, clash the pan and feed your kids. Feed yourself as well." Eli shook his head and scowled. "Ten thousand for a scrawny old hen like you. The rancher feller has more money than sense. An' feed O'Brien. He's damn near as scrawny as you."

Constance was busy with the children and the three brothers were off in a corner talking in whispers. Jacob sat at a table and ate, glad to be left alone for a spell.

He chewed on a slice of salt pork wrapped in a stale tortilla and figured that he'd ended the danger to the woman, at least for now. As for himself, Eli would keep him alive so long as he believed the colonel would pay a ransom.

Jacob had considered talking Eli into heading for Dromore first. But the colonel would never pay a ransom and Eli could get mad clean through and shoot his prisoners, figuring they were worthless to him. Better to take his chances with Rafe Kingston—slight as they were.

The Rafter-K was a ways off, and a lot could happen on the way there. What he needed to do was get hold of a gun, but the odds on that were also mighty slim.

Jacob's depression had fled as the danger around him mounted. But the gloom returned as he figured he was facing a stacked deck without a hole card.

He watched Eli walk to the door and look into the street. He cursed. "Will this storm never end?"

"Anxious to get your mitts on all that money, huh?" Jacob smiled.

"Yeah, or put a bullet in you, whatever comes first."

"You're a first-rate fellow, Eli. True blue. Anybody ever told you that before?"

Eli shook his head. "No, nobody ever did."

"Gee, I wonder why," Jacob said.

"Keep talking, scarecrow man," Eli said, his bearded face ugly. "Your time will come real soon. Depend on it." He stepped to the door again and after a few moments turned and kicked a rickety chair with such force it splintered apart. "I've had enough of this. Ezra, Enoch, saddle up, we're riding."

"In a sandstorm?" Enoch looked at Eli like he was crazy.

"Yeah, in a sandstorm. Saddle O'Brien's horse and one for the woman. The brats can ride behind them."

Enoch shook his head. "Eli, I hope you know what you're doing."

"Better than you do. Now saddle them horses."

* * *

The wind tore the words from Jacob's mouth, but Constance heard them. "I'm holding up just fine," she yelled back. She looked at the kids, then leaned from the saddle closer to Jacob. "I don't know about the children."

The girl was up behind Jacob and had her face buried in his back. Adam clung to his mother, his arms around her waist.

Eli rode about a hundred yards ahead, but Ezra and Enoch rode close behind Jacob, rifles across their saddle horns. Both men had their heads bent against the wind and looked miserable, but they were alert and ready. Jacob had no doubt about that.

Eli chose the trail west, leading the others through broken, timbered country. Around them, pines tossed in the wind, scattering needles, and higher, above the aspen line, a ponderosa cracked like a rifle shot and broke in half.

Sand drove against the riders and after an hour talk became impossible, drowned out by the roar of the unceasing wind.

His face covered thick with dust, Jacob looked like a gray ghost, his half-closed eyes red and inflamed. None of the others were faring any better, and behind him he heard one of the brothers curse, a brief, rough yelp of anger before the wind dragged the words away.

Squinting ahead of him, Jacob saw Eli's horse get hit by a gust of wind, stumble, and go down.

And he took his chance.

Chapter Twenty

Jacob O'Brien pushed Martha into Constance's startled arms, and kicked his black into motion. He charged directly at Eli who had scrambled to his feet. Behind him he heard a surprised yelp, then a bullet cracked the air an inch from his right ear.

Eli reacted quickly. His hand dropped to his gun and he got off a quick shot—a miss—before Jacob was on top of him. He slammed his horse into Eli's left side. The man staggered back and fell. He fired again, but his shot went wild.

Jacob launched himself from the saddle, landing boot-heels-first on Eli's belly. The man gasped as his breath blasted out of him and for a moment he lay still. Rolling off Eli, Jacob quickly got to his feet, aware of Enoch and Ezra galloping toward them, Colts in their hands. Eli got to his hands and knees and scrambled around until he found his gun. He tried to push himself erect, but a savage kick to the face from Jacob put the scalp-hunter down, blood spurting from his nose and mouth.

With no time to assess the damage he'd done, Jacob dived for Eli's revolver, wrenching the gun out of the man's hand and thumbing the hammer. There was no triple click. The Colt's cylinder was stuck fast with grime and sand. Cursing Eli for a dirty scoundrel, Jacob turned and ran for the man's horse and booted Winchester. He felt the burn of a bullet across his right shoulder.

Ezra fought his rearing mount and tried to bring his Colt to bear for a second shot. To Jacob's surprise, Enoch had turned and was riding after Constance, who was galloping to the west with a child in front and a child behind her.

Driving sand lashing at him like a cat-o'-nine-tails, Jacob dodged the flying hooves of Ezra's horse and made a grab for the man. Ezra swayed in the saddle, easily avoiding Jacob's grasp and again bringing down his Colt for a killing shot.

Fighting a rising surge of panic, Jacob made a grab for the rifle under Ezra's knee. The Winchester slid clear and Jacob stepped around the front of the horse—and got a painful kick in the ribs for his pains.

With Ezra broadside to him, Jacob racked a round into the chamber and fired.

Ezra fired at the same instant. Firing off the back of a restive horse, a .44-40 round in his belly, he managed to get off a shot that came dangerously close to Jacob's head.

Jacob pumped two more shots into Ezra and watched him fall.

The man had shown sand and Jacob O'Brien

appreciated that. Later, he would grudgingly admit that Ezra had done well.

After a quick glance at Eli, who was again on all fours, strands of bloody saliva from his mouth bending in the wind, Jacob rushed to his own mount and went after Enoch.

Enoch was a hundred yards away and had dragged Constance onto the back of his horse. The children stood watching, the girl crying. To Jacob's horror, Enoch drew down on them. The man obviously considered Constance the valuable prisoner and her kids just a nuisance.

Unlike his brother Samuel and Luther Ironside, Jacob was no great shakes with a rifle, but he had to take the shot—and make it. He yanked his horse to a halt and fired from the shoulder a split second later.

Constance screamed as Enoch's hat blew off and with it the top of his skull. Blood and brain splattered over the woman's face as Enoch toppled from the saddle and thudded, a dead weight, to the ground.

Jacob galloped to Constance. Ignoring her shrieks as her hands came bloody from her face, he swung out of the saddle and gathered up the kids. He threw them on the back of Constance's horse, grabbed the reins, and remounted. Gathering up the reins of Enoch's mount, all three horses trotted in the direction of Eli, who was on his feet but staggering.

Holding her hands out to Jacob, Constance said, "Look, I'm covered in blood and . . . and . . ."

"You can wash," Jacob said bluntly.

"But it got in my mouth!"

"Woman," Jacob shouted, the storm pummeling him, "quit your whining. When we get to Dromore you can take a bath."

"I'm done, O'Brien." Eli's hands hung at his sides. His nose was pulped from Jacob's kick and both his eyes were black.

"You were done a long time ago," Jacob said.

"Let bygones be bygones, I always say." Eli looked up at Jacob. "Will you give me the road?"

"Letting bygones be bygones isn't my style." Jacob triggered a rifle shot into Eli's chest and the man dropped to his knees, his expression a mix of disbelief and fear.

"You ain't a forgettin' man, right enough," Eli gasped and fell on his face, dead when he hit the ground.

Already hysterical from her experience with Enoch, Constance's voice was shrill. "Did you have to kill him like that?"

"He had his chance," Jacob said.

"You're . . . you're a killer like he was."

"There isn't too much doubt about that, lady."

Chapter Twenty-one

The wind dropped, the turbulent sand fell back to earth, and the late afternoon sun reappeared.

"The sandstorms in Egypt are much worse. In late March to mid-April they sweep in from the desert and kill people and livestock." Miles Lazarus turned and looked at Lucy Masters. "Hundreds of people sometimes."

"You loved Egypt, didn't you?" Lucy smiled. "The great deserts and the blue Nile River."

Lazarus stood at the parlor window of the Kingston ranch house, watching punchers outside mount up to inspect the range for storm damage. "Loved it and hated it. The Nile isn't blue, it's kind of muddy brown, and the desert . . . well, if it kills someone we love we can grow to hate it." He returned Lucy's smile. "I guess the ancient Egyptians felt the same way."

"At dinner last night you said you'd entered tombs," Lucy said. "That must have been a most singular thing to do."

"It was. Of course they'd all been looted, but in some cases the mummies were still intact."

"Robbers?" Lucy asked, surprised. "I thought Egyptians would . . . what's the word? . . . revere the tombs."

Lazarus nodded. "Many did, but the lure of gold and jewels, easy money, can overcome piety. The ancient Egyptians themselves, often at the behest of their pharaohs, robbed the tombs. So did the Greeks, Romans, Arabs, French, and British." He smiled. "And a few Americans."

"I would've liked to have been an Egyptian princess. Wear gauzy dresses and live in a marble palace."

"And die from parasites and disease before you were thirty? I don't think you'd like that. And the palaces were built from mud bricks and limestone, not marble."

Lucy laughed, a pleasant peal of sound in the overly ornate room. "No, you're right. I don't think I'd have liked that."

The parlor door opened and Rafe Kingston stepped inside. Big, blond, and handsome, his powerful presence filled more than its fair share of space. "What are you two talking about?"

"Ancient Egypt," Lucy said. "I've been telling Miles that I wanted to be an Egyptian princess, but he told me I'd be dead by thirty, only ten years older than I am right now."

Kingston waved a dismissive hand. "All them people over there die young." He poured himself a bourbon and flopped into a chair. "I want you on the range bright and early tomorrow, Lazarus."

"I'll ride out with the herd at first light. But I don't punch cows. I don't know how."

"Men who come a lot cheaper than you will do that. I want a gun, not a puncher." Kingston sipped his drink then lit a cigar. "You know what you have to do?"

"I caught your drift last night." Lazarus nodded.

"Just remember, don't put a bullet into an O'Brien. I don't want old Shamus to get too mad and play hob."

"I wish he was dead," Lucy said. "He's lorded it over this part of the territory long enough."

"That," Lazarus said, "can be arranged."

"No!" Kingston pounded his fist on the arm of the chair. "I don't want the colonel in the ground, I only want him to see reason."

"From what Miss Masters tells me, Colonel O'Brien is not a reasonable man," Lazarus said.

"He's not," Kingston agreed. "But like any man he can be made to see reason if I pressure him enough. You need to make it look good, Lazarus. Don't leave yourself open to a murder charge."

"Only shoot in self-defense, you mean?"

"Make it look that way. Other than that, I don't care how you do it. Just do it."

Lucy, pert, pretty, and petite, smiled. "From . . . what do you call a man who digs up old stuff?"

"Archeologist," Lazarus said.

"Yes, that's right. From archeologist to hired gunfighter is quite a trip."

"It was. Quite a trip."

"Will you tell us the whole story sometime?"

"No."

Lucy was surprised. "No?"

"There are things a man keeps to himself."

"Lucy, I've got nearly two dozen hands out there right now and every one of them has a story to tell," Kingston said. "Go speak to them if you want to hear stories. Just don't believe everything they say." He spoke a barb motivated by jealousy. "Don't believe what any man says."

Lucy grinned. "Except you, Rafe."

Kingston smiled. "Including me."

Lucy Masters woke with a start, moonlight filtering into her room through the lace-curtained windows. She became aware of the prairie night's chill.

For a while she lay still, eyes open, listening into the darkness.

She heard the sounds that had wakened her, a series of soft noises, rhythmic, monotonous and solemn, like the *tick, tick, tick* of a courthouse clock.

Swinging out of bed, she slipped a pink velvet robe over her nightgown. After a moment's hesitation, she picked up a Remington derringer from the night table and put it into her pocket.

Coyotes yipped in the distance and the curtains

billowed in the breeze like bridal veils. Outside, the *tick, tick, tick* went on and on.

Her hand on the derringer, Lucy stepped to the window. She drew back the curtain and looked outside, and her eyes widened in surprise.

By the corral, Miles Lazarus stood alone in the moonlight. His eyes fixed on a fence post a few yards from him, he drew his Colt, dropped it back on the holster and repeated that single movement over and over. *Tick . . . tick . . . tick . . .* the sound of blue metal leaving leather.

Fascinated, Lucy watched the revolver spring into Lazarus's hand again and again with stunning rapidity. Raised among rough men who lived by the gun, she had never seen anyone skin iron that fast, even Rafe. And she doubted anyone else had either.

Such amazing gun skills were rare, as rare as clean socks in a bunkhouse, as her father would put it.

Curiosity is one form of female bravery, and it drove Lucy to open the window to take a better look. But the snick of wood against wood alerted Lazarus and he swung around, his Colt coming up fast.

For a moment Lucy froze, too scared to move. But then she saw Lazarus smile and walk toward her, holstering his gun.

"Why are you up so late, Miles?" Lucy said after she'd found her voice.

"I'll kill a man tomorrow. I can't sleep on that."

"It troubles you that much? I mean . . . killing?"

"It troubles me some," Lazarus admitted.

"Then why do you do it?"

"It's my job."

"Can't you do something else?"

"No, there is nothing else."

"You can be an archeologist again."

"That's in the past. It's over and done with."

"Was it a woman made you feel this way?" Lucy asked.

Lazarus smiled. "Why do women always say that?"

"Because it's so often true. An unfaithful woman can break a man's heart and cause him to do strange things."

"Well, you're right, it was a woman. The desert killed Vicky . . . and me."

"She died of thirst?"

"No, she was killed, murdered really, by Tuaregs, a tribe of desert raiders and warriors."

"And now you hate them?"

"I did, once. But then I realized that Tuaregs are a force of nature. How can you hate the wind or the rain?"

Lucy smiled and shook her head. "You're a strange man, Miles. I can't even begin to understand you."

"Then don't try. I'm a force of nature myself."

"Well, I'm going back to bed." The last sound Lucy heard was the *tick, tick, tick* of Lazarus's Colt as he drew down on enemies only he could see.

Chapter Twenty-two

Shawn O'Brien looked at his brother. "Jake, every time you leave Dromore you bring back waifs and strays. We're going to have to build an annex to house them all."

"That will do, Shawn," Shamus said. "Let your brother explain why he returned with a woman and two children and not my bull and two cows."

"Hey, maybe he's married." Patrick winked. "Did you get hitched out on the range somewhere, Jake?"

"I swear," Jacob said, "there are two O'Briens in this parlor who think the sun comes up just to hear them crow."

"That is true, Jacob," Shamus said. "But remember that the man who can't take a word of criticism hears it the most. Now, tell us what happened, and, if you can remember where you left him, inform me of the whereabouts of my Hereford bull."

"It could be long in the telling, Pa."

"I have time."

Pruning words as he spoke, Jacob told of his gun

battle with Newt Dunn and his gang in the ghost town and his desperate battle with the scalp-hunting Cotton brothers.

"Jake, you've only been gone a couple days and you killed six men?" Samuel's face was stiff with shock.

"Five. Constance done for one of them."

"I'm sure those men needed killing," Shamus supported Jacob. "I won't argue the right or the wrong of it, at least not now."

"There's more," Jacob said.

"Jesus, Mary, and Joseph, not more dead men?" Shamus crossed himself.

"No, Colonel, it's about putting a noose around Rafe Kingston's neck."

"Well, boy, speak up," Shamus said.

"Constance and her kids escaped Kingston's fence." Jacob waited a few moments for that statement to register in the colonel's mind. "She saw her husband shot down by Kingston's riders before she got away. And she's willing to testify in court about what she experienced."

"We have him, by God." Luther Ironside drove a fist into his open palm.

"Do you trust this woman, Jacob?" Shamus asked.

"Her hair turned from black to gray overnight. She's been through it, all right. To answer your question, Colonel, yes, I trust her."

Shamus sat in silent thought, but Ironside, never one to hold back from intruding on another man's ruminations, said, "Colonel, all we need now is the marshal and we're in business."

"I am aware of that, Luther."

"Well?"

"Well, what?" Shamus glared at the man.

"When does the marshal get here?"

"Your guess is as good as mine," Shamus said. "Soon, I hope."

"I've got an idea, Colonel," Ironside blurted.

Watching the conversation between the two men, Shawn turned to Ironside. "Let's hear it, Luther."

"We've got the goods on Kingston, thanks to this Constipation woman."

"Constance," Shamus said. "C-o-n-s-t-a-n-c-e."

"Well, whatever she's called. Anyhoo, here's what we do, Colonel. We ride to the Rafter-K, grab good ol' Rafe, an' string him up. Then, when the marshal gets here and says, 'Why did you boys stretch Rafe Kingston's neck?' we say, 'Because we had the goods on him, and here's poor little Consti . . . Constance to prove it.'" Ironside sat back in his chair and beamed at the others. "Ol' Rafe is hung. The marshal is happy and we're free and clear." He slapped his hands together. "Done and done."

Shamus brooded for a while before saying, "Luther, how did you ever survive the war?"

Ironside was crestfallen. "You don't like my plan, huh?"

"It stinks," Shamus said. "If we do what you say the law will call it a lynching. We'll all be arrested for murder."

Suddenly Ironside brightened. "Then we don't hang him, we just gun him."

"Same result." Shamus looked at Patrick. "Get Luther a drink. He's overexcited."

"Nobody listens to me around here anymore," Ironside grumbled.

"We will, Luther, when you talk some sense," Shamus said.

Ironside muttered to himself, a few stray words escaping into the room. "Darned shame . . . good advice . . . be sorry . . . don't listen."

"What did you say, Luther?" Shamus asked, his face stern.

"Nothing, Colonel, I didn't say nothing."

"Just as well," Shamus said.

"I hope the marshal gets here pretty quick," Jacob said. "Constance is determined to move out of Dromore. She says she wants to raise her kids in her own place. If she leaves, we might have a time trying to round her up again to testify in court."

"Tie her to a tree until—" Ironside stopped abruptly. "Oh, I forgot. Nobody wants my advice any longer."

"Not that kind," Shamus said. "Luther, why are you on the prod? Did you get up on the wrong side of the bed this morning?"

"Right side, wrong side, I know what's best for Dromore." Ironside looked like an old shaggy bear teased by puppies.

"We all do, Luther," Shamus said. "But I don't want to make a move of any kind until the U.S. marshal gets here. We need the law on our side in this."

"Suppose the marshal sides with Rafe," Ironside questioned, "then what?"

Patrick pushed up his eyeglasses. "I think that's highly unlikely. Kingston's claim to Dromore has no validity, and he knows it. The marshal will see his play as a barefaced land grab."

"And peg him as a murderer?" Jacob asked.

"We have the proof right here at Dromore," Patrick said.

"If we can keep her here," Jacob said. "Constance Baker is a mighty strong-willed woman."

"Samuel, in what kind of shape is the old miner's cabin down by Barbero Canyon?" Shamus had given his question much thought.

"Last I looked it was still standing, Colonel. It's got a good roof and there's a spring close."

Shamus turned to his youngest son. "Can we bribe her with the cabin, Jacob?"

"It could work, Colonel," Jacob said. "But Samuel better talk to her. I don't set well with her."

"Imagine that." Shawn grinned. "And you such a dab hand with the ladies."

Jacob ignored that and rose to his feet. "Pa, I'm going to collect the Hereford bull."

"Samuel already sent a couple of vaqueros," Shamus said. "We were afraid that you'd come back with the Lost Tribe of Israel in tow."

"Jake's taste runs more to ladies in distress, Pa," Shawn said. "Or haven't you noticed?"

"Shawn, don't tease your brother," Shamus said.

"He did what he thought was right and I won't fault him for that."

Suddenly Jacob felt uneasy. He turned his battered black hat in his hands. "Sam, who's carrying the iron?"

"Saul Vasquez," Samuel said, his face puzzled.

"He'll do."

But Jacob's sense of impending disaster refused to leave him.

Chapter Twenty-three

The sky blazed with fire, ribbons of scarlet and jade stretched to the western horizon, turning men and horses into statues of copper.

The land around Miles Lazarus and two Rafter-K riders stretched silent and empty. The coming evening was already painting lilac shadows among the pines.

For two hours the three riders had seen no other travelers, not even a passing cowhand or a raggedy-assed Indian leaving nowhere, headed for nowhere.

Jubal Saturday spat a stream of tobacco juice over the side of his horse. "Hey, Lazarus, looks like them Dromore hands have given us the slip. Gonna be dark soon."

Lazarus said nothing, but he stood in the stirrups and his eyes scanned the shadowed range. Trees, grass, sky . . . and nothing.

"Jubal's right," Mordecai Tanner said, "we should head back."

Lazarus finally spoke. "Seems like."

Ten miles to the north the remainder of the hands had pushed a small herd onto Dromore range, but they'd encountered no opposition. Disappointed, Lazarus had taken two men and headed south where he figured there might be better hunting.

All he'd found were cold trails and a lonely land echoing emptiness.

"Chuck wagon stew for supper tonight," Saturday said. "The cook told me that his ownself."

"I wouldn't want to miss it," Tanner said. "Sticks to a man's ribs, that stew does."

"Don't worry on it, boys," Lazarus said. "Looks like we'll all be home for supper."

But in the blink of an eye everything changed . . . when the twilight gloom betrayed a man and ensured that he'd never eat supper again. Lazarus, a far-seeing man, caught a brief glimmer of light to the south that flared for an instant, then was gone.

He smiled to himself, his mouth tight and grim under a mustache clipped close in the British army officer style.

Vaqueros were smoking men, and one of them had just lit a cigarette.

His mistake. Maybe the last one he'd ever make.

"Follow me, boys. I believe the hunt is on." He kneed his horse into a gallop, the Rafter-K riders thundering close behind him. Lazarus grinned. It was like riding to hounds.

* * *

The Rafter-K riders drew rein in front of two young vaqueros who rode tight herd on a Hereford bull and a couple of heifers.

Their eyes suspicious, the Dromore men halted and the older of the two, a man with black hair to his shoulders, smiled warily. "*Buenas noches, señores.*"

Jubal Saturday spat. "Greaser, do you speak American?"

"*Sí,*" the vaquero said, "I do, but my friend does not."

Lazarus let his eyes roam over the man, noting the hardness in his mouth and his brass studded, two-Colt rig. He would be the fast one.

"You're trespassing on Rafter-K property," Lazarus said.

The vaquero shook his head. "No, *señor*, you are mistaken, I think. This is Dromore range."

"It was, but is no longer," Lazarus said. "I'm confiscating your cattle and I advise you to ride on. If I catch you on Rafter-K range again, I'll hang both of you."

He saw fight in the older vaquero as he knew he would. The man rode for the brand and would die for it.

"I don't think you will take my cows, *señor*," the vaquero said.

The younger man seemed frightened and he said something quick in Spanish. Saul Vasquez irritably waved away the vaquero's comments, his anger rising.

"Who is the gun?" Lazarus asked.

"*Qué?*" Vasquez said, not understanding the question.

"Pistolero," Lazarus said. "Which of you is the pistolero?"

"That would be me, *señor*," Vasquez said.

"I took you for a back-shooting, greaser yellow-belly," Lazarus said.

The vaquero knew he was being railroaded, but there are some insults a man can't walk away from. Vasquez snarled and went for his guns.

Lazarus put two bullets into the man's chest before he cleared leather.

After he watched Vasquez fall dead to the ground, Lazarus turned icy eyes to the younger man. Almost paralyzed with fear, his eyes bugged out of his head.

"Go," Lazarus said.

The man needed no second bidding. He swung his horse away and galloped north, frantically slapping his mount's flanks with the reins.

Jubal Saturday let rip with a rebel yell. "Yeeeehah! Lazarus, I ain't never seen a man skin iron that fast."

"Me, neither," Tanner said. "Never in all my born days."

Now that the hunt was over and the prey dead, all excitement died in Lazarus replaced by a flat, empty feeling, as though his guts had been torn out and thrown to the wind. He looked at Saturday, his eyes bleak. "Taking another man's life doesn't make for a soft pillow at night."

The puncher's flushed, excited face paled to puzzlement. "What do you mean by that?"

Lazarus smiled. "It means nothing. Absolutely nothing."

"Well, Miles, do you like it?" Lucy Masters poised her fork halfway to her mouth as she smiled across the table at him. "It's the best stew you'll ever eat."

"It smells like a dead horse." Lazarus wrinkled his nose.

"Try it, you'll like it," Rafe Kingston said, chewing. He had a white bib tucked under his chin.

"What's in it?" asked Lazarus, his suspicions aroused.

"Simple ingredients really," Kingston said. "Beef, marrow gut, heart, liver, kidneys, sweetbreads, some pig and deer meat, I reckon, and whatever else the cook could find to throw into it."

Lazarus pushed his plate away from him. "I reckon I'll pass."

"It's an acquired taste," Lucy said. "Why don't you eat some bread and butter, Miles? And there's apple and raisin pie for dessert."

Kingston helped himself to more stew. He was a big man and it took a lot to fill him. "What did them old Egyptians you're always talking about eat for supper, Lazarus?"

"Bread and beer, and maybe a little dried fish if they were lucky."

"No beef?"

"Only on special occasions and little enough of it at that."

"That's not grub for fighting men," Kingston said. "No wonder they all died young."

Lazarus chewed on a piece of bread. "In a lot of cases the peasants were worked to death, building pyramids or temples for their pharaohs."

Kingston smiled. "I wish my boys worked like that, eh, Lucy?"

"Rafe, treat cowboys like that and they'll light a shuck. I suppose the Egyptians couldn't do that . . . quit I mean."

"No, they couldn't," Lazarus said. "Laze around on the job or quit and you were liable to get your hands cut off. Maybe even your head."

Kingston chewed slowly, his eyes on Lazarus. Then, for the first time he asked about the shooting. "He didn't give you any trouble, huh?"

"The vaquero? He was slow, way too slow."

"This will bring Shamus O'Brien to heel," Kingston said. "Make him forget all this nonsense about the cholera wagons."

"It might," Lazarus allowed, "but I hear tell the old man is a fighter."

Kingston sneered. "Does he scare you?"

"No, not in the least." Lazarus stared at the piece of bread in his hand. "What about Jacob O'Brien?"

"What about him?"

"He's a gun, or so I'm told."

"You can take him. On his best day you can take him." Kingston sat back in his chair. "I can take him if it comes to that."

Lazarus didn't seem to move, but suddenly a Colt was in his hand, pointed at Kingston's chest. "If I was Jacob O'Brien, bang, you're dead."

Kingston didn't flinch. He didn't even raise an eyebrow. "I won't let O'Brien get the drop on me like that."

Lazarus nodded as he reholstered his revolver. "No, I don't suppose you would. But if Jacob O'Brien is as good as he says he is, you won't have much time to think about it."

"That's why I hired you, Lazarus, to take care of minor details like O'Brien."

"I can't be your shadow, but if the ball opens, I'll stay close." Lazarus's eyes held a warning. "Just be careful, Mr. Kingston, that you don't corner a critter a lot meaner than you."

"You mean Colonel O'Brien?"

"That would be the man I'm talking about."

Kingston laughed. "If the old gent wants to play rough I'll accommodate him. But I reckon he'll fold, on account of how he's got too much to lose."

Lucy had watched this exchange in silence, her eyes moving from man to man as though she was a spectator at one of the newfangled tennis games that were all the rage up north. "Well, now that's over, shall we have pie?"

* * *

Sleep would not come to Miles Lazarus. A black depression hung on him like a damp cloak and tore all the—what had Sir Richard Lytton called it?— ah yes, *joie de vivre,* the love of life, out of him. He got out of bed and stepped to the window.

A starlit sky and waxing moon cast a mother of pearl light on the dusty ground outside the ranch house. Shadows gathered everywhere, brooding and mysterious. To the west, the peaks of the Manzano Mountains stood like ebony cutouts against the stars. There was no sound and no movement. The night held its breath.

Vicky came from the direction of the horse corral. She glided across the ground, her beautiful head held high, with that careless, aristocratic grace that came so naturally to her and that Lazarus had so often admired. Gone were the drab khakis and pith helmet of Egypt, in their place a ball gown of yellow silk that left the top of her breasts and shoulders bare. A plain black ribbon circled her slender throat. Atop her piled-up hair was a glittering diamond tiara that was already a hundred years old the day she was born.

Lazarus remembered the dress and tiara well. Vicky had worn it in London at a Coldstream Guards' victory ball the night they first met. Their star-crossed love affair began that evening, and, as far as Lazarus was concerned, it had never ended.

Standing still, almost afraid to breathe lest Vicky

disappear, he watched her glide closer to his window. She smiled at him and raised her hands, cupped around a bright green apple.

Suddenly, where Vicky had been, there was only moonlight and shadow.

Lazarus hesitated a moment. Lucy and Kingston didn't sleep together and he'd have to pass both their rooms to get outside. Rather than risk waking them, he opened the window and dropped onto the dirt. He looked around him, but there was no sign of Vicky, no lingering scent of her perfume or the marks of her feet.

It was a trick of the light, Lazarus told himself. Only the teasing moon playing tricks. A cold, empty feeling inside him, he turned to step back to the bedroom window, but his bare foot kicked something in the dirt that rolled away from him.

It was a bright green apple.

"No, I didn't drop an apple out front. But a Mexican fruit vendor was here yesterday morning and he and the cook spent some time outside haggling over prices. Probably the Mexican dropped it." Lucy poured coffee for Lazarus and herself. "Why do you ask?"

"I found it," Lazarus said.

"Ah, well give it to the cook. I'm sure he'll bake it in a pie."

"I think I'll keep it."

Only half-interested, Lucy said, "Yes, eat it. It's good for you."

Lazarus smiled. "I wish I could be sure of that."

Chapter Twenty-four

Great was the lamentation at Dromore.

Riding under a gibbous moon, vaqueros brought home the body of Saul Vasquez. His wife, fair and slim, cut off her hair and wailed her grief as she watched other women wash her husband's body as they prepared to lay him in the ranch chapel.

Saul's wife kissed his blue lips before six vaqueros carried him to the chapel and laid the dead man, wrapped in a shroud, on his bier. Women, their faces as somber as Renaissance saints, lit wax candles that guttered scarlet flame and issued thin smoke rising straight as blue ribbon to the rafters. The ancient señoras, their faces like wrinkled parchment, kneeled in the front pews of the chapel and their rosary beads *click-clicked* against polished oak.

There was no priest, only the great wooden crucifix hanging over the altar. Christ's bloody, agonized face looked down on the mourners and it seemed to all present that he shared their suffering.

The chapel smelled of incense and long-withered

prairie flowers. To Colonel Shamus O'Brien it seemed grief had its own odor, musky and damp, like leaves rotting on a forest floor. He was not angry, not yet. Let the mourning and the respect due a fine man and a top hand—attributes Shamus considered synonymous—come first. He looked around him, at the grieving vaqueros and their woman and children, and then at his own sons, united by blood yet so different in character.

Samuel, a family man and co-owner of the ranch, kneeled in solemn prayer, his eyes closed, head bowed. Beside him, Patrick, slim, bespectacled, intellectual, had his face raised to the face of Jesus. There was no way to tell what he was thinking. Shawn, handsome, laughing, and carefree, had his head bowed like the others, perhaps in prayer, but more likely he was thinking about the pretty señorita that glanced at him now and then with knowing black eyes.

And then there was the dark, brooding figure of Jacob.

He sat in a pew at the back of the chapel, his craggy face looking like it had been chiseled by an unskilled stonemason. His great beak of a nose gave him the appearance of a bird of prey and his still hands gripped the back of the pew in front of him like talons.

Shamus was touched by fear, not for himself, but for his son and the man he planned to kill. In this holy place, amid mourning, he knew Jacob's thoughts were not turned to Judgment Day and eternity, but to vengeance . . .

An eye for an eye, a tooth for a tooth.

The reckoning to come.

Shamus shivered, as though an icy hand had just passed down his back. He pulled his black mourning garment closer around him and again tolled the rosary beads in his hands.

The chapel was small, hot, and smoky, thick with the horse, leather, and tobacco smell of the vaqueros and the strange, musky odor of female grief. Outside, coyotes approached the lit chapel on hesitant feet, then stood and listened into the night, their eyes gleaming like gold coins in the darkness. A night bird called, and called again.

The dead man lay on his back like a marble statue, stiff, cold, unmoving. Earlier, Samuel had sealed the eyes of Saul Vasquez with silver dollars and had pushed a metal crucifix into his hands. Shamus wondered if the ferryman would take the coins and cross as payment.

Spurs chimed at the back of the chapel as Jacob got to his feet. Luther Ironside, who'd been sitting next to him, also rose. Ironside tapped the shoulder of the vaquero who'd been with Vasquez when he was killed, and all three men stepped outside.

Shamus was alarmed when he saw Jacob and Ironside leave. Both were loose cannons and there was no telling what they'd do next. He motioned to Samuel's wife Lorena to push his wheelchair in the direction of the altar. Lorena passed her young son to Sarah, then got behind Shamus and wheeled him along the aisle between the pews.

They stopped at Vasquez's young wife and Shamus took her tiny hand in his great paw. "If there's anything you need, anything at all, you only have to ask."

The girl nodded, but said nothing, too numbed by grief to speak.

Lorena took the woman in her arms and hugged her close, but the women were separated by temperament and culture. Lorena thought that her gesture had helped very little, if at all.

Shamus said, "Lorena, take me outside, please." Then, as though he'd read his daughter-in-law's mind, he smiled. "You did well."

Jacob, Ironside, and the vaquero stood under a wild oak. Saber blades of moonlight slanted between the tree branches and turned the faces of all three men pale, as though they'd seen a ghost in the darkness.

Although Jacob knew some Spanish, Ironside was fluent in the language and acted as the interpreter.

"Ask him to describe the man who killed Saul," Jacob said.

Ironside rattled off the question, then waited until the vaquero finished his answer.

"He says the man was as tall as you, Jacob, slim, with the face of a poet or great artist."

"How fast was he with the iron? Ask him that."

Ironside repeated Jake's question.

The vaquero's reply was that the man was a pistolero. He added nothing else.

Ironside's eyes met Jacob's in the gloom. "It's got to be Miles Lazarus. None of them Rafter-K hands look like poets, I can tell you that. They're a tough bunch. Not a nose that hasn't been broke among the lot of them."

"What's going on here?" Shamus asked as Lorena pushed him under the tree. He turned to her. "You can go back to the chapel, Lorena. I'll be just fine here."

Lorena frowned and looked from Jacob to Ironside, two tall, booted, and belted men with hard, unforgiving faces. "Are you sure you'll be safe?"

Shamus said nothing, but satisfied with her dig. Lorena turned on her heel and walked, stiff-backed, toward the chapel.

Ironside shook his shaggy head. "Poor Sam."

"Well, God help us, you do look like a couple of desperados who just rode in from the badlands." Shamus told the vaquero to go back to the chapel and continue his vigil. To Jacob he said, "Well, what did you learn?"

"Saul Vasquez was killed by Miles Lazarus, as I suspected all along."

"On Kingston's orders, no doubt," Shamus said.

That statement needed no further comment and Jacob remained silent.

"Then it's war to the hilt." Shamus pounded the arm of his wheelchair. "I can't let such a direct attack on Dromore pass."

"Now you're talking, Colonel." Ironside nodded his agreement. "It's high time we wiped out that nest of killers."

"Jacob, we ride at dawn for the Rafter-K," Shamus said. "The vaqueros are spoiling for a fight and we'll take the war right to Kingston's doorstep."

Ironside beamed. "Sounds just like the old days, Colonel. Dromore rides again!"

But Shamus's bleak stare stopped Ironside cold. "Luther, this time tomorrow we'll be mourning more dead men, good men. I don't see that as a cause for celebration. Do you?"

Ironside shuffled his feet and stared at the ground, for once stumped for words.

Jacob got him off the hook. "How do you plan to play it, Colonel?"

Shamus shook his head. "I don't know yet. Sometimes the terrain and the disposition of the opposing forces dictate how the battle will be fought. I will fight on ground of my own choosing."

It was an answer, but no answer at all, and Jacob was not reassured. Taking the Rafter-K would not be easy and Miles Lazarus was a force to be reckoned with.

"Take me back to the house, Jacob, and see to your arms," Shamus said. "There will be no sleep for anyone at Dromore this night."

Chapter Twenty-five

It could have been any peaceful evening at Drom-ore. As the clock in the hall outside Shamus's study struck eleven, the O'Brien brothers, Luther Ironside, and Lorena were gathered inside the comfortable room. There was little talk but much thought, as there always is on the eve of a war.

Shawn, ever the dude, sat in a chair by the fire, lit against the chilly night air. He wore a scarlet smoking jacket and Persian slippers of the same color. Little Shamus was in his arms and the child looked up at him with adoring eyes as Shawn crooned a lullaby in his fine, high tenor voice.

"Beautiful dreamer,
  Wake unto me.
  Starlight and dewdrops
  Are waiting for thee . . ."

Jacob admitted to himself that he felt a twinge of jealousy. On the few occasions he'd held the boy,

Little Shamus had kicked and screamed, his little face bright red, until Jacob handed him back to Lorena. But the child loved his Uncle Shawn and was as happy in his arms as he was in Lorena's.

"Maybe," Jacob said to himself, "I smell bad."

"Sounds of the rude world
  Heard in the day
  Led by the moonlight
  Have all passed away . . ."

Shamus was silent, sitting in his wheelchair with his head bent. He could have been listening to Shawn's beautiful voice or perhaps he heard the sounds of distant gunfire.

Jacob could not decide which.

"Beautiful dreamer,
  Queen of my song,
  List' while I woo thee
  With soft melody . . ."

Lorena, who'd been sitting quietly watching her son in Shawn's arms, suddenly buried her face in her hands and her shoulders shook with sobs.

Jacob, no hand with crying women, sat in his chair and looked for others in the room to comfort Samuel's wife. Shawn, as though he hadn't noticed, brought his song to an end.

"Gone are the cares of
Life's busy throng.
Beautiful dreamer,
Awake unto me.
Beautiful dreamer,
Awake unto me."

Lorena dropped her hands and stared at Shamus with tear-stained eyes. "Colonel, is there no other way?"

Shamus continued to sit with his head bowed for a long moment. When he finally looked up, he said, "No, Lorena, there is no other way. A great wrong has been done Dromore and as God is my witness I will not let it pass."

"It's pride, foolish male pride, the deadliest of the Seven Deadly Sins," Lorena declared.

"Is that what killed the vaquero lying stiff and cold in the chapel? Pride?" Shamus asked. "I thought it was a forty-five ball from a murderer's gun."

"I don't want my husband lying in the chapel, too." Lorena swung on Jacob. "You're a violent man. Tell them what will happen when we ride on the Rafter-K tomorrow."

"Men will die," Jacob said, the darkness on him. "All the green apples will fall from the tree."

"Jake, that's enough," Shawn interjected. "You're spooking me and you'll wake the baby."

"Jacob speaks the truth." Shamus nodded. "But we will fight for what is ours."

"Lorena." Samuel stood. "It's time Little Shamus was in bed."

The woman looked around the room, her red eyes frantic. "Will no one put a stop to this insanity? Luther, tell them."

"Tell them what, Miss Lorena?" Ironside said. "I ride for the brand. We all do."

Lorena opened her mouth to speak again, but there was a knock at the door and the butler stepped inside. "Colonel, there's a gentleman to see you. He says he's a United States marshal."

"Then show him in," Shamus said. "Better late than never, I suppose."

The marshal was a tall, melancholy man that Luther Ironside described later as, "So down in the mouth he could eat oats out of a churn."

Of early middle age, the man was dressed for the trail in canvas pants, a faded blue shirt, and his star was pinned to a scuffed leather vest. His boots were old, his hat shapeless. A three-day growth of beard covered the lower part of his face. He wore a Colt in his waistband and its cold blue metal matched the shade of his eyes.

"Name's Red Hart," he said, standing hat in hand in the middle of the room. "You sent for me."

"Would you be the Red Hart out of Wichita, Dodge, and Ellsworth?" Jacob asked.

"As ever was, and out of a lot of places besides," Hart answered. "And you'd be Jacob O'Brien." He noticed Jacob's look of surprise. "You were described to me, and a heap of folks set store by your nose. It's not as big as they say."

"Big enough," Jacob said.

Hart nodded. "Well, I ain't gonna argue that point."

"Take a seat, Marshal." Shamus pointed to the chair vacated by Samuel. "May I offer you a drink?"

"You may, but I'm missing my last three meals and I'm a mite peckish. Whiskey could go right to my head, like."

"I'll get you something, Marshal," Lorena said, rising. "Sandwiches all right?"

"That'll suit me just fine, ma'am, and I'm obliged to you."

Lorena actually smiled and when she left the room her step seemed lighter, as though she expected the presence of the marshal would put an end to plans for an attack on the Rafter-K.

"Now, since food is in the offing," Hart said, "I feel I can partake of a glass of ardent spirits. To wit, whiskey."

Samuel poured the marshal his drink. Shamus watched Hart take his first sip, and then said, "As to why I brought you here—"

Hart raised a silencing hand. "Please, Colonel, after I enjoy a repast, then my mind will be clear. You understand, I hope."

Shamus didn't understand in the least, but since the lawman was a guest in his home, he said, "As you wish."

Jacob was puzzled. Red Hart had built a reputation as a town tamer and he'd come up against some of the toughest hard cases in the west. It was said, perhaps truthfully, that he'd put the crawl on John Wesley Hardin and in 1884 had outdrawn and killed the Montana gunfighter Lucas Blanche in an Abilene saloon. But this man, with his long Yankee face, looked nothing like the fighting Red Hart of legend.

Further undermining Jacob's opinion of him, Hart was a talking man, holding forth about ladies' undergarments. "I was still city marshal of Ellsworth when I became entranced with short bloomers, a wonderful invention for ladies of fashion."

Shamus was horrified and Shawn kissed the top of the sleeping baby's head to hide his smile. Like Jacob, Samuel was stunned and Ironside looked as though someone had just kicked his favorite hound dog.

Hart seemed blissfully unaware of the male consternation in the room and charged right ahead. "A drummer in ladies' corsets and undergarments introduced me to his short bloomer line, and he told me, 'Marshal, each pair comes with one standard row of lace, gathered with elastic at the bottom, and a satin ribbon for tying. As for size, they come in—if you'll excuse me using the word—thigh or knee length. For fall and winter wear, we have both models in velvet, corduroy, or flannel to trap the lady's body heat and keep her warm as toast. For summer, muslin or cotton will keep her comfortable and cool.'"

The marshal looked around the room. "You can imagine that I was impressed by such a step forward in ladies' under apparel, and when he told me Queen Victoria had bought several pairs in all materials, well,

I was sold. Naturally, when he offered me a job with his company I jumped at the chance."

"Is that," Shamus asked, his voice iced, "what you do, sell knickers?"

"Oh no, that's all behind me now. Mrs. Hart took exception to my new profession. She said that selling bloomers to the opposite sex was an occasion for temptation and carnal sin. She hinted, in a most singular fashion, that our marital bliss might be threatened if I continued on my reckless course. Naturally, when the job of U.S. marshal was offered, Mrs. Hart ordered me to take it, declaring that it would keep me out of further mischief."

Shamus exchanged glances with every man in the room. "You know that you've arrived on the eve of a range war?"

"No, I wasn't aware of that." Hart looked up as Lorena entered the room, a tray in her hands. "Ah, here is a most beautiful young lady with the comestibles. Bravo!"

Lorena smiled. "It's a humble repast, Marshal, I'm afraid. Roast beef sandwiches and a wedge of green-apple pie."

"It looks and smells divine."

The lawman had eaten one sandwich and was working on another, when he looked at Shamus. "Tell me."

Jacob was startled. The man's voice had changed. The two words he'd just spoken bladed from his mouth as though they'd been forged on an anvil.

Chapter Twenty-six

Shamus O'Brien was not intimidated by Red Hart, but the man irritated him immensely. He kept his account of the wagon train massacre, the attempts on his life, and the shooting of Saul Vasquez short. He mentioned Rafe Kingston's claim to his land as a matter of no importance.

Then he wound it up. "Since Rafe Kingston gives the orders, I want you to arrest him on a charge of murder." He could have said, "I'll take care of Miles Lazarus myself," but he didn't, though that was his intention.

"Colonel O'Brien," Hart said, "I was in Ellsworth when the rails reached the town in the summer of '67. The railroad carried new faces to town and they brought the cholera with them. Before it was over, there were so many dead the gravediggers had to work in shifts to bury them all. The town fathers said three hundred died, but I reckon it was twice that number. I saw the bodies with my own eyes."

"What does something that happened in Kansas

nearly twenty years ago got to do with what I just told you?" Shamus asked, his irritation rising.

"Just this. The sin-eaters were headed north where they could ply their disgusting trade and the first major city on their route was Santa Fe. If the wagons hadn't been stopped, hundreds would've died, maybe thousands."

Shamus's anger flared. "Are you trying to tell me that Kingston should get a medal for killing those folks?"

"You've told me yourself that he only killed those who were trying to escape and spread their contagion."

"It was murder, Hart, and I have an eyewitness to prove it. They tried to kill her and her child"

"While escaping?"

"Of course she tried to escape the fence. Wouldn't you?" Shamus looked at Lorena. "Would you please bring Mrs. Baker? I believe she should tell the marshal what she experienced."

"No, not yet," Hart said. "Once I've talked to Mr. Kingston and got his side of the story, I'll interview witnesses."

"His side of the story . . ." Shamus was beside himself. "The man made two attempts on my life and his hired gun killed my vaquero. You have the facts, now act on them, or—"

"Or, what, Colonel?"

"Or I'll do your job for you and bring Kingston to justice myself. Then you can go back to selling corsets."

If Hart was annoyed he didn't let it show. "Colonel,

there is no proof that the attempts on your life were made by Mr. Kingston. A man in your position must have many enemies."

Shamus opened his mouth to speak, his face black with anger, but Hart held up a silencing hand. "We also can't prove that Miles Lazarus works for the Rafter-K, if there is such a person."

"He's real all right," Jacob said. "Depend on it."

"The vaquero may have been killed in self-defense." Hart continued to argue his point. "That is something I'll have to determine."

"You're taking Kingston's side." Samuel couldn't believe what he was hearing.

"I'm taking no one's side," Hart said. "Once I gather all the facts, then I'll decide who I'll arrest and who I won't."

"And in the meantime?" Shamus glared at the marshal.

"You will do nothing, Colonel. Depend on it. I'll kill any man who unlawfully tries to hinder my work."

"Big talk from a corsets salesman," Shamus said, his eyes blazing.

"I can back up my talk, Colonel. Don't let my past profession lure you into thinking otherwise."

"What do you reckon, Jake?" Ironside said. "Do we take this carpetbagger seriously?"

"Luther!" Shamus yelled. "You will not speak in those terms about a guest in my house. Apologize to Marshal Hart at once."

Hart shook his head, as unsmiling as ever. "No

need, Colonel. I can understand Luther's frustration, but he must allow the law to take its course."

"I guess I spoke out of turn," Ironside said, his face sullen.

Jacob smiled. "Don't blame yourself, Luther. There are at least ten hard cases planted in Boot Hills across the west that didn't take Red Hart seriously. He's a very easy man to underestimate."

"I've heard similar words spoken about you, Mr. O'Brien. And from men of reputation." The marshal shook his head. "If Miles Lazarus does indeed exist, the talk is that he spent years digging up tombs in Egypt. And you, Mr. O'Brien, are a gifted pianist. What a strange world we live in."

Jacob said, "And Red Hart, the gun-slinging marshal who tamed a dozen cow towns, sold ladies' bloomers. I'd say that's stranger still."

"I apologize for the word Mr. O'Brien just uttered," Hart said to Lorena. "It is not my habit to mention ladies' intimate undergarments in mixed company."

Lorena shrugged. "We all wear them."

"Ah, just so." Hart held up his glass and said to Shamus, "May I have another libation, Colonel. After riding a night trail a man needs to steady his nerves."

Jacob did the honors, and Hart sampled his drink. "I would also like a place to bed down, Colonel. A dry corner of a barn, perhaps?"

"We have guest rooms, Marshal," Shamus said,

struggling mightily to be civil. "I'll see that you're conducted to one right away."

Shawn grinned. "Not that you've worn out your welcome or anything."

Hart rose to his feet. "I understand. I'll ride out at first light."

"I'll show you to your room, Marshal." Lorena threw Shawn a dagger look. "I'm sure you'll find it quite comfortable."

"Well, Colonel," Luther Ironside said, "where do we go from here? I say we mount up now while the corsets drummer is asleep and bust ol' Rafe wide open."

"For a change, Luther, your suggestion is not without merit," Shamus said. "But I think we should err on the side of caution and let Hart conduct his investigation. If he sides with us, that will be fine. If he sides with Kingston, we'll wait until he's gone and then carry out our original plan."

"I agree with Luther," Shawn said. "Let's get it over with and do our explaining later."

"Jacob, do you have anything to say?" Shamus asked.

"Red Hart is a man who's always been willing to die to uphold the law as he sees it. You can explain all you want, but he'll clap us all in irons. The only way to avoid that is to kill him, and he's not an easy man to kill. Besides, it's no small thing to gun a U.S. marshal."

"Jake, who said anything about killing him?" Shawn said. "All we say is that we rode out to the Rafter-K to make peace talk, but Kingston's men attacked us. You said Hart will uphold the law. Well, self-defense is the law. Hart said that himself."

"Samuel?" Shamus said.

"I say we wait."

"Patrick?"

"I side with Sam on this one, Pa."

"Lorena, you're a member of this family," Jacob said. "What's your opinion on this?"

"You know my opinion, Jacob. I agree with my husband and Patrick."

"Well, Colonel, do we open the ball tonight or not?" Jacob looked at his pa.

"No. We'll wait three days and no longer."

"This will make us look weak, Colonel," Ironside said. "One of our own killed and we do nothing about it. Every rustler and bandit in the territory can sense weakness like the coyotes they are."

"If Hart doesn't make an arrest within three days, we attack." Shamus repeated his decision. "After Rafe Kingston is no more, nobody will accuse us of weakness."

"Suppose ol' Rafe guns Hart, what then, Colonel?" Ironside asked.

"I don't catch your drift, Luther."

"It ain't hard to follow. Rafe guns Hart, then has a dozen of his boys say they saw one of us kill him. Next thing you know we'll have the army camped on our doorstep and gallows going up all over the place."

Shamus thought that through, then looked at Samuel. "Can we spare the Kiowa from his black-smith's forge for a couple of days?"

For a moment Samuel looked doubtful. "I guess so, Pa. But only for a few days."

"It will be enough. Bring him to me."

The Kiowa's name was Setangya, but since no one at Dromore cared to wrangle with the pronunciation he was called Seth. A man of medium height, stocky, with handsome, regular features, he dressed in the white man's garb of collarless shirt, black pants, and vest. A necklace of hammered silver discs hung on his broad chest, and his hair was fashioned in two thick braids, bound with soldier blue ribbon.

"You will protect the white peace officer," Shamus told him. "But at a distance. You must not be seen."

The Kiowa, a man of few words, nodded.

"Do you have a rifle?"

"Winchester."

"Belt revolver?"

"Colt."

"Seth, don't let any harm come to the white man, do you understand?"

"He will be safe. I will see to it."

"He rides out at first light. You will follow."

Again the Kiowa nodded. Like the Apache, his

tribe had no word for good-bye. He merely turned on his heel and walked out of the room.

"Talkative feller, that Injun," Ironside said. "I've known him for ten years and in all that time he's said maybe a dozen words to me."

"He's a first-rate blacksmith." Samuel gave his father a sidelong look. "I'd sure hate to lose him."

Chapter Twenty-seven

As Red Hart saddled his buckskin, moonlight still glanced off the rocky parapet of Glorieta Mesa and coyotes barked in the shadowed distance. Jacob, an early riser, had made coffee and Hart's cup smoked in the morning cool as he stood relaxed and easy beside his horse. He watched Jacob build a cigarette. "Mind if I borry the makings?"

Jacob obliged.

His head bent over tobacco and paper, Hart said, "What am I facing?"

"Probably not much. Rafe Kingston won't gun a marshal. He's way too smart for that."

"And Miles Lazarus?"

"He kills on orders, and like I said, Kingston won't give that order." Jacob thumbed a match into flame and held it to Hart's cigarette.

The marshal drew deeply, and then lifted his cup to his lips. "You make good coffee."

"Black as sin and bitter as gall," Jacob said, smiling. "That's how Luther Ironside taught me to make it."

"He doesn't like me."

"Luther doesn't like anybody he doesn't know."

Hart's blue eyes lifted to Jacob. The glow of the lantern hanging on the barn door cast an orange glow over both men. "I don't know what's coming down, Jacob. I can't make any promises to your father or anyone else."

"Kingston is a murderer. That's the bottom line."

"I'll decide that for my ownself," Hart said. "If he's guilty, I'll arrest him."

"Step wide around Miles Lazarus," Jacob advised. "If only half what I hear about him is true, he's a handful."

Hart's slight smile lasted as long as frost on a summer leaf. "How good is he?"

"Maybe the best with the iron that's ever been."

"Faster than you?"

"I reckon."

The marshal took a second or two to absorb and analyze that. "I'll be careful." He passed his empty cup to Jacob. "Thanks for the coffee."

"Here." Jacob passed Hart the makings. "You may need this."

Hart touched his hat brim. "Much obliged."

"Ride easy," Jacob said.

A few minutes after Hart rode out under a scarlet sky, Seth appeared from behind the barn riding a dun pony. To Jacob's surprise the Kiowa was dressed and painted for war, wearing the traditional breech-clout, moccasins, and otter skin turban, a feather fan in his right hand. Apart from the hammered silver necklace, his chest was bare.

He rode past Jacob at a walk, nodded, then faded into the shadowed dawn.

A few moments later Jacob got another surprise.

Seth's wife followed in her husband's tracks, then stood in front of the barn, the oil lamp touching her hair with shimmering bands of red. She wore the Kiowa woman's battle dress, the first time Jacob had ever seen her in it. The dress was of elk skin, heavily beaded, and of great value.

"Adoerte," Jacob said, using the woman's name, "what does Seth see?"

The Kiowa turned to him and for the first time he saw that the right side of her face was painted black. "Setangya is a great warrior and he saw a terrible vision in the flames of his forge."

"What was that vision, Adoerte?"

"He saw the man you call Red Hart. He stood amid the fire and scarlet coals and called down thunder, lightning, and a black rain."

"Did Setangya know what his vision foretells?"

"Thunder is the roar of men in battle. Lightning is the bringer of death. The black rain is the blood that will flood the earth."

"Do you fear for your husband, Adoerte?"

"My husband is dead."

The woman turned and stepped away so softly her feet made no sound.

"Jake, she's an Injun," Luther Ironside said. "Injuns are always saying stuff that don't make a lick o' sense."

Shamus tapped the top of his boiled egg with the back of his spoon, then looked at his son. "Adoerte troubled you, Jacob, I can tell."

Since the attack on the Rafter-K had been postponed, Samuel, Shawn, and Patrick were out on the range. Lorena was in the nursery with young Shamus, and only Jacob, Ironside, and the colonel sat at the breakfast table.

Outside a couple of vaqueros broke grade horses in the corral, their hoots, hollers, and Spanish curses loud in the morning quiet, borne to the house by a long wind.

"Seth has the gift, Pa. And so does Adoerte."

"Benighted heathens is what they are," Ironside said. "Seeing pictures in a fire, my ass. What that Kiowa needs is more work, and when he gets back I'll give him plenty."

Jacob watched his father spoon yellow egg yolk into his mouth. "Adoerte is convinced her husband is a dead man."

"Jacob"—Shamus swallowed the egg—"Hart is not for us, I can tell that. But he ain't agin us either. United States marshals don't make range wars worse."

"A woman's foolish fancy, if you ask me." Ironside scowled at Jacob. "Jake, eat some o' them braised kidneys and put some meat on your skinny bones."

"Even as a kid he wouldn't eat," Shamus said.

"I know," Ironside agreed. "And many a time I tanned his hide for leaving good meat on his plate when kids in foreign countries were starving."

Jacob smiled. "Just to please you, Luther, pass me the kidneys and some of the bacon."

"Now you're talking, boy," Ironside said, pleased. "Get stuck in and you'll grow big and strong like me."

In truth, Jacob had lost his appetite right after his talk with the Kiowa woman. But he ate enough to please Ironside, who was watching him like a crouching buzzard, then poured himself coffee.

"Well, that was little enough, Jake," Ironside said. "But it'll do."

Shamus laid his napkin on the table. "Luther, I know you're still recovering from your wound, but it sounds to me like the wranglers are having trouble out there."

Ironside had tucked his own napkin under his chin. He pulled it away and rose to his feet. "I'm recovered enough to teach them youngsters how to break a horse, Colonel."

"Tell them, Luther. Don't show them," Shamus said.

"Ha, that'll be the day." His spurs ringing, Ironside walked to the door and stepped outside.

Shamus looked at Jacob. "If Seth has the gift, this

is serious, Jacob. He saw something in the fire that troubled him enough to tell his wife about it."

"It could be nothing, Colonel," Jacob said.

"You're right, it might just be superstitious nonsense, but I want you and your gun out there."

"Trail Hart and Seth to the Rafter-K?"

"Just that. I already sent a guardian angel after Hart, now I'm sending a demon."

Jacob laughed. "Is that what I am, Colonel, a demon?"

"With a gun, yes." Shamus sat back in his wheelchair and lit his first cigar of the day. "Jacob, all I want you to do is keep an eye on things," he said though a haze of smoke. "Don't ride onto Kingston's range, but drift west. I understand there's a heap of country to cover between Dromore and the Rafter-K, but I'd feel better knowing you're out there. I gave Hart three days and that's how long you'll be gone."

Jacob nodded. "I'll do my best to keep our marshal safe, Colonel."

"Not the marshal, Jacob, I want you to keep Dromore safe."

"I'll get some grub from the kitchen and ride out." Jake rose to his feet and moved toward the door.

Shamus stopped him. "Wait." He made a sign of the cross in the air. "In the name of the Father, and of the Son and of the Holy Ghost." Shamus smiled. "May my blessing protect you, son."

Shamus had never done that before and it caused

Jacob to feel perplexed and anxious. "What do you see, Pa?"

"In my dream last night, I saw a green apple on the branch of a tree, but when I tried to pick the apple it fell to the ground because of the wind from a great thunderstorm." Shamus shook his head. "What could be the meaning of such a strange dream?"

"I don't know, Pa. I just don't know."

Chapter Twenty-eight

Gunfighter. Miles Lazarus pegged the man on the tall buckskin as such. Studying him from the corner of the barn, he decided the rider was past his prime. Age would slow him, but he'd still be arrogant and confident enough to be dangerous.

"Howdy," Lazarus called out.

The man drew rein and turned his head. "Right back at ya, young feller."

"Looking for somebody?"

"Yes, Mr. Rafe Kingston by name."

"He's out visiting his future in-laws with his bride to be. Should be back soon, I reckon."

"And who might you be?" Red Hart asked.

"I might be John D. Rockefeller, but I'm not."

"Name's Red Hart, United States marshal. And I want to know who you are, mister, not who you might be."

The lawman didn't lack for sand and Lazarus respected that. "Miles Lazarus is the name."

"I've heard of you."

Lazarus nodded. "Men talk, but usually they've no idea what they're talking about."

"You're the feller who used to dig up dead folks in that Egyptian country, wherever it is."

"That sounds like me."

"Mind if I light and set? I'll wait for Mr. Kingston."

Lazarus pointed a forefinger at Hart and then at the ground.

"Much obliged." Hart swung out of the saddle.

And Lazarus noted the Colt in the man's waistband. It was as good a way as any to carry a gun, and faster than most.

Hart stood with the reins dangling in his hand, obviously undecided about his next move.

Lazarus solved the problem for him. "Take your horse into the barn. There's hay and a sack of oats. When you've taken care of your mount, come to the house and I'll see if the cook can rustle up coffee."

"Good coffee," Red Hart said, "but the Dromore stuff was better."

Miles Lazarus smiled. "Don't let it sway your opinion of us."

"I won't. I form my opinions on factors other than coffee." Hart stared at Lazarus over the steaming rim of his cup. "Serious charges have been leveled against you, Mr. Lazarus."

"Such as?"

"The murder of a Dromore vaquero for one."

"That was a clear case of—"

The marshal held up his hand. "Not now. I will do my questioning when Mr. Kingston gets here."

Hart let a silence stretch for a few moments. "Tell me about Egypt."

"Sand, heat, and flies. You want to hear more?"

"A man has to take a giant step to move from . . . what's the word?"

"Archeology."

"Is that what digging up dead folks is called? Well, I never. Anyhoo, it's a big step from that to gun-fighter-for-hire."

"I discovered that I had a natural talent with firearms."

"It seems you also had a natural talent for archeology."

Lazarus noted that Hart did not stumble over the unfamiliar word. The man was smarter than he seemed. "Circumstances change a man, push him in a different direction."

"Ah, yes, I know that only too well. For a while I left law enforcement to sell ladies' undergarments."

"Safer than marshalling, I'd say."

"It was, but my lady wife objected, and I perforce hastened back to my old profession."

"Too bad."

"Indeed, but there is a certain satisfaction in bringing killers and outlaws of all stripes to justice."

Lazarus smiled again. "You think I'm a killer, Marshal?"

"You've killed often. I can see it in your eyes."

Lazarus made no comment and the men sat in silence for a few minutes.

Hart spoke first. "For some men, the more they kill the easier it gets. Others are the very opposite. Taking a man's life becomes harder and harder. That's how it is with you, Mr. Lazarus. You've killed so many your eyes are dark with pain."

"Quite the philosopher, aren't you?" Lazarus said, an edge to his voice.

Hart shrugged. "I see what I see."

"Just fine to see the law in this part of the territory," Rafe Kingston said after the pleasantries that hospitality demanded had been issued. "Now perhaps we can all settle down to what we do best, ranching."

"Indeed, Mr. Kingston," Hart said, "we all wish for peace."

"I'm a peace-loving man, Marshal, whatever you may have heard to the contrary," Kingston said. "Shamus O'Brien and his violent brood have made my life a hell."

"Ah," Hart said. Only that and nothing more.

A glass of bourbon in hand, Kingston sprawled in his sofa. Lazarus sat by the window, staring outside.

Hart thought Lucy Masters, perched at the edge of her chair, knees pressed together, hands knotted in her lap, looked unnecessarily prim. Her pretty mouth was shut tight, like a steel purse. He decided

Kingston was indeed a handsome man, with the flashy good looks of a frontier dandy. But as yet, Hart had not discovered any depth or substance to him. "I understand you and Miss Lucy are betrothed. May I offer you my congratulations?"

"Thank you," Lucy said, "but my father does not approve of our union. Rafe visited him today and he was practically kicked out of the house. I went with him, of course, but I fear Papa and me are even more estranged."

"Hugh Masters is like Shamus O'Brien," Kingston said. "Pig-headed and set in his ways."

"And you, Miss Lucy, will inherit the ranch on that sad day when your father passes to his reward?" Hart asked.

Lazarus thought that a strange question to ask, and looked hard at Hart, trying to read an explanation in the marshal's bland, empty face.

"I hardly think your question is of the greatest moment, Marshal," Lucy answered. "But yes, I stand to inherit the Three Aces Ranch."

"Just call it idle curiosity, dear lady. As you say, my question was of little import." The marshal held his whiskey glass to the light of the window, and then took a sip. He savored the taste for a moment. "Dromore serves better bourbon, Mr. Kingston. Smoother and more mellow I would say."

"He doesn't like your coffee either, Mr. Kingston," Lazarus said, grinning.

The big rancher was not in the least annoyed. "Then I'd better upgrade my cellar and my cook."

"Tell me about the cholera wagons." The tone of Hart's voice signaled an abrupt change in attitude.

Suddenly defensive, Kingston sat up. "What did the O'Briens tell you?"

"At the moment that's neither here nor there. I want to hear your version."

"The truthful version, you mean."

The marshal smiled but said nothing.

"The wagons were just south of the San Pedro Mountains, headed north, carrying their dead and dying with them." Kingston leaned his elbows on his knees.

"How many wagons?" Hart took another sip of bourbon.

"I don't remember that."

"Six, I was told."

"Then it was six."

"Please continue, Mr. Kingston, and I apologize for the interruption."

"Well, I rode down there and smelled cholera."

"Like rotten fish," Hart said.

"Yeah. How did you know that?"

"Up Kansas way I saw cholera at work."

"Well, anyway, I told them to stay right where they were and go no farther. But the men trained their rifles on me and told me, 'By God, we're headed for Santa Fe or bust.' I said, 'Over my dead body,' but I had only a couple of my men with me and was forced to retreat. I was in fear of my life, you understand."

"Did you see dead bodies at this time?"

"Oh sure, maybe two dozen were lying outside the

wagons, men, women, children." Kingston pinched the bridge of his nose. "It was a terrible sight."

"Go on, Mr. Kingston," Hart said after a while. "I know this must be very painful for you."

"Well, I rode back with a dozen of my men and a wagon, and we built a fence around those plague wagons. We were under fire the whole time, but my boys stuck to their task, though one was killed. They knew as well as I did what death and suffering those sin-eaters could visit on Santa Fe if they were not stopped."

"You knew they were sin-eaters at that time?"

"No, I learned that later."

"What about the men you and your riders killed?"

"They were trying to break out and spread their contagion." Kingston continued his story. "And as I told you already we were under fire. We fought back and, yes, some men from the wagon train died. But they were justified killings."

"Shamus O'Brien says he has a witness who can testify against you in court."

"There were no witnesses left." Realizing he'd gone too far, Kingston gave a hasty explanation. "I mean, by then only the men who shot at us were alive."

"You said you killed the men to stop them spreading their cholera. But men who could pick up rifles and fight were obviously not diseased. Cholera weakens a man before it kills him. I've seen it happen, and believe me, victims don't have the strength to get into a gunfight. Why, they couldn't lift a rifle let alone shoot it." Hart smiled. "Strange that, is it not?"

"Marshal, are you implying my fiancé is a murderer?" Lucy's eyes flashed. "You've been listening to that devil Shamus O'Brien's lies."

"Men lie, Miss Lucy, that's a natural fact," Hart said. "My job is to find just who is lying and who is not."

"Rafe doesn't lie. He's a brave man who stopped a threat to this territory the best way he knew how."

The marshal nodded. "Perhaps. That remains to be seen." Hart's melancholy eyes moved to Kingston. "On my ride out to your ranch I came across Hereford cattle and longhorns. As far as I could tell, they were both on Dromore range and the longhorns were wearing a Rafter-K brand. How do you explain that, Mr. Kingston?"

"I have title to all the Dromore range," Kingston said, his face stiff. "I moved some of my herd onto fresh grass is all."

"The validity of your title will be decided in federal court. And that could take months if not years. Until a determination is made, I would pull your cattle off Dromore range." Hart smiled. "As a peace gesture, like."

"If that's what it takes to keep the peace, then I'll do what you say," Kingston said. "But I will not tolerate any attack on my men by Dromore ruffians."

Hart nodded. "That sounds like a fair pledge." He rose to his feet and placed his empty glass on the table beside him. "I'm only a little way into my investigation, Mr. Kingston, but I do foresee arrests."

Kingston's eyes were the color of knife blades. "Arrests? Who do you plan to arrest?"

"I haven't yet made that determination, Mr. Kingston, but when I do, you'll be the first to know."

"Is that a threat?" Lucy eyed the marshal.

"Bless your heart, miss, no. I'm merely being polite. Sociable, you might say."

The marshal stepped to the door, then stopped and turned to Kingston. "Please, see to the cattle thing. The sooner they're gone from Dromore range, the better for all concerned."

After Red Hart rode out, Kingston turned to Lazarus. "What do you think?"

"I think the marshal doesn't like you."

Kingston turned to his betrothed. "Lucy?"

"Rafe, I don't want to think about it right now. I want to smooth things over with my father. Can I borrow a horse?"

"Of course you can. What's mine is yours, Lucy. But take the surrey."

"No, I think riding will clear my head."

"I'll have one of the boys saddle up the paint mare."

"No, I'll do it myself." Lucy stepped outside.

Kingston watched her go, then turned his attention back to Lazarus. "We may have to kill the marshal. Blame it on Dromore."

"It could come to that."

Kingston thought for a moment. "I'll kill him myself. I didn't like the way the upstart talked to me."

"A word of advice," Lazarus said. "Do it at a distance."

"What? You think I can't take him?"

"I know you can't take him, not in a straight-up gun fight."

"Well then, I'm a good hand with a rifle," Kingston snapped.

"There's your answer," Lazarus said.

Chapter Twenty-nine

Jacob O'Brien rode deeper into the gathering darkness, a lost, lonely figure in a far-reaching land. Knee-high to his horse, a gray mist lay on the ground and the surrounding spruce and piñon looked as though they were rising out of a lake. The night was coming in clean after the heat of the day and a light breeze carried the distant scents of pine and cooling mountain rock.

Jacob was a fair thirty miles from the front doorstep of Dromore House in rolling grass and brush country north of El Cuervo Butte, and he badly needed to find a place to camp for the night. The burlap sack tied to his saddle horn clanked with every step of the horse, the sound of the coffeepot butting against the frying pan loud in the silence.

His eyes searched the shadowed terrain ahead of him as he swung south in the direction of the butte. Ten minutes later, he drew rein when he heard the first shot.

Then another.

The rifle's echoes racketed around him, but Jacob was sure it came from the west. He kneed his horse in that direction, slid the Winchester from the boot, and rested the buttplate on his thigh. Not a man to gallop headlong into trouble, he rode at a distance-eating walk and his horse's head came up as though he, too, was wary of what lay in front of them.

The rising moon soon silvered the wide land, making the shadows long and dark. Stars appeared in the dark sky like diamonds strewn on lilac velvet. As they began their hunt, coyotes called out to each other. The breeze grew stronger and the air Jacob breathed was cool as mountain water.

Emerging from the low mist, Jacob was suddenly upon a pale pinnacle of rock, a tall cottonwood growing at its base. Near the tree a scarlet fire winked, as though one of the stars had fallen to earth and turned into a glowing cinder.

Jacob pushed his horse past a line of willows that drooped over a small stream, some of their branches trailing into bubbling water. He pulled into a patch of deep shadow and drew rein.

"Hello, the camp."

There was no answering call.

Jacob heard a faint rustle, like a man's booted foot sliding across gravel. He waited a long minute, but heard no other sound. Swinging out of the saddle, he shoved the long gun back into the leather. If he was about to walk into an ambush it would be close work, revolver work.

On a hunch, he yelled again. "Hart, is that you?"

He heard only the wind and the babble of the stream.

Colt up and ready in his hand, Jacob walked toward the campfire. He stayed in the shadows, every jangling nerve in his body alert.

Then he saw the man sprawled facedown beside the guttering fire and whispered, "Oh my God."

Red Hart had taken a bullet high in his back. When Jacob turned the man over, he saw that the bullet had exited under Hart's left collarbone, punching out a wound as wide across as a teacup.

Hart groaned as Jacob laid him on his back again. The man was alive . . . barely. His eyes were shut and his mouth was filled scarlet with blood. Nothing about his wounds looked good. But lawmen of his stamp were as tough as old boot leather.

Kneeling beside the marshal, Jacob lifted his head. "Red, can you hear me?"

When he got no answer, Jacob left the marshal and brought his horse closer. He undid his bedroll, folded the blanket, and placed it under Hart's head. Only then did he walk behind the spire of rock and the cottonwood into the darkness. Jacob was not a night-seeing man, but it was obvious there was no cover for a bushwhacker. Beyond the rock the land was flat. Before night fell, Hart must have seen his attacker at a distance. He'd obviously not been on his guard and had turned his back on his assailant. It was a greenhorn's mistake, probably the first the marshal had ever made, and it might well have cost him his life.

There was one other thing—if Hart was not on his guard, then he'd welcomed somebody he knew into his camp.

Jacob asked himself the obvious question. *Who does he know in this part of the territory?*

The answer was troubling. Hart knew only the O'Briens of Dromore and Rafe Kingston. No one from Dromore had shot the marshal in the back, so it had to have been Kingston. Or Miles Lazarus.

The coffeepot simmered on the dying coals of the fire and Jacob poured himself a cup then built a cigarette, trying to figure his next move. Hart was in no shape to ride; that was obvious. The marshal's breathing was irregular and gray shadows had gathered under his eyes and in the hollows of his cheeks—the harbingers of death.

Smelling blood in the air, the coyotes called closer, their yips more urgent.

Jacob lit his cigarette. He'd stay with Hart until the man died and then try to bury him deep enough to keep predators away.

He sat by the fire and listened to the marshal's labored breaths.

An hour passed.

Jacob added sticks to the fire and took a pot at a

coyote crouching just beyond the rim of the light, its eyes glittering. The animal yelped and ran away and he reckoned his bullet had either burned its hide or he'd put the fear of death into it.

Bacon sizzled in the frying pan when a clamor out in the moon-raked darkness made the hair on the back of his neck stand on end. Not much afraid of ha'ants and boogermen and the like, Jake was nevertheless a little spooked. The clank and creak he heard was made by something bigger than a coyote . . . and it was headed his way.

Reluctantly, he removed the half-cooked bacon from the fire, rose to his feet, and stepped into the shadows.

Haloed by mist, a yellow light bobbed toward him and the clanking grew louder, like a fettered ghost rattling its chains.

"Who's out there?" Jacob yelled. "I can drill ya from here."

A man's voice, muffled by distance, called back. "And why would you drill me, a poor peddler man who means harm to nobody?"

"Come in slow and keep your hands away from your gun."

"Am I not a peddler?" the voice answered. "What do I know from a gun?"

"I'm not a trusting man," Jacob called out. "Come in smiling, like you were visiting kinfolk."

"Am I not doing that? Am I not coming in?"

The clank and creak grew louder, the light brighter, and after a few moments a mule-drawn, two-wheeled wagon drove into the arc of the fire-light, a small man with gray threads in his long beard at the reins.

Pots and pans hung from hooks along both sides of the wagon and they clashed and clanged as the man reined the mule to a stop. The wagon looked as though a carpenter who didn't know his business had hammered it together from scraps of driftwood, and one wheel canted at a crazy angle. The mule was old, slatted in the ribs, and its only eye was mean. A lantern guttered on the canvas cover above the driver's seat, illuminating the bearded man with orange light.

"What and who are you?" Jacob stepped out of the shadows.

"As I already told you, am I not a poor peddler?"

"What are you doing out here?"

"Do I not travel from place to place selling my wares? Do I not have pots and pans, needles and threads, ribbons and calico cloth, salt and coffee, molasses and syrup in jugs, stick candy for the children, medicine for the adults, and farm tools of all kinds?"

"What's your name?" Jacob asked brusquely. "And don't make any fancy moves."

"My name is Shelomo Silverstein," the peddler said. "And do I look like I make fancy moves? At my age I can't even make plain moves."

"You're a Child of the Book."

"And does that trouble you?"

"No, I guess not."

Jacob made up his mind about the peddler and holstered his gun. "I've got a dying man here. Unhitch your mule and set it to graze beside my horse. There's good grass over there. I've got coffee in the pot and bacon frying." Jacob smiled. "Oh, sorry, you can't eat bacon."

"Is it not trout?"

"No, it's bacon."

"Just between the two of us, it's trout."

Silverstein climbed down from the wagon. "First, let me see the dying man."

"He's in bad shape." Jacob led the peddler to Hart.

"Dying men usually are." Silverstein kneeled beside the marshal and examined the man's wounds front and back. Muttering to himself in a language Jacob did not understand, the peddler's words were interspersed with much shaking of the head and whispers of, "Oy, oy, oy," that he did understand.

The little man looked up at Jacob, his brown eyes wounded. "Did you shoot this man?"

"No, I found him this way. He's a United States marshal by the name of Red Hart, and I don't know who shot him, through I have my suspicions."

"Then suspicion some more, because there's a dead man back there in the trees, and he looks like an Indian to me."

"Seth!" Jacob said. "Show me where he is."

Silverstein led the way through the darkness about ten yards and pointed out the body half-hidden in undergrowth.

Jacob kneeled beside the dead man and rolled

him on his back. Seth's lifeless eyes stared at him, but saw nothing. He'd been shot in the chest, probably as he ran to Hart's rescue.

Another death laid at Rafe Kingston's doorstep.

Silverstein stepped to his wagon and returned with bandages, a bottle, and a small alabaster ointment box. He took a knee beside Hart again, unscrewed the lid of the box and held it up to Jacob.

"Green as an apple, is it not?"

"What is it?"

"It is a mysterious nostrum brought from Cathay to San Francisco by a sailorman. As to what it is, I have no idea, though it's said to heal wounds, running sores, and the croup."

"Can't hurt, I guess." Jacob shrugged.

"In this case, I agree with you." Silverstein nodded. After he spread ointment on Hart's wounds, he bandaged the lawman tight, and then held his head as he pressed the bottle to his lips.

"What's in the bottle?" Jacob asked.

"Another mysterious nostrum, this time from the West Indies," the peddler said. "It will cure venereal disease, tuberculosis, cancer, cholera, neuralgia, epilepsy, scarlet fever, necrosis, mercurial eruptions, paralysis, toothache, abscesses, and female complaints."

"Must be powerful stuff."

Silverstein winked. "Since it's mostly Jamaica rum, it should be."

Hart coughed as he swallowed the rum, then the peddler laid the lawman's head back on the blanket.

"All you can do now is pray for your friend," Silverstein said.

"He's not my friend," Jacob said. "And besides that, I'm not exactly on speaking terms with God."

"Then we'll wait."

Jacob shook his head. "That's not the plan, Shal . . . say, what's your name again?"

"Shelomo. It means peaceful in Hebrew."

"Well, Shelomo, my name's Jacob O'Brien and my family ranch is northeast of here. We'll load Hart into the wagon and take him there."

"Ah, but that was not my plan," Silverstein said. "You see, I—"

"It's your plan now."

The peddler sighed. "You are the man with the gun."

Jacob drew, spun the Colt in his hand and extended it, butt-first to Silverstein. "Take it."

Like a man reaching out to pet a rattlesnake, Silverstein took the revolver from Jacob's hand with his fingertips.

"Now you're the man with the gun," Jacob said. "I'm asking you to take Hart to Dromore as a favor to me. It's a favor you can call in anytime."

Silverstein passed the Colt back to Jacob. "Am I not a reasonable man? All right, as a favor I'll take him to your ranch."

"There's womenfolk aplenty at Dromore who'll buy your wares, so your trip won't be wasted."

The peddler brightened. "When do we leave?"

"Now, while Hart is still breathing. Can your mule make the trip?"

"She'll walk all day and all night, especially if there's oats at the end of the journey."

"I'll see she gets all she needs," Jacob said.

Suddenly Hart groaned and beckoned to Jacob with a weak, bloodstained hand. Taking a knee beside the lawman, Jacob leaned close to his mouth.

Hart whispered something, then returned to unconsciousness.

"What did he say?" Silverstein whispered.

Jacob looked up at the man and shook his head. "'Goose.' He said, 'Goose.'"

"What does that mean?"

"Shelomo, I have no idea.

Chapter Thirty

Red Hart was still alive, when Jacob O'Brien led Shelomo Silverstein's wagon up to the big house at Dromore. The day was waning and Samuel and Shawn, dusty and tired, had just returned from the range.

Shawn was delighted to see the wagon and the little man who drove it. "What have you brought us back this time, Jake? Looks like some kind of peddler to me."

Silverstein lifted his flat-brimmed hat. "Shelomo Silverstein at your service, young sir."

Jacob swung out of the saddle. "Marshal Hart is in the back of the wagon," he said to Samuel. "He's been shot up real bad."

"Did you gun him, Jake?" Shawn asked.

"No, not me. It was somebody else. He says it was a goose."

"A goose shot him?"

"So he says."

"I always reckoned geese were dangerous." Shawn grinned. "All that hissing and stuff."

A crowd had gathered outside the house and Jacob was relieved to see Lorena among them. "Lorena, it's Red Hart, he's—"

"I heard." Lorena turned to the gawking servants. "A couple of you men get him inside and into a bed."

Constance Baker, looking the better for regular food and a roof over her head, stepped beside Lorena. "I have some experience with wounded men, Mrs. O'Brien. Can I help?"

"Of course you can. Please come with me."

The women passed Shamus in the doorway. His butler pushed him outside and he beckoned to Jacob. "What happened?"

"I found him a few miles northwest of El Cuervo Butte, Colonel. He'd camped for the night and somebody shot him in the back. I reckon it was somebody he knew, because there was no sign of a fight."

Quick anger flashed in Shamus's eyes. "Kingston?"

"I'd say him or one of his boys." Jacob nodded.

"Did Hart say anything?"

"Only one word."

"What was it?"

"Goose."

"Goose?"

"Goose."

"Jesus, Mary, and Joseph, what does that mean?" Shamus threw up his hands.

"I don't know, Pa."

Shamus's eyes moved to Silverstein who had stepped beside Jacob. "And who is this gentleman?"

The peddler lifted his hat. "My name is Shelomo Silverstein, sir. At your service."

"Shelomo tended to Hart's wounds, Colonel, and that's his wagon." Jacob pointed over his shoulder.

"Welcome to my house, Mr. Silverstein," Shamus said. "Though you be a Child of the Book, you'll find no prejudice at Dromore."

"Thank you, sir. And though you be an Irishman, you'll find no prejudice in my wagon should you ever feel the need to ride in it."

For a moment, Shamus was taken aback. Then he laughed and slapped the arms of his wheelchair. "Well, that's a fair go, Mr. Silverstein, and no mistake. Indeed I'm an Irishman, and a Catholic to boot, but I still bid you welcome."

"You are too kind, Mr. O'Brien," Silverstein said. "Does your welcome extend to my mule? She's much worn from her journey. Marshal Hart is not a small man."

"Of course it does." Shamus turned to Samuel. "Will you see to it that Mr. Silverstein's mule has the best of care?"

"Of course, Colonel." Samuel took a step toward the mule.

Jacob put a hand on his brother's arm. "Sam, I promised her oats."

"Then oats she shall have."

"How is he, Lorena?" Shamus asked when the woman entered his study.

"He's still alive. We'll know better if he has a chance when the doctor gets here."

"This is a dire situation" Shamus glanced around the room at Luther Ironside and his sons. "Things have reached crisis point, have they not?"

"Damn right they have, Colonel," Luther said. "When do we ride?"

"Luther is right, Pa," Shawn agreed. "It's time we wiped Kingston and his hired-gun trash off the map."

"If Hart regains consciousness he can tell us who shot him," Jacob said. "It would justify our attack on the Rafter-K."

"Jake, he says a goose shot him, for God's sake." Ironside shook his head. "We'll never get a lick o' sense out of him. I say we ride and ride now."

Patrick stared at the ceiling. "Deuce . . . moose . . . loose . . . juice . . ."

All eyes turned to him, and Shamus said, "What on earth are you doing?"

"Colonel, Hart didn't say *goose*, he said a word that sounds like *goose*."

Patrick stared at the ceiling again. "Foose . . . hoose . . . koose . . . loose . . ."

"You've already said *loose*," Shawn said.

"Goose . . . loose . . ." Samuel started repeating the words. "Wait a minute, Hart could've been trying to say Luce . . . Lucy."

"Jacob, you were there," Shamus said. "Is it possible Hart tried to say Lucy?"

"It's possible, Colonel. He was pretty far gone and his voice was a whisper."

"Hart trusted whoever shot him," Samuel said. "If he met Lucy Masters at the Rafter-K he would've welcomed her to his camp, thinking she carried a message from Kingston."

"She carried a message all right," Ironside said. "A .44-40 ball in the back."

Shawn grinned. "What do we do with her, Luther? Hang her?"

"If she's a murderer, yes, we string her up alongside Kingston."

"Then we'd have to fight old Hugh Masters," Samuel said. "And he'd be a handful."

"The first tenet of armed conflict is not to fight a war on two fronts," Shamus said. "And perhaps worse, I count Hugh Masters among my friends."

"Well, we fight ol' Rafe first, and when we're sure that partic'lar wolf is skun, we take on Masters," Ironside said.

"Luther, I just said that Hugh is my friend." Shamus scowled.

"A man loses friends in a war, Colonel," Ironside reminded him.

"Yes, and he loses sons. And that is why I'm so reluctant to fight another one," Shamus fired back.

"Like the last scrap, we got no choice but to fight, Colonel." Ironside was adamant.

"I fear you tell the truth." Shamus suddenly looked old.

Jacob got to his feet, tall, lanky, and terrible. "I'll fight this war alone."

"You will not." Shawn rose so quickly his chair

tumbled under him. His face blazing, he said, "This is a Dromore war and we'll all fight in it."

"You're needed here, Shawn," Jacob said. "You and Pat and Sam and little Shamus. I'm not needed anywhere."

"Sit down, Jacob." Patrick pointed at him. "You've said enough. We all ride on the Rafter-K and we do it now. Pa, can we have your blessing?"

"No." Lorena spoke before Shamus could answer. "I don't want to see my husband brought home over his saddle." Tears sprang into her eyes. "Jacob is a gunfighter and war is his business. Don't you see that? Are you all so pigheaded and proud you don't see it?"

"Lorena, go join the other women and see what Mr. Silverstein is selling," Samuel ordered.

"Don't patronize me, Samuel," Lorena snapped. "I'm not some little brainless chippy you picked up in a saloon." She looked at Jacob. "Tell them, Jacob. Tell them how they'll all die."

"My brothers know what they'd face."

"Then good!" Lorena cried. "Jacob, let you be the one to die."

"Lorena!" Patrick yelled, rising to his feet. "Don't talk to my brother like that. Not now, not ever again."

"You're angry because you know I'm telling the truth, Patrick. Sooner or later Jacob is going to die by another man's gun. Best to get it over with."

"Lorena, let it go." Shamus's head drooped, chin on his chest as though he was taking an after-dinner nap.

When he looked up again, he seemed like a man being torn apart by iron claws. He spoke into a silence as taut and fragile as a spiderweb. "Earlier, Jacob told me he saw Rafter-K cattle all over our southern range. If for no other reason, this makes war unavoidable.

"Saraid and I raised four fine sons and now I have to choose between them. God forgive me, I must sacrifice one to save the others." He stared at Jacob with anguished eyes. "Jacob, do what you have to do. And may God have mercy on my soul for saying so."

"Colonel, that choice is not yours to make." Ironside rose to his feet, a tall, hard old man with sand. "I'm riding with Jacob."

"No, you're not, Luther," Shamus said. "I need you here."

"I never disobeyed an order from you before, but I'm disobeying this one." Ironside held his ground.

Shamus's anger flared. "Luther, if you go with Jacob, don't come back here, ever."

"So be it." Ironside crossed his arms.

"Pa, I guess that means I won't be coming back either," Shawn announced. "I'm riding with Jake."

"That goes for me, too." Patrick mimicked Ironside by crossing his arms.

"And me," Samuel added.

"I made my choice, now we live with it." Shamus shook his head. "Sit down, all of you."

"Ready to ride, Jake?" Ironside said, turning his back on the colonel.

"You boys know what you're getting into?" Jacob looked at his brother and the foreman of Dromore.

"Of course they know." Lorena was surprisingly composed. "But the O'Brien pride won't let then do anything less." She looked at her husband. "Samuel, come back to me." She turned to the others. "All of you come back, each and every one of you magnificent O'Briens."

"You're singing a different tune, Lorena," Shawn said.

"You're brave, loyal men—and you too, Luther. I was wrong to think I could change that. Jacob, can you forgive what I said to you?"

Jacob smiled. "Lorena, I think if it wasn't for little Shamus you'd ride right along with us."

"Would you have me?"

"I can't think of anyone else I'd rather have at my side."

"You're very kind. But I think you'd rather have Luther or one of your brothers backing your play when you meet Kingston and his gunmen."

Shamus looked around the room, his eyes sharp under his lowered white eyebrows. "Will no one obey me?"

"Not this time, Colonel." Samuel looked his father in the eye.

Shamus's three younger sons fixed their gaze on their father, ready to add their own defiance to Samuel's.

For the first time in his life, Shamus capitulated. "I can't go with you. I'd slow you down."

"We need you here, Pa," Patrick said.

"Then take the vaqueros." Shamus insisted.

Samuel shook his head. "The widow of one vaquero is already grieving and I won't ask more of them."

"They'll fight for the brand." Shamus knew they would.

"Yes, they will and they'd fight well, but they're not gunmen. This is a job for the brothers O'Brien, Colonel. Kingston's on the prod and his threats against Dromore and his killings have gone on long enough. We'll handle him ourselves. We've got it to do."

"What about Miles Lazarus?" Shamus asked.

"I'll take care of him," Jacob said.

"He's fast on the shoot."

"So am I."

Shamus turned to Ironside. "Luther, take care of my boys."

"I'd do that anyway, Colonel, but you fired me, remember?"

"I didn't fire you."

"Seems to me that you did," Ironside said.

"Well, I've hired you again. Look out for my sons like I told you, Luther. And no more sass."

Ironside grinned. "It's good to be back, Colonel."

Chapter Thirty-one

Rafe Kingston stood by his horse. Beside him was Miles Lazarus. A dozen hard-bitten Rafter-K riders stood around, waiting for the order to mount up and ride.

The sky was the color of gunmetal and the sun had not been seen for an hour. To the east, thunder rumbled over the Manzano Mountains and lightning touched the edges of the clouds with bands of silver. A few drops of rain tumbled in a rising wind and men glanced at the glowering sky and then at their boss to see if he took account of the weather as they did.

"It's your play, Mr. Kingston," Lazarus said. "Anything changed since last night?"

Kingston shook his head. "Nope, it's still just as I took it out of the box. We'll spend the morning looking for the marshal and if we find him, I'll kill him. Then we ride on Dromore, like I said."

Lazarus looked around him. "Half these boys will be dead by sundown."

"Do you care?"

"Not particularly."

"I can't have this noose hanging over my head any longer." Kingston moved his head back and forth. "It's keeping me awake o' nights."

"Then you'll sleep well tonight," Lazarus said.

"You and me will concentrate on the O'Briens, especially old Shamus. Let the boys take care of the Dromore riders." Kingston looked hard at Lazarus. "You sure you can take Jacob and that brother of his? Shawn, they call him. He's no slouch with a gun either and he's killed his share of men."

"I can take them," Lazarus said firmly.

"Then listen up. We'll have to kill every living soul there, including women and children, like I did with the sin-eaters. I don't want any loose ends." Kingston's eyes held a challenge. "You got the belly for that?"

"I've got the belly for ten thousand dollars," Lazarus answered. "That much money pays for a lot of killing."

Lucy Masters stepped out of the house, glanced at the sky, then stood next to Kingston. "Did you remember to take your slicker, Rafe?"

Kingston nodded absently, his mind on other things.

Then, as through she was making casual conversation at a ladies sewing circle, she said, "I already took care of the marshal for you."

Lucy saw the confusion and shock in Kingston's eyes. "I succeeded this time in ridding you of a worry, Rafe. I tried a couple of times to do away with that mean old Colonel O'Brien, but my shooting wasn't up to the task." She smiled. "But with Hart, well, even I can hit a man in the back at five paces."

"You shot him in the back?" Kingston asked, aghast.

There were men, including Lucy's father, who considered the rancher close kin to a skunk. But, no matter how he warped its meaning, he lived by the western code that when a man faces an enemy he looks him in the eye.

Lucy was genuinely puzzled. "Rafe, did I do wrong? Hart welcomed me to his camp and I took my chance."

"You shot him in the back," Kingston said, more to himself than the woman.

Lucy took a step back, swallowing hard. Her surprise was suddenly replaced by a pang of fear. "Rafe, I did it for you, for both of us. Don't you see? The marshal was in cahoots with the O'Briens and he planned to see you hang. I got rid of him and you reward me with a coldness of a most distressing nature." She slid her eyes to Lazarus. "Miles, talk to Rafe. Make him see reason."

But Lazarus, a man who affected the mores and manners of the frontier gambler/gunfighter, considered the woman had crossed a line. "It seems to me, Miss Lucy, that a young lady of good breeding who can shoot a United States marshal in the back, might do the same thing to a husband."

Kingston's head snapped in Lazarus's direction. "You're right about that, by God."

Lucy's hand flew to her forehead. "Am I the only sane person here?" She stepped closer to Kingston and put her hand on his arm. "It was all for us, Rafe, to clear the way for our wedding."

The Rafter-K hands shuffled their feet and looked at each other. Dealing with a hysterical woman was outside their experience.

One tall, rangy man whispered to the towhead at his side. "We got to ride before the rain hits."

The towhead nodded and scowled at the gray and black sky. "Why don't the boss just send her inside and tell her to keep her yap shut?"

As thunder banged to the west, Kingston got everybody's undivided attention. "Lucy, there isn't going to be a wedding."

Lucy Masters took a step back, her eyes wild. "What do you mean?"

"I mean just that. There will be no wedding. I've got other plans."

"But . . . but you love me."

"No, I loved your pa's ranch. That's the only reason I aimed to wed and bed you in the first place. But he's made it pretty clear that if you marry me, you won't inherit the Three Aces."

"Rafe, we don't need the Three Aces. We . . . we have each other."

"It isn't enough. Not for me." Kingston turned his back on her and said to his riders, "Listen up, all of you. I want you to hear this." He waited until a crash of thunder growled into silence. "When we stopped the sin-eaters and their pestilence, I learned a lesson that affects me, you, every man jack of us."

"Let it outta the box, boss," a rider yelled, a laugh in his voice.

"Is it about wimmen?" another man asked.

"Maybe, but not directly." Kingston looked down at his feet, then looked up at his men. "It's about power."

"I'd ruther it was about wimmen," the rider said.

"Jamey, shut your trap," Kingston said, annoyed. "Pay attention to what I'm telling you."

Lazarus, intrigued, led his horse closer and listened.

"I first knew I had power when we wiped out the wagon train," Kingston began. "Oh sure, we all heard high and mighty Colonel O'Brien huff and puff, but what did he do about it? Huh? Not a darned thing!"

A few of the punchers cheered and Kingston continued. "He was running scared and that's why he sent for a marshal." Kingston grinned. "A fat lot of good he did. And now the poor sod is dead."

More huzzahs, and Kingston spoke into them. "Shamus O'Brien knows I have the power and it scares him bad. He knows I can take Dromore and every acre, every cow, even the house he lives in."

Kingston threw up his arms. "And that's what I intend to do!"

The yells of approval grew in intensity and even Lazarus felt himself swept up in the tide of enthusiasm.

Kingston was caught up in his own fervor. "But I won't stop there. By God, not me. Old Hugh Masters treats me like dirt, says I'm a piece of white trash unfit to marry his daughter."

"For shame," a man said.

"Aye, shame. But it will not stand." Kingston's voice rose to a shout. "Men, I say we take Dromore today and the Three Aces tomorrow. After that, we'll be the biggest ranch in the territory and each and every one of you motherless hellers will have a share in it."

The cheers were so loud and so prolonged the horses danced in alarm and tugged on their bits.

After the clamor died down, a man questioned Kingston. "Hey, boss, what about the law?"

"The only law in this part of the territory is *my* law," Kingston answered. "Colonel O'Brien learned that years ago, and though I've come late to it, I've learned it, too. We know how to handle any lawman who pokes his nose too deeply into our affairs, don't we, boys?"

As he knew they would, more loud cheers erupted, the boom of the thunder a more timid counterpoint.

"Mount up, boys," Kingston yelled. "Tonight we'll eat supper in hell or the O'Brien parlor!"

"Rafe, wait," Lucy called out. "Tell me you didn't mean what you said. Tell me you love me."

"Go home to your pa, Lucy," Kingston grunted. "I don't need you any longer."

"You can't mean that, Rafe."

"Honey, I meant every word of it."

"But what will I do?"

"Do? You can start by going to hell." Kingston waved his arm and his riders clattered after him.

Lazarus drew rein on his horse and looked down at Lucy. "Hell being in love with somebody who doesn't love you in return, huh?"

The woman looked up at him, the falling rain mingling with her tears. "I'm lost." She attempted a smile. "But sometimes when a man says good-bye, it really means, 'I love you.' It doesn't mean that Rafe has stopped caring for me, does it?"

"For your sake, Lucy," Lazarus said, "I sure hope that's the case. You hold onto that because it's all he's left you."

"No," Lucy said, "there's one thing more."

"And what's that?"

"I can kill him . . . then myself. We can go to hell together . . . hand in hand."

Chapter Thirty-two

Shawn O'Brien yelled above the roar of the storm. "Jake, we need a place to hole up until this passes."

Sheets of rain hammering on his hat and the shoulders of his slicker, Jacob glanced at the sodden sky and nodded. "Seems like." His words were torn away by the wind and Shawn didn't hear him.

Patrick emerged through the tossing gray curtain of the storm and walked his horse toward his brothers and Luther Ironside. He cupped a hand to his mouth and hollered, "Shelter up ahead." Turning in the saddle, he pointed southwest. "That way."

Jacob motioned for Patrick to lead the way and he and the others fell in behind him. They rode up a steep rocky rise between stands of ponderosa pine and onto a grassy mountain meadow, a low-lying section to their right under a pool of rainwater.

As lightning glimmered around him, Jacob reckoned they were seven thousand feet above the flat and still climbing. The rawboned peaks of the Sandia Mountains towered on all sides of the five riders, dwarfing them into insignificance. The wet slopes shimmered with every lightning flash and the pines bowed their heads to the prevailing west wind.

Patrick angled across the hanging meadow and pointed ahead of him to a ruined stone cabin, only two of its walls still standing, forming a right angle. Beyond the cabin a break in a sheer rock face looked like a narrow cave. Only when the riders got closer did they make out the rectangular entrance to a mineshaft.

In the lee of the cliff the wind blew with less bluster and Patrick was able to speak in an almost normal tone of voice. "Take your pick, boys. The cabin or the mine?"

"Anywhere to get out of this rain," Ironside said, his face sour.

Patrick pushed his rain-spotted glasses higher on his nose. "I reckon the mine is the better bet. At least it's got a roof."

"Yeah, and lets hope it's roof enough to keep the whole mountain from coming down on top of us." Ironside kicked his horse forward.

"Well, this is cozy." Patrick smiled. "I reckon I'm a better scout than Dan'l Boone."

Because of the rain, Luther Ironside's rheumatisms were acting up and he was not in a mood to be complimentary. "We're stuck in a mine shaft with two dead men when we should be burning down the Rafter-K like Sherman burned Atlanta. What kind of scouting is this?"

"We needed a place to shelter, Luther," Samuel said.

"You did, Sam. I didn't."

Shawn grinned. "Rheumatisms troubling you again, Luther?"

"You mind your manners, boy." Ironside scowled. "You ain't so old that I can't take down your breeches and tan your hide with my belt."

"As soon as the rain quits we'll move out," Samuel said. "We can plan a dawn attack and maybe catch the Rafter-K when everybody's still asleep."

"Now somebody is talking sense." Ironside glared at Shawn. "And it's about time."

Jacob had explored farther into the mine and returned holding a burlap sack. He held it up for everyone to see. "I reckon there's five thousand dollars in here in notes and coin."

Ironside nodded to the two skeletons sprawled behind Jacob. "Did it belong to them?"

"I doubt it." Jacob shook his head. "Those boys have been dead for years, but the sack is new."

There was no way to tell how and why the miners had died, but both skeletons were surrounded by mildewed brass cartridge cases, suggesting they'd fought for their lives.

"What do you think, Jacob?" Samuel asked.

"Stashed here by robbers, probably," Jacob answered.

"I guess we should take the money and hand it in to the law."

Jacob shook his head again. "No, we'll leave it. The robbers might be friends of mine."

Ironside nodded his approval. "That's true blue, Jake, just like I teached you."

Samuel shrugged. "Lawman would probably keep it for himself anyway."

Patrick and Shawn managed to rustle up enough dry wood in the mineshaft to make a fire and Ironside, to make the point that he was spry as ever, went outside and filled the coffeepot from the stream that ran past the ruined cabin.

After an hour there was still no letup in the rain and spiky lighting scrawled across the sky like a hanging judge signing a death warrant.

Patrick stepped to the entrance of the cave to check on the horses. Tethered in the ruined cabin under a partial roof, they seemed to be doing all right.

As he turned to move back into the cave a movement at the top of the rise leading into the meadow attracted his attention. Through the sheeting rain he saw two riders draw rein, then slide rifles out from under their knees.

"Jacob," he said without turning, "if these two are friends of yours, you'd better start grinning and making like kissin' kin."

Jacob joined his brother at the entrance. The riders were coming on at a slow walk, their heads up and wary. Rain wheeled around them and thunder rolled across the black sky.

The men entered a stand of ponderosa and when they emerged, Jacob smiled. "Yup, just as I expected. That's One Wing Jack Norwood and Lake Anderson. I heard they were running together in this part of the territory."

Shawn stepped beside Jacob. "I heard Lake Anderson had been hung for a cow thief up Colorado way."

"So did I," Jacob said. "But that's him all right, as ever was."

"Jake, are you friends enough to those hard cases to talk pretty, or do we get ready to make a play?" Patrick looked sideways at his brother.

"They're coming in open. Just nod and grin and act friendlylike."

"Does that include me?" Ironside joined the brothers at the entrance.

"Especially you." Jacob grinned.

The riders drew rein ten yards from the mine entrance, the rain falling around them. Both were tall, grim-faced men, sporting huge untrimmed dragoon mustaches suggesting days on the scout.

"Howdy, Jack, Lake. It's been a long time," Jacob called out.

"How you been, Jake?" Anderson called back. "I heard you went crazy."

"Maybe a little, Lake. I heard you'd been hung."

Anderson nodded. "Heard that my ownself, Jake. Seems the law hung the wrong Anderson. How I was told it, they strung up a circuit preacher by mistake. Once they realized what they'd done, they gave him a nice funeral though, with a brass band and the town all draped in black bunting. I heard they roasted a pig and there was ice cream and cake." Anderson shook his head. "Sorry I missed that funeral, even though it was my own."

"Well, I'm surely glad they hung the preacher and not you, Lake." Jacob moved his eyes to Norwood. "Good to see you again, Jack."

The left sleeve of Norwood's slicker hung empty, but his right hand remained on the rifle across his knees. "It's coming down hard times, Jake. What with the telegraph and the law everywhere, it's gettin' harder for an honest outlaw to make a living."

Jacob nodded. "Sorry to hear that. Hard times all right."

"You find a poke in the mine, Jake?" Norwood asked.

"Been keeping it safe for you, Jack."

"That's mighty kind of you." Norwood glanced at the others standing around Jacob. "Me an' Lake found it on the trail, like." He blinked. "Stashed it in the mine while we was looking for the rightful owner."

"Man can't do any better than that." Jacob smiled. "Light and set. We've got coffee inside. You can put up your horses in the cabin over there if you have a mind."

"We'll keep them hosses close, Jake, if'n you don't mind," Anderson said. "Man never knows when he'll need them in an almighty hurry."

"Hard times," Jacob repeated.

"Ain't that the truth." Anderson sighed. "You know what me and Jack got when we robbed the Katy Flier a three-month ago? A bunch of bananas and thirty-five cents. Man can't even prosper in the train-robbing profession no more."

After Jacob made the introductions and Luther Ironside complimented Anderson on not getting hung, the outlaws sat with their backs to the wall, the burlap sack safely stashed between them.

After a while, Anderson looked at Jacob over the rim of his tin cup. "You boys on the scout?"

"No," Jacob said, "we've got business to attend to, is all. After this rain stops."

"We seen something." Anderson looked at his partner. "Didn't we Jack?"

"We did at that." Norwood took time to light his pipe with a brand from the fire. "Twelve, maybe fourteen riders over to White Bluffs or thereabouts."

Samuel looked alarmed. "Where were they headed?"

"They wasn't headed nowhere." Norwood shook his head. "They was holed up. Only fools and poor outlaws ride across flat ground in a lightning storm."

"Could it have been a posse?" Ironside asked. "No offense, Jack, but them riders could've been after you an' Lake."

"Could've been," Norwood allowed, "but me and Lake ain't exactly fourteen-man posse outlaws. Usually we get chased by a deputy and his dog."

Silence followed his statement.

"Just thought you'd like to know." Norwood spoke into the silence. "But since you boys ain't on the scout, you've got nothing to worry about."

"Our worries are just beginning." Samuel looked at Jacob. "Kingston?"

"Could be. And if it's him, the only place he could be headed is Dromore."

"Are you talkin' about big Rafe Kingston, owns the Rafter-K?" Norwood asked.

"Yeah," Jacob answered. "That's him."

Norwood looked at Anderson. "Lake, you mind about three years ago Kingston hung ol' Cooper Hunt and his two half-grown sons fer lifting a slick-eared calf?"

"Yeah, I mind it well." Anderson nodded. "Ol' Coop was never right in the head after his jenny mule kicked him that time. Afore that, he ran with Frank and Jesse and them, and Frank always said that Coop was true blue an' did just fine. You don't string up a man who rode with the James boys fer stealing a slick-eared calf. At least not in my book you don't."

Ironside shouldered off the wall. "Sorry, Lake, the time for talk is over. What are we waiting for, boys? Let's mount up."

Anderson glanced out at the teeming rain that glittered like steel needles in the lightning flashes. "If this Kingston feller is an enemy of your'n, Jake, you can hit him afore he gets a chance to get set. He ain't going to expect to get an attack in the rain."

Patrick pushed his glasses higher on his nose. "How do we play it, Jake? You're the war lord."

"We ride," Jacob answered. "And like Lake says, hit him when he least expects it."

"Sorry we can't ride with you, boys," Norwood said. "But me and Lake are on the scout, so you see how it is with us."

"This isn't your fight," Samuel said. "We'll handle it."

The outlaws rose to their feet and exchanged handshakes all around.

Ironside stepped to the cave entrance, then stopped and turned around. "How did you lose that wing, Jack? While you were wearing the gray?"

"While I was wearing another man's wife."

Chapter Thirty-three

"So he sent you back to me, damn his eyes." Hugh Masters looked at this daughter.

"Rafe doesn't want me, Father, he wants this ranch," Lucy said.

Masters' mouth was set in a hard line, the muscles of his jaw bunched. "I'll kill him, Lucy. He has dishonored you and disgraced me and it cannot stand. I'll take that from no man."

Masters took his holstered Remington from the gun rack beside his front door and buckled the cartridge belt around his waist.

"Pa, it's raining hard." Lucy looked out the window.

"Good, then we'll fight in cool weather," Masters answered. He was a short stocky man with close-cropped iron-gray hair. His mustache was full and thick in the fashion of the times and his brown eyes glowed with golden fire. Before he flung out the door, he yelled, "I'll round up the hands, and then I'll bring back Kingston's head on a spike."

Lucy ran to the door. "Pa, he's headed for Dromore!"

Masters stopped, rain pelting over his hat and slicker. "Dromore, you say?"

"Rafe plans to kill Colonel O'Brien."

"Then I'll fight him there."

Ten minutes later Lucy watched her father and four of his hands ride out under a leaden sky. She knew right there and then that she'd never see him again.

She crossed the polished wood floor of the cabin to the battered old campaign table that held her father's decanters. She poured herself a brandy, tossed it off, and then poured another. A hand-tinted portrait of her parents hung above the mantel. Her father stood stiffly in his gray uniform, corporal of artillery chevrons on his sleeves, and her late mother, small, demure, and pretty, sat in a chair beside him.

Lucy raised her glass. "To both of you. But it would have been better if I'd never been born."

She sat in a chair beside the fire, lit to rid the cabin of dampness. She emptied her glass again, refilled it, and returned to the chair.

The door opened and Alonsa Rios stuck her shawled head inside. After the death of Lucy's mother, Hugh Masters had appointed Alonsa his daughter's nurse. She'd taken her duties seriously and continued her duties into Lucy's adulthood, acting as a surrogate mother and a best friend.

Alonsa, wrinkled by sun, had had a hard early life as Masters battled weather, low cattle prices, and nesters to establish his ranch. She walked across the room and put her hand on Lucy's shoulder. "Child, you're soaked. You'll catch a death of cold."

"I'll be fine, Alonsa."

"I saw you ride in, and you weren't even wearing a cloak," the old woman said. "Come, let me get you out of those clothes and into something dry."

"It doesn't matter," Lucy whispered. "Nothing matters, not a thing."

"That's the brandy talking now," Alonsa said. "Why, if your father finds you drinking in the middle of the day he'll take a stick to me, and you."

"Leave me, Alonsa." Lucy looked up into the woman's eyes and read a mix of love and compassion in their black depths. She rewarded Alonsa's caring with a smile. "I'll change my clothes directly, I promise."

"I suspect a lovers' quarrel." Alonsa smiled.

"Yes. Just that."

"Do you wish to talk to me about it?"

"No, not now. Perhaps later."

"I'll come by again soon, after I've fed Carlos," Alonsa said. "You know how that husband of mine has never missed a meal in his life."

Lucy smiled. "A blacksmith works up an appetite."

"*Sí*. My blacksmith certainly does."

The woman gently took the brandy glass from Lucy's hand and laid it on the table. "Now, no more brandy. Get changed and I'll come back and check on you, and we'll talk about you and your intended." Alonsa kissed Lucy on her forehead. "Everything will work out, you'll see. Mr. Masters is a stubborn man, but in the end he'll give your marriage his blessing. You must be patient with him."

Lucy nodded. "Do you have your rosary with you, Alonsa?"

"Why, bless you, child, I always carry it."

"May I borrow it for a while?"

"Of course you can."

Alonsa dipped into the pocket of her dress and produced a rosary of pink coral. As she handed it to Lucy she said, "Pray to the Madonna of Good Counsel. She will give you sound advice."

"Yes, I will, Alonsa. And thank you, thank you for all you've done for me over the years."

"Lucy, are you feeling quite well?" the older woman asked. "You don't seem yourself today."

"I'm fine. Just a lovers' quarrel, as you said."

"Broken hearts do mend, Lucy. Now, get changed and I'll see you soon."

After Alonsa left, Lucy filled her glass with brandy again and stepped to the window. The sky looked like coal in a scuttle and the relentless rain rattled on the panes, streaming tears. She struggled in thought for a while, then made up her mind, crossing the floor to sit at her father's desk.

Lucy found writing paper, dipped a pen in the inkwell and wrote . . .

My Darling Rafe,

She wrote nothing else. No words came to mind, at least none that could explain her sense of loss, her utter hopelessness, and the bruises on her conscience over Red Hart and the Indian's unnecessary deaths.

After crumpling the paper and throwing it on the floor, Lucy drank more brandy. The alcohol worked on her, numbing her for what was to come.

The pink rosary in her left hand, she stepped to the gun rack where the blue rifles stood end on end. Under the rifles was a rectangular drawer. She opened it and smelled the familiar odor of gun oil. Three revolvers lay in the green baize bottom of the drawer. She chose the engraved Smith & Wesson .45 caliber Schofield, for no other reason than it looked pretty.

Lucy carried the gun into her bedroom, drained the last of the brandy from her glass, and then stripped off her clothes. She dressed in a lacy nightgown that had come all the way from Denver, brushed out her luxuriant hair and tied it up again with bright scarlet ribbons. That done she applied her makeup, taking pains to get it just right.

The big Schofield in her right hand, the cascading rosary beads in her left, she lay on the bed, settled herself, and arranged the fall of her hair on the pillow. Modestly, she pulled the nightgown over her ankles.

Lucy placed the muzzle of the revolver against her temple, thumbed back the hammer, and pulled the trigger.

Thunder roared.

Chapter Thirty-four

"We're moving out," Rafe Kingston hollered. "This storm looks like it will last all day."

"I'm with you," Miles Lazarus agreed. "We're getting nothing done squatting in the trees."

Rain from the pines ticked around the Rafter-K riders and lightning flashes lanced across the sky, thunder roaring its approval.

"Derned hundred year storm, if you ask me." Kingston looked at Lazarus from under his dripping hat brim. "Is it a good or bad omen?"

"Bad for Shamus O'Brien and his sons. Good for us."

Kingston agreed and waved to his men. "Mount up, boys."

Cowboys are even more superstitious than sailors, and the Rafter-K hands were no exception. Not a man of them had experienced a storm like the one raging around them. Unlike Lazarus, most of them took it as a bad sign. Maybe it was not a good day to die.

Grumbling, the riders swung into the saddle and followed Kingston and Lazarus down the shallow rise from the trees onto the flat. Rain and wind tore at them as they glanced fearfully at the sky where lighting threatened to crack it open like a rotten egg.

"What was that?" Lazarus drew rein so suddenly Kingston trotted past him.

Turning his horse around, the Rafter-K boss came back. "What was what?"

"I thought I heard a gunshot," Lazarus said.

"I didn't hear anything." Kingston turned in the saddle and asked his men, "Any of you boys hear a gunshot?" He was met with blank stares and said to Lazarus, "You're hearing things."

"I was sure I heard a revolver shot," Lazarus said, his face puzzled.

"Just the thunder," Kingston replied.

"Yeah, I guess that's what it was." But Lazarus felt uneasy, as though a goose had just flown over his grave.

Kingston and his men were in the high timber country ten miles south of Dromore when the rain grew colder, a sure sign it was falling from a higher altitude than the clouds suggested.

Without warning, a lightning bolt hit.

The man riding drag disappeared in a flash of blinding light. Thunder crashed. Horses screamed and reared. Riders nearest to the flash were thrown.

The riderless horses galloped in a panic across the flat, their stirrups flying.

Lazarus jumped out of the saddle and ran to the man who'd been struck. The tough-looking young puncher lay pinned under his dead horse. Other than a red flush on his face he looked unhurt.

"He's all right," Lazarus said to the men gathering around him.

A moment later he realized he was very wrong. The puncher was stone dead, his heart stopped by a terrifying electrical blast that had lasted less than a tenth of a second.

"Young Tom was dead afore he even knowed he was dead," a puncher mumbled.

He was right. The young Texan never knew what hit him.

As the two thrown riders got painfully to their feet, Kingston and another man left to round up their scared horses.

At that moment Lazarus knew what Kingston did not—that all the fight had gone out of the Rafter-K men. They were beaten before they'd even fired a shot.

The rest of the men dismounted and clustered around Tom's body, their faces grim. The storm still roared around them, but lost in the tragedy of the moment they seemed unaware of the rain and wind.

Kingston rode back with the loose horses, aware that all was not well with his men. "Boys," he yelled above the racketing storm, "you know what hap-pened here? Colonel Shamus O'Brien called down the powers of hell against us and made the lightning strike."

"Then it's time to head back," a man yelled.

Steamrolling over murmurs of agreement, Kingston roared, "That's what O'Brien wants us to do, but we won't. We will ride on to Dromore and fall on him like the sword of God."

Kingston's speech was deliberately biblical, but met with little enthusiasm. He upped the ante, speaking in terms his men could understand. "Men," he roared, "I will pay a bounty of five hundred dollars for the ears of Shamus O'Brien. For the ears of any of his sons, his vaqueros, and any woman and child who calls Dromore home I will pay a hundred in gold." He waited until his riders absorbed that. Then he upped it again. "For each ear!"

There were a few cheers and no mutters of dissent. Money is the international language and Kingston was speaking it fluently.

Sensing that he had them, Kingston yelled, "Well, boys, are you with me?"

Most everyone cheered. The exception was one man who asked, "What about Tom?"

"We'll come back this way and bury him decent," Kingston answered. "I can't say any fairer than that."

This seemed to satisfy the riders and to a man they swung into their wet saddles.

Lazarus kneed his horse beside Kingston. "You're spending big."

Kingston nodded. "Maybe. But for Dromore I'd sell my soul, and yours and everybody else's."

"They'll cut and run at the first volley," Lazarus predicted.

"There won't be any first volley," Kingston said. "Dromore is taking a nap in the rain. We'll be on them like a pack of wolves before they get a chance to wake up."

"Mr. Kingston, I don't like the feel of this. It seems all wrong to me, like I'm in the middle of a bad dream."

"If you've suddenly developed a yellow streak, ride on out of here," Kingston spat out.

"I'll stick." Lazarus gritted his teeth, his anger flaring.

"Then stick, and keep your trap shut. These men are boogered enough as it is."

Chapter Thirty-five

"You don't have much time, Shamus," Hugh Masters said. "I reckon Kingston and his men are right behind us."

Masters' word was good enough for Shamus, or any man come to that. The colonel immediately summoned his butler and ordered him to bring the vaqueros to the house. "As many as you can round up, mind. And be quick about it."

Shamus turned to Masters. "How many men with Kingston, Hugh?"

"He'll have a dozen at least, and that Galveston gunhawk is with him."

"Miles Lazarus?"

"Yeah, and they say he's worth a dozen men all on his lonesome."

"I've heard that about other men," Shamus said. "Usually they don't pan out."

"This one will, Shamus, depend on it."

Impressed by the butler's urgency, eight vaqueros

crowded into the parlor. All wore belt guns and carried rifles.

"Where are the rest?" Shamus cried.

"Out on the range, *patrón*," a man said.

"Then we'll make do with what we have." Shamus turned to Masters again. "How many hands did you bring, Hugh?"

"Four. They're punchers, not gunmen, but they'll stand."

"Then we have about equal numbers."

"How do we play it?" Masters, the sergeant of artillery yielded command to the colonel of horse.

Shamus didn't hesitate, as though he gave the matter no thought. But the ability to make instant decisions was bred into him on a dozen battlefields. "Hugh, take two vaqueros and your own men and establish a position on the ridge opposite the house. Lie low and allow the Rafter-K to pass. I don't want you to be seen."

"Yes, Colonel," Masters said, the war coming back to him.

"They'll try to surprise us and when that fails they will act like cavalry always does when fired upon," Shamus said. "They'll fall back to regroup and that's when you'll attack from the ridge. We'll have them between us and God help Kingston and the poor souls with him."

An old soldier like Masters needed no further orders. He picked out two vaqueros and told the men to follow him.

After he left, Shamus posted his remaining vaqueros at the windows of the house and ordered them to lie low until Kingston attacked. "Shoot to kill, boys. We're facing lads with sand and there will be no quit in them."

He motioned the nearest vaquero to push him to his open parlor window. As the cowboy returned to his post the colonel set his rifle across the arms of his wheelchair. To his surprise Lorena joined him, carrying her own Winchester.

"Lorena, this is no place for you," Shamus said. "Go to the back of the house with the women and take care of little Shamus."

"In a pig's eye, Colonel." She moved to the other window and stared outside. Without turning, she said, "This is my fight as well as yours."

Shamus knew that further argument would be useless. "Then keep your head down and shoot only if there's danger of us being overrun."

After a few moments of silence, he smiled. "You'd make one hell of a soldier, Lorena."

"I'm fighting with one hell of a soldier, Colonel."

As Dromore waited, the rain fell in sheets, tumbled by a blustering wind. Iron gray clouds hung heavily on the summit of Glorieta Mesa and the lighting made itself known, flickering inside them.

Shamus knew old Hugh Masters and his men must be suffering up on the ridge because the rain was

cold and the keening wind relentless. Under those
conditions, even in summer, a man could get chilled
to the bone.

Where is Kingston?

"Lorena, you've got young eyes," Shamus said. "Do
you see anything?"

"I saw a man on the ridge, Colonel. Just a
moment, then he was gone."

"I told Masters to lie low. I never met an artillery-
man yet that could follow orders."

"I wish he had a couple cannon up there." Lorena
voiced what she had been thinking.

"Or a Gatling gun," Shamus mused. "That would
be better still." As an afterthought he added, "Or two
of them."

The Rafter-K attack was determined, violent, and
sudden. Rafe Kingston led his men through the rain
and charged directly at the front of Dromore, his
riders firing into the windows, shattering glass and
wood frames.

As guns and men roared, Kingston rode for the
door. He was already halfway out of the saddle, his
left foot in the stirrup, when the first Dromore volley
crashed into the Rafter-K riders.

Two men and three screaming, kicking horses
went down.

Alarmed, Kingston regained his seat and pumped
shots into the window where Shamus sat in his

wheelchair. A bullet grazed the colonel's left bicep and a second slammed into the grandfather clock against the wall behind him. The clock chimed its mortal wound and groaned with a sound of twanging springs and mangled flywheels.

The Dromore vaqueros fired in earnest and another of Kingston's riders threw up his hands and slammed onto the muddy ground, rainwater splashing around him. Already shaken by the lightning bolt, the Rafter-K men were unsteady in the attack. To a man, they wheeled their horses and trotted back toward the ridge. Kingston followed them, cursing.

This was not Miles Lazarus's kind of fight. He fired into two of the upper windows and retreated with the others, in time to be met by the volley of Masters' riflemen on the ridge.

Bullets raked the milling Rafter-K riders and two more men hit the ground, one pulling his horse on top of him.

Suddenly, it was nobody's kind of fight.

Vaqueros poured out of the front door of Dromore and worked their rifles steadily, firing into the tangled, panicked mass of men and horses.

It was enough. What was left of the Rafter-K broke and ran.

Unwilling to take part in a slaughter, Shamus yelled at his vaqueros to cease firing. But a man with his blood up will keep killing long after the need is gone.

Joined by the men on the ridge, the vaqueros ran

out onto the flat in front of the house where they were joined by Masters and the others.

Two more of the fleeing riders were shot out of their saddles until rain and mist mercifully shrouded the few survivors.

Lazarus and Kingston were first-rate fighting men and kept up a steady fire as they retreated. Later, talking men would say that Lazarus accounted for the pair of vaqueros who were killed in the battle and that he also mortally wounded one of Masters' men, shooting off his lower jaw.

The vaqueros also claimed that Lazarus and Kingston were both hit before they disappeared into rain and distance.

Shamus listened to their report but paid little heed to the possible fate of Kingston and his hired gun. He was worried about Lorena, who lay slumped in a chair attended by Sarah and Mrs. Baker. Blood reddening the sleeve of his shirt, he wheeled toward the women. "Well, how is she?" he demanded. "Ladies, tell me something."

"She has glass fragments in her neck, Colonel," Sarah said. "But she's not hurt badly."

"No, she's not," Constance Baker added. "Lorena will be just fine."

"You know, I can talk for myself." Lorena raised her head so that Shamus could see her bloody neck. "It's just a scratch, Colonel."

"At least a dozen scratches," Sarah said. "If the truth be told."

Hugh Masters thudded inside, his spurs ringing. "Shamus, it was a close run thing."

"It wasn't a close run thing at all," Shamus disagreed. "It was a slaughter. Pour yourself a drink, Hugh, and for anybody else who wants one. And pour three fingers for me." He pushed closer to Masters. "What's the butcher's bill?"

"Seven of Kingston's men dead." Masters looked away as though pouring whiskey suddenly demanded all of his attention. Without meeting Shamus's eyes, he said, "There were no wounded . . . that lived."

He handed Shamus a glass. "You lost two vaqueros, Colonel, and my man Elias Thorne will last until midnight."

"A steep price to pay for one man's stupidity," Shamus pointed out.

"And his treachery," Masters said. "As we speak, my daughter sits in my house nursing a broken heart. It may take her years to recover from it." He raised his glass. "Here's to a battle won, Shamus."

Shamus raised his own glass. "And to your daughter, Hugh. May her poor broken heart soon mend."

The brothers O'Brien and Luther Ironside rode up as vaqueros dragged away the dead horses and gathered the dead for burial. Shamus sat outside in his wheelchair to supervise the work. A black umbrella protected him from the rain and there was a fat bandage on his left upper arm.

"Looks like we missed a scrap," Ironside said. "I told you boys not to dillydally, but nobody ever listens to me."

The riders swung out of the saddles. Samuel stepped to his father's side. "Pa, are you hurt bad?"

"I got winged was all. But go inside and see to your wife. She was cut by flying glass."

Alarmed, Samuel ran inside.

Jacob looked at his pa. "How bad is she, Colonel?"

"She'll be fine, just a few scratches." Shamus glared at Ironside. "A tad late to the party, huh, Luther?"

"Sorry I missed it, Colonel," Ironside said, writhing in shame and regret.

"I would've liked you at my side." Shamus looked at his sons. "And that goes for the rest of you."

"Kingston?" Jacob asked.

"Got away clean, him and Lazarus. Some of the boys say they were hit, but I don't know about that."

Jacob's eyes roamed over the Rafter-K dead who'd been laid out under canvas tarps, only their booted feet showing. Wailing women were already carrying away the bodies of the two dead vaqueros. "Looks like you had yourself a ball."

"Hugh Masters joined me with four of his hands, and now one of them isn't expected to live through the night. But, God bless him, he and the rest of them made the difference."

"It isn't over, Colonel," Jacob said. "Not so long as Rafe Kingston casts a shadow on the earth."

"Masters is out looking for him, but he won't find him. His hands are pretty well done after today's work." Shamus smiled. "And they've each drank a bellyful of my best whiskey."

Chapter Thirty-six

Hugh Masters looked older than he'd ever had, older than he'd ever felt before. Numb, his eyes stared into the distance but he saw only the vision of his daughter on her bed, blood and brains staining the lace pillow under her head.

He stepped out of the cabin into the rain and, like a sleepwalker, stumbled toward his men, his boots dragging deep ruts in the mud.

The hands saw Masters from the livery stable, then stood at the door and watched him. They'd say later that it was like looking at a dead man.

Happy Harry Monroe, a woebegone man of middle age with the long, downhearted face of an overworked mule, was more sensitive to sadness and loss than the rest of the punchers. He left the barn at a fast walk and stepped in front of Masters. "Boss, what's the matter?"

Masters' unfocused eyes finally hardened into a

direct stare. "She's dead, Harry. My daughter took her own life."

For a moment Monroe looked like he'd been slapped. His mouth opened, shut, opened again. His prominent Adam's apple bobbing, he said, "Boss . . . oh my God, boss."

Masters eyes were relentless and lanced into Monroe like shards of shattered glass. "She's already in hell, Harry, burning in the lake of fire as we speak."

Monroe shook his head. "No, boss, no. The Bible is silent on suicide. My ma told me that after my pa hung hisself to end the pain of the belly cancer. Whether Lucy is in heaven or hell is between her and her God."

"You believe that?" Masters asked.

"Yes, boss, I do."

"Then I'm the one in hell. Do you believe that?"

"Boss, I—"

"Am I in hell, Harry?"

The puncher hesitated, his brown eyes bleak. "I reckon so, boss. It's a hard thing for a man to lose his child."

"And hard is the vengeance I will bring down on the Rafter-K and the head of Rafe Kingston."

Masters looked beyond Monroe. "Clem, saddle a fresh horse and one for me. Shorty, you and Harry hitch up the buckboard and bring shovels." He stared at them, a grim, unforgiving old man who stood alone in mud and rain. "We'll have burying to do before this day is done."

* * *

Hugh Masters carried his daughter's body from the cabin. Lucy's face, as white as marble, was turned to the rain and her blue eyes were open but saw nothing. The bullet had shattered her skull and the running rain turned the front of her gown pink.

Helped by the hands, Masters laid the body in the bed of the buckboard then covered it with a canvas tarp.

"Mount up, boys," he said, swinging into his saddle. "By God, if I don't bring fire and sword to Rafe Kingston, then bury me deep because I'll be dead."

Masters moved out, the man called Clem riding next to him, Monroe and Shorty up on the buckboard seat. Behind them, Lucy's body rocked back and forth with the motion of the wagon. Harry Monroe, a Bible-reading man, whispered prayers for the dead—and for himself.

Shorty handled the ribbons, his round, freckled face bent to the wind and rain. Without looking at Monroe, he said, "What do you reckon, Harry?"

"About what?"

"Well, here's how it goes. Oncet me and another puncher got drunk down San Antone way and we wandered into a lantern lamp prayer meetin' in a tent. As I recollect, it was raining like this and it hardly ever rains in San Antone."

"So what happened?"

"Well, the preacher made us sit in front on what he called a mourning bench on account of how it's reserved for folks grieving fer a loved one."

"Who were you mourning fer?" Monroe asked as

lightning scrawled across the sky and the mule team tossed their uneasy heads.

"We wasn't grievin' for nobody, but poor sinnin' cowboys always get to sit on the mourners bench with the crying folks. I don't know why that is, but it's a natural fact."

"And then what happened?" Monroe asked again, only vaguely interested.

"Well, how it come up, the preacher lit into me and this other feller, saying we was killin' ourselves with demon drink. He said, 'There's a serpent in every whiskey bottle and it biteth like the viper.' Biteth like the viper. I always remembered that."

"Shorty, you're a storytelling man, an' no mistake. So what did the preacher do?"

"Do? He didn't do nothing. But he said a man who kills himself with whiskey commits suicide." Shorty shivered and jerked a thumb over his shoulder. "Suicide, mind, just like she done."

"And that's it? That's the story?"

"No, not all of it. See, then the preacher said that the souls of suicides can never find eternal rest and they wander the earth forever, moaning and groaning and begging God for forgiveness. Scared me so much, I swore off whiskey and whores for a month after that."

"She ain't going to wander the earth, Shorty," Monroe said.

"How do you know? She looks pretty lively back there to me."

Thunder rolled across the heavens and around

the wagon and riders, and shredded pine needles tossed in the wind. The buckboard creaked and gobs of black mud slopped off its iron-shod wheels.

Shorty, a talking man, was not done. "Why are we taking her to the Rafter-K, Harry? I mean, if there's gun work to be done."

"I don't know, Shorty. I surely don't."

"The boss ain't gonna bury her there, is he?"

"Naw, that would be too strange."

"Then why are we taking her to the Rafter-K, Harry?"

"I don't know, Shorty."

"You ain't much for a knowin' man, Harry."

"Sometimes it's better not to know things."

Chapter Thirty-seven

Rafe Kingston knew the wound was bad. The rifle bullet had entered his right armpit, ranged upward, and exited close to his shoulder joint, shattering the collarbone on its way out.

The pain was intense and when he removed his slicker from collar to chest his shirt was glistening scarlet with blood. He poured himself a drink, then looked out the window, hoping to see his hands ride in. His eyes met only rain and wind and emptiness.

Roughly handled at Dromore, the boys had lit out for places unknown, putting as much git between them and the O'Briens as a galloping horse would allow.

Kingston gulped the raw whiskey, then grimaced as a fresh wave of pain hit him. He needed a doctor real bad.

There was no question of him remaining at the Rafter-K. Too many enemies would be hunting him. He had to get away, and soon before they caught up with him.

Kingston crossed the room, opened his safe, and removed the money and negotiable bonds he'd stashed over the past few years when times were good. He found an empty flour sack in the kitchen and stuffed the money and bonds inside. He reckoned he'd around thirty thousand dollars, enough to make a fresh start somewhere else. Later, when he was set, he could return and deal with the O'Briens.

"Going somewhere, Kingston?"

Startled, Kingston turned, aware that his gun hand was next to useless. "Lazarus, you surprised me."

"Obviously."

Kingston didn't like the curious, feral light in Lazarus's eyes. It scared him. The archeologist had the Egyptian statue jammed into his pants above his gun belt and looked like an avenging god.

"I thought you'd run with the rest," Kingston said, pretending a bravado he did not feel.

"Not while you owe me ten thousand dollars," Lazarus stated.

"The deal is off, Lazarus. You didn't kill Shamus O'Brien or any of his sons. But I'll see if I've any pocket change and give you a grubstake."

Lazarus smiled and Kingston didn't appreciate it one bit. It was a cold smile, like the grin on a skull.

"How much in your poke there, Kingston?" Lazarus nodded to the sack.

"Only enough for me. I need this money to make a fresh start."

"How much?"

"I don't know."

"How much?"

Kingston hesitated, then said, "Maybe thirty thousand in banknotes and bonds."

"It's enough." Lazarus held out his hand. "I'll take it."

"This money is mine, Lazarus.

"Big talk from a one-armed man."

Kingston saw the logic of that. His brain worked feverishly. There must be a way out before he bled to death. He'd compromise, or pretend to, then wait for his chance to shoot Lazarus in the back. "Half. You can have half. That's fifteen thousand, Lazarus, more money then you'll ever see in your life." Kingston tried his best to look sincere. "All you have to do in return is help me get to a doctor."

"Why did you kill the sin-eaters, Kingston?" Lazarus spoke softly.

The comment was so unexpected Kingston was stuck for words. But after opening and closing his mouth a few times, he managed to say, "You know why. They were carrying the cholera."

"The wagons were headed north, away from your range. You had no call to kill them."

"I did it to save Santa Fe. The diseased trash planned to enter the city and they'd have killed thousands. I stopped them."

Lazarus smiled. "Kingston, you didn't care about Santa Fe, not then, not now. You killed them because you could. It gave you a sense of power and boosted your ego."

"What does that mean?"

"Killing those people made you feel like a big man. Even the fence was unnecessary. You and your boys could've stood off and shot the pilgrims down with rifles, but the barbed wire was a symbol of the power you wielded and it pleased you mightily."

"And what about you, gunfighter? How many men have you killed because you could?"

"Too many."

"Then you're no better than me."

"I know, and it troubles me. I meet a lowdown, murdering guy like you and it's as though I'm looking into a mirror, seeing what I've become. Now, before I leave, I'm going to smash that mirror."

Lazarus's gun was suddenly in his hand. "Kneel down, Kingston, and keep your eyes on mine. See it coming and die like a man. Now kneel!"

Kingston was horrified. "You're going to kill me over a bunch of dirty sin-eaters?"

"No, I'm going to kill you because you're the man in my mirror."

Holding up a pleading hand, Kingston dropped to his knees. "Don't kill me, Lazarus." He grabbed the money sack. "Here, take it all, every penny. Just don't shoot."

Lazarus pushed the muzzle of his Colt between Kingston's eyes and thumbed back the hammer. Outside thunder roared and Kingston winced at the sound, then whimpered, repeating "*no*, no, no."

A half-minute passed before Lazarus lowered the hammer and reholstered his revolver. He leaned over, jerked the sack from Kingston, and pulled the man's Colt. Opening the loading gate, he rotated the cylinder and allowed the rounds to thud onto the floor.

He tossed the revolver into a corner, then said, "Kingston, you're not worth killing, and I guess that means I'm not worth killing either."

Lazarus stepped to the door and behind him Kingston pleaded for at least some of the money. The door slammed shut and broke off the rancher's words like a snapping branch.

Sick to his belly, Lazarus wiped rainwater from his saddle and mounted. For a few moments he sat deep in thought, and then glanced at the black sky, a man with a past, a present, but no future he cared to face.

He felt the Shabti in his waistband, warm, as though the woman the figurine represented was alive.

"Miles, I'll be very jealous if your handmaiden ever comes to life," Lady Victoria Lytton once told him. And he'd said, "No matter, she could never compare to you."

But Vicky was dead, with no warmth in her. She lay under the hot dry sand of Egypt and all her dazzling beauty had long since moldered away to bone.

Lazarus swung his horse away from the ranch house and rode into the somber gloom of the day, a man in hopeless search of a star.

Chapter Thirty-eight

Rafe Kingston's time was running out fast and he knew it. He was losing blood at an increasing rate and his head had already begun to swim.

Ignoring his discarded Colt, he hobbled to the rifle rack. After fumbling the key in the lock a few times he finally opened the glass doors and took down a Marlin Model of 1881 in .38-55 caliber. The lever-action rifle was a tack driver and he chose the beautiful weapon because his shattered right shoulder would allow him only one shot. The recoil would do even more damage. He knew and accepted that a second shot would be out of the question.

Good with a long gun, Kingston reckoned he could take down Lazarus with one bullet and get his money back.

But if he missed . . . Kingston refused to consider that. Lazarus's back was broad enough, he couldn't miss.

Kingston winced in pain and cried out aloud as he struggled into his slicker. Rifle in hand he stepped to the door then lurched outside. His horse had gone to the barn and cursing, he went after it.

The horse was tired and didn't want leave the dry barn, but Kingston managed to mount, then savagely roweled the animal into a run, following Lazarus north before the rain washed out his tracks.

His eyes scanning the rain-lashed ground ahead of him, Kingston calculated Lazarus would head for Albuquerque where he could spend his ill-gotten gains. But the man seemed to be keeping close to the timbered foothills of the Manzano Mountains, riding clear of the rolling flat lands and a direct route to the city.

Kingston slowed his faltering horse to a trot. Ahead of him he saw only the raking rain and pines tossing in the wind. The wet land around him shimmered searing white in the lightning flashes, but of Lazarus there was no sign.

Hell's Canyon curved into the mountains to Kingston's east and his gaze searched the area. Nothing moved but the wind and trees, and the rain hammered at him, drumming on his hat and shoulders. He felt an ache in his right hand and realized he was clutching the Marlin so tight it pained him.

Where is Lazarus? Kingston worried the gunfighter could be up on one of the high ridges with his sights lined up on the rancher's chest. Shuddering from a combination of pain and loss of blood, he was glad to ride into a stand of juniper and piñon where he could take stock of his situation without fear of getting blasted from the saddle.

Branches pitched around Kingston, showering rain-water down on him as he considered his options. It took him only a second to make his decision. His wound needed a doctor's care and he could easily make Albuquerque before dark. He'd ignore Lazarus and swing northwest toward the city. When his shoulder was healed enough for him to hold a gun, he'd go hunting the man he now hated with a burning passion.

His mind made up, Kingston rode out of the trees—and into a nightmare that spoiled all his plans.

Ahead of him, coming on through the weather, two riders rode point for a wagon with two up on the seat. Kingston recognized the lead horseman and his blood froze. It was Hugh Masters and the last person he wanted to meet was Lucy's angry father. The man had steadfastly refused his daughter's hand in marriage, but he could be mad as all get out because she'd been dumped and betrayed.

Angry papas with heartbroken daughters were not big on logic and tended to reach for horsewhips.

Kingston considered that he might brazen it out, confront Masters and blame his breakup with Lucy on him. Then, if all went well, ask him for his help to get medical care for his shoulder and his pledge to help hunt down Lazarus. The old man was a nonentity and stupid, and stupid nonentities could be talked into anything.

Smiling, Kingston rode toward Masters, his good hand raised in a friendly greeting.

Masters' rifle shot took off the middle and ring fingers of that hand.

Kingston screamed and stared in horror at his mangled, bloodied stump. He dropped his rifle, useless now, and tried to spur his horse away from the oncoming riders.

A second shot dropped the horse and Kingston went down with it, the cartwheeling ground hurtling up fast to meet him.

He lay on his back and opened his eyes, looking up at Hugh Masters' hard, unforgiving face.

"Lucy is dead," Masters said. "She took her own life."

He was joined by all four of his men and Kingston felt a spike of panic and fear. He'd seen expressions like those on the faces of men before, as though each feature had been chipped from granite . . . the faces of a hanging posse.

"The fault is not mine, Masters," Kingston said, his voice unsteady. "All the blame is yours."

Masters nodded. "There is some truth in what you say, and it's a thing I'll have to live with. But it was you who cast Lucy aside like a worn-out boot and it was you who destroyed her will to live. For that, there must be a reckoning."

"Masters, you shot my fingers off, and maybe it was you who put a bullet into me at Dromore," Kingston wailed. "There's already been reckoning enough."

Masters shook his head, the rain and the stark

lightning flashes making him look more terrible, like an Old Testament prophet ordering the stoning of an adulteress. "Kingston, I will punish you like I've never punished any man. And may God forgive me."

"Don't hang me, Masters, for pity's sake." Kingston held up his bleeding stump of a hand. "Look, there's the reckoning. It's done."

"No, the reckoning is still to come." Masters turned to his men. "Bring the shovels and find a loamy spot in the earth where the soil is deep. Dig a grave of great depth and make it wide."

"Boss," Happy Harry Monroe said, "we gonna hang this man?"

"Dig the burial pit, Harry, like I told you."

"Masters," Kingston whined, "what are you going to do? Have mercy on me. Please, have mercy on poor Rafe Kingston."

Masters placed his hand on his chest. "There is no mercy here. I cannot give you what I don't have."

"After this is done, Mr. Masters, you're going to have to live with yourself for a score of years and maybe more," Monroe said.

Masters nodded. "Yes, a score of years in hell, I know that." He looked at Monroe, into the puncher's sad, hound dog eyes. "Dig, Harry."

It took the Three Aces hands an hour and a half to dig a hole on top of a hogback rise where the unyielding wet soil was tangled with juniper roots. When the men were finished, they returned to Masters' side.

"Put Lucy in the ground, boys," Masters said.

Monroe looked hard at his boss, but said nothing. To the others he nodded. "Let's do as he says."

Kingston tried to rise to his feet, but the muzzle of Masters' rifle prodded him back to a sitting position.

"Now I understand. You're burying Lucy then taking me to the O'Briens," Kingston said, hope gleaming in his eyes. "That's the reckoning, isn't it?"

Masters said nothing, his weather beaten mahogany face revealing as much emotion as a cigar store Indian.

"Well, you're right, Masters. Let the O'Briens deal with me. That's only right." The rain had lessened and so had the fear in Kingston's eyes. "Colonel O'Brien is a hard man, but he's fair. He'll find me a doctor and then impose a fair punishment." Despite the pain from his mangled shoulder and shot-up hand, Kingston managed a slight smile. "That's the way it's going to be, Masters, isn't it? That's the way it's going to be?"

Masters said nothing. He glanced at the sky, then to the south where a black and gray shelf of cloud, shaped like a gigantic fan, heralded a coming squall front. The old man nodded to himself. The hundred-year rain was not through with this part of the territory yet and it would benefit his grass.

Monroe interrupted his thoughts. "Boss, we've laid Miss Lucy to rest. Do you want to say the words now?"

"There are no words for a suicide, Harry. My daughter is surely damned." He nudged Kingston with his rifle. "Tie him up, boys. Bind him tight hand and foot."

"Boss, do you mind if I say the words for Lucy?" Monroe asked solemnly.

"Bind him!" Masters screamed. "Bind this piece of trash."

"I know what you're going to do, boss," Monroe spoke softly. "And I'll have no truck with such an obscenity."

"That goes for me too, Boss," Shorty said. "I ride for the brand, but this here is stretching it mighty thin."

"Well, if you don't have the bellies for it, take the horses and go back to the ranch." Masters was harsh. "When I get back, you can draw your time."

"Sorry, real sorry," Shorty said.

"We're all sorry, Shorty." Masters nodded.

Monroe jammed his lips together, his throat working. Finally he said, "May God forgive you for what you're about to do, Mr. Masters." He looked at Clem. "You comin'?"

"I'll stick," Clem said.

"Your funeral, Clem Lander," Monroe said.

Rafe Kingston didn't start screaming until he was dragged to the top of the rise.

The squall hit and the rain fell heavier than before, but there was no thunder, only the venomous hiss of the downpour.

The slickers of Masters and Clem Lander glistened in gray light as they dragged Kingston closer to the hole. Lying on his left side, he looked into the grave and saw Lucy's body. Dirt spotted her face and her open eyes stared up at him, impervious to the spattering rain.

It was then that Kingston knew what Masters had in store for him. The man who'd delighted in bringing fear to others shrieked and begged for his life. "Masters, for the love of God, don't do this. Don't do this to me," he cried.

"Lucy wanted to be with you in life," Masters said. "Now she'll be close to you for all eternity."

Bound hand and foot, Kingston couldn't move, but he turned his head and yelled to Lander, "Stop him! He's crazy, don't you see? Crazy!"

But Lander's face was like stone. As a boy he'd watched his mother and three sisters raped and tortured by a Ute war party and since that day no horror could touch him. Whatever feelings he'd once possessed had long since withered and died inside him. Kingston's plight did not touch him.

"Rafe Kingston," Masters said in a terrible voice, like a judge announcing a death sentence, "you are about to enter the ground. The dirt will fall on you and cover your eyes and your ears and your mouth, but you won't be dead. That will take time."

A glint of Kingston's old cruelty shone in his eyes. "Masters, I'll see you in hell," he screamed. "You'll watch as I use your daughter like a fifty cent whore."

As though he hadn't heard, Masters continued.

"Perhaps in your last seconds, before the earth smothers the life out of you, you'll see the light and beg God for his tender mercy. I hope that is the case."

Masters looked at Clem. "Throw him in the hole and cover him up."

Kingston thudded on top of Lucy's body and he smelled the vile beginnings of her corruption. Beyond words, he screamed until the wet dirt filled his mouth and throat and he could scream no longer.

Clem Lander filled the grave with earth and then patted it flat with his shovel. There was no movement of the soil and the only sound was the *tick-tick-tick* of the rain.

Masters dropped his rifle and pulled his revolver. "Clem, tell them how it was."

"Boss, I—"

Hugh Masters shoved the gun barrel into his mouth and pulled the trigger.

Chapter Thirty-nine

When Lorena O'Brien stepped out of Red Hart's room, the first person she saw in the hallway was Ironside. "Luther, quickly. He wants to talk with someone urgently."

"Me?" Ironside looked confused.

"You'll do. Now come. I don't know how long he'll stay conscious."

Ironside stepped into the room and smiled at Hart, who was lying on his back on the bed, his head propped up on a pillow. "How are you doing, Marshal?" Ironside shook his head. "You don't look so good, pale as a ghost."

"Listen," Hart whispered. "It . . . it was Lucy Masters who shot me."

"We thought it was a goose."

"Arrest her. Find a local sheriff. I'll talk to her when I feel better."

"You ain't gonna feel better lying in that bed," Ironside stated flatly. "Can I get you a whiskey?"

Hart shook his head.

"How about a beefsteak and maybe half-a-dozen fried eggs on the side? Do you good, old feller."

"Luther!" Lorena cried. "Marshal Hart is very ill. He can't drink whiskey or eat beefsteak."

"It's all this female fussin' makes a man ill," Ironside claimed. "He says Lucy Masters shot him. Did you hear that?"

"Yes, I did."

"Stupid that. I mean stupid for any man to turn his back on a woman who knows you intend to arrest her beau."

Lorena stepped to the bed. "He's passed out again."

"I knowed he should've had that whiskey," Ironside grumbled. "I'll go tell the colonel what he said."

"Yes, do that. I'll be down directly." Lorena glared at the tall old man who wore chaps, spurred boots, a gun belt, and seemed to fill the entire room. "And Luther, one more thing."

"What's that, Miss Lorena?"

"Don't ever visit me when I'm sick."

"Is he still conscious, Luther?" Shamus O'Brien asked.

"No, Colonel. He told me about Lucy Masters shooting him, then conked out again."

"Luther, did you pester him?"

Ironside blinked. "No, I sure didn't."

"Sometimes you get to talking to a man and he's glad to conk out."

"Marshal Hart is very ill." Ironside echoed Lorena's words, knowing how sympathetic they sounded.

"Yes, he is." Shamus said. He turned his attention to Jacob. "Bring her in. Take Patrick and Shawn with you and if Kingston's still breathing I want him as well."

"What about Lazarus?"

"And him. In both cases, dead or alive."

"Pa, what about old man Masters?" Shawn asked. "He's a good man not to mess with. Ran me off his place one time for coming within a mile of his daughter. Back then I didn't even know he had a daughter."

"Hugh is a reasonable man. Just explain the situation, tell him what Hart said, and take it from there." Shamus thought for a moment and added, "Hugh will use the law to free his daughter, not a gun."

"Then we'll head for the Rafter-K first and deal with Kingston," Jacob said. "Then we'll head to the Masters place."

"I'll go with you, Jake." Ironside gave Shamus a sidelong glance. "There's a certain party in this house who doesn't think I'm fit company for a sick man."

"You can go, Luther," Shamus said. "But when you're around Hugh Masters keep your mouth shut. The last thing I want is for you to bend his ear into a bow knot and start another range war."

Jacob quickly fended off what he guessed would be an ill-considered Ironside retort. "Good to have you, Luther, sack up some grub from the kitchen, will you? I don't think we'll reach the Rafter-K before nightfall."

"Gladly," Ironside said, scowling at Shamus.

Jacob rose to his feet. "We'll ride, Colonel."

"Jacob, and this goes for Patrick and Shawn, too. Be careful around Lazarus." Shamus eyed his sons. "If it comes down to it, kill him any way you can. Don't try to take him in a straight up draw and shoot."

Patrick smiled. "Gun him in the back, Pa?"

"You heard what I said, all of you. Kill him any way you can . . . and I mean it."

The rain had stopped as Jacob and the others rode through the high timber country south of Lone Mountain. Ahead of them the San Pedro peaks lay under a vast brick red cloud shaped like an anvil. Behind the anvil, rising higher, soared a mighty parapet of gold-tinged clouds, incredibly beautiful but a harbinger of more thunderstorms to come.

The wind had free rein and it drove hard and long, mean as a curly wolf. The pines bent to the blast and ripples swept across the long grass and shredded pink and white petals from the wildflowers.

"Jake," Ironside said, "I can smell rain in the wind. Best we hole up for the night, huh?"

Jacob glanced at the lowering sky. "Shawn, Pat, what do you think?"

"Luther's right," Shawn said. "The darkness is coming down fast."

"And I could use some coffee," Patrick said.

Jacob nodded. "All right, then we'll look for a likely spot."

Luther Ironside was not a man who had trouble sleeping and staying asleep, nor was he easily spooked, so when he sat bolt upright in his blankets and cried out in fear, the O'Brien brothers woke and went for their guns.

"What is it, Luther?" Jacob whispered.

"Over there, by the cottonwood." Luther's pointing finger shook.

Jacob thumbed back the hammer of his Colt and stepped toward the tree on cat feet. Around him rain ticked through the pine canopy and lighting flickered in the sky.

"Come on out of there," Jacob called, his revolver pointed into darkness. "I can drill ya square."

The only answering sound was the rush and rustle of wind and rain.

"See anything?" Shawn stepped to his brother's side. He too had his Colt up and ready.

"Too dark," Jacob said. "I can't see a thing."

"A coyote or a bear, maybe?" Shawn spoke softly.

"Maybe."

Ironside joined them, his eyes scanning the trees.

"What did you see, Luther?" Shawn turned his head.

"A woman," Ironside said. "I'm sure it was a woman."

"What kind of woman?" Shawn whispered.

Ironside shook his head. "Not the usual kind."

The trees rustled and Patrick called out from the darkness. "I'm coming in. Hold your fire."

"That's a good way to get yourself shot," Ironside yelled, taking out the anger he felt at himself on Patrick.

"I looped around to come up behind him, but I saw nothing," Patrick explained.

"Luther claims he saw a her, not a him," Shawn said, holstering his Colt.

"It was a woman, I tell ye," Ironside said. "She stood there by the cottonwood, all green an' scary."

"That's all you saw, a green, scary woman?" Shawn was skeptical.

"She wore a long dress and she'd black hair down to her waist," Ironside said.

"I thought you said she was green," Patrick argued.

"She was. I mean she glowed green like a railroad lantern, but her hair was black and she looked at me as though she hated my guts or I smelled bad or something."

"Ah, then your green woman certainly had discerning taste." Shawn grinned.

"What does that mean?" Ironside eyed Shawn suspiciously.

"Nothing, Luther," Jacob said. "It means nothing at all. You had a bad dream is all."

"But she looked real, Jake. Kinda stared right through me, hating me, like."

Shawn opened his mouth to speak, but Jacob cut him off. "Don't." He gave his brother a look.

"I say we get back to sleep. Be light soon." Patrick turned back toward the camp.

"You boys can sleep," Ironside offered, "and I'll stand watch. I don't want to doze off an' see that green woman again."

"I don't want you to see her, either." Jacob said. Then he wondered why he'd said that.

Chapter Forty

"Plenty of blood, Jake," Luther Ironside said. "Looks like ol' Rafe was hit hard and bled out some."

"Yeah, but he didn't die in his own living room," Jacob answered. "He left here in such a hurry he didn't even close the door to his safe."

"It's empty," Shawn said. "As you'd expect, I guess."

The bed in a room that had obviously been used by Lucy Masters was made up and she'd laid out a white lace nightgown before she'd left in a hurry.

The brothers O'Brien had ridden into an empty ranch.

There were no horses in the corral and even the ranch dog was gone, leaving behind food in its bowl.

The bunkhouse door stood open, and inside it looked as though the hands had just gone to break-fast. The small treasures punchers accumulate over the years still lay in the apple boxes tacked to the wall over their bunks and a guitar stood forlornly in one corner. Clean shirts hung on nails and dress-up boots stood two-by-two, polished up and waiting for their owners to return.

Luther Ironside stood in the middle of the bunkhouse floor and summed it up. "Seems like them as weren't killed at Dromore didn't even take time to come back here. They just lit a shuck."

"Kingston was wounded, probably badly, and he'd need a doctor." Shawn looked around. "I'd bet the ranch he headed for Albuquerque. Right now he might be lying between white sheets in a hospital with a pretty nurse taking care of him."

"Or he's dead," Ironside said. "Takes a badly wounded man to bleed that much."

"Well, there's no point in staying around here." Jacob turned toward the door. "We'll ride to the Three Aces and do what we have to do."

"I hope old man Masters doesn't cut up nasty." Shawn followed Jake. "He could be a handful."

"But then, so could we." Ironside smiled as he exited the bunkhouse behind the brothers.

"And that's the story, gents," Harry Monroe said. "At least it's the way Clem Lander tells it."

"I told you it's true." Lander nodded. "Ain't Hugh Masters lying stiff and cold in his bedroom prove the truth of it?"

"Looks like he blew his brains out, just like his daughter done," Ironside said.

"He put the gun barrel in his mouth and pulled the trigger," Lander said. "A man doesn't survive that."

"A hell of a thing," Shawn said. "I mean . . . to be buried alive."

"Rafe screamed and begged for mercy," Lander explained. "He did that for a long time afore the dirt . . . silenced him."

Jacob looked at Clem. "After Masters shot himself, why didn't you dig Kingston out of there?"

"It would've been too late. A man suffocates in wet dirt pretty fast. At least, I guess he does. Besides, he was shot up so bad, he wasn't gonna live anyhow. Then old Hugh blowed two fingers off Kingston's left hand and made things a sight worse."

Jacob continued the questions. "Did you see anything of Miles Lazarus?"

"Not after we fought off the attack at Dromore," Lander said. "I took a pot at him, but I don't think I hit him."

"So what are you boys going to do now? We can always use top hands at Dromore."

"Especially when we take over this ranch and the Rafter-K." Shawn frowned. "Why are ya'll looking at me like that? Better we take it than somebody else."

"Shawn, you're just like your pa," Ironside said. "Them words you just used are what the Colonel would say. We'll take it all right. It's a lot of prime range."

"Maybe Masters and Kingston have kinfolk," Patrick said.

"Do they?" Jacob said to Monroe.

"I don't know about Rafe Kingston, but Miss Lucy was Hugh's only kin."

"Well . . . kin or no kin, we'll take the land anyway," Ironside stated.

Jacob knew that Luther was speaking the truth. Dromore had paid a price in blood for both ranches and it had a right to take them.

At least, that's how the colonel would see it.

"You boys can stay on," Jacob said.

Harry Monroe shook his head. "Me an' Shorty will drift, I reckon."

"How about you, Clem?" Jacob asked.

"I took my wages that were due, so I'll head for some town and drown out Kingston's screams with whiskey and the voices of whores."

Monroe looked directly into Jacob's eyes. "We all took what we were due . . . no more, no less. If you look at the tin box in the boss's desk, you'll see maybe a hunnerd dollars still there."

"You're honest men," Ironside agreed. "There are them who'd have taken it all."

"Yeah, well that's their way," Monroe said. "It ain't my way."

"Anybody think we should find the grave and dig them up?" Patrick said.

"Why?" Ironside frowned.

"To give them a proper Christian burial," Patrick answered.

"Let them lie in peace," Monroe said. "They couldn't be together in life but they're together in death."

"Seems to me they'll make pretty uneasy grave

companions," Ironside said. "Seein' as how it all came down an' all."

"We'll let them alone where they are," Jacob said. "I don't think these boys would show us where the grave is anyway, would you?"

Harry shook his head. "No. Some things are better left dead and buried."

After the three punchers rode out, Shawn volunteered to remain at the Masters ranch and Patrick was willing to return to the Rafter-K.

"Tell the colonel we're holding the land," Shawn said. "Tell him to get some hands over here and we'll check on the range and the cattle."

Jacob looked at him. "Shawn, if we seize the ranches are we any better than Rafe Kingston? Where is the difference, because I don't see it."

"The difference is Dromore, Jake," Shawn answered. "In a nutshell, whatever Dromore does is right. That's just the way of things."

"Shawn is telling the situation like it is, Jake," Patrick said. "We won the war and the ranches are ours by trial of arms. We'll surrender them to no one."

Jacob studied the faces of his brothers.

Shawn, a man who made light of everything and anything, stood unsmiling, the planes of his handsome face hard and calculating. When it came to land and cattle all the humor in him fled, leaving the inflexible steel backbone of the robber baron.

But it was Patrick who surprised Jacob the most.

Bookish, bespectacled, and mild-mannered, Patrick revealed the same resolute will as Shawn. He stood in the rain, his legs spread, boots firmly planted on the ground, as though defying anyone to try and take the land away from him.

Jacob turned to Ironside. "Luther, what do you think?"

"I don't think, I know, Jake. I know that we have claimed the ranches for Dromore and that's how it will stand."

"You think it's right?"

"I don't think it's wrong. Ask the colonel and he'll tell you the same thing."

"What about you, Jake?" Shawn stared at him. "Where do you stand?"

Again Jacob was struck by the hardness in his brother's eyes. This was not the laughing, loving Shawn, but a complete stranger, a man to whom land and cattle meant everything.

"Dromore, right or wrong, Shawn," Jacob answered firmly. "That's how it's always been."

"And how it will always be," Shawn said.

Ironside spat. "Damn right."

Jacob was an O'Brien but he felt he stood in the midst of men and manners he'd never really understood . . .

Cattlemen to the bone.

Chapter Forty-one

"It was my wish that you'd remain at Dromore and take on the management of our new range." Shamus O'Brien watched his youngest son closely.

Jacob shook his head. "I've got to be riding on, Pa."

"Ride? To where?"

"I'm going after Miles Lazarus." Jacob smiled. "He's a green apple on the tree that I should have picked but didn't."

"Son, you speak in riddles." Shamus shook his head.

"Lazarus is as guilty as Kingston ever was," Jacob said. "Our women mourned husbands and sons because of him, and his reckoning is long overdue."

"Samuel"—Shamus held out his hand—"pass me the newspaper." He folded it into a rectangle and gave it to Jacob. "Bottom of the page. Read it."

Jacob scanned the headline and words.

NEWS OF A BOUNTY KILLER

We have news from colleagues in Texas that Giles Lazarus, who recently graced us with

his presence during the recent Manzano
Mountains War, is back enjoying the good
life in his native Galveston. We hear that
the gentleman enjoyed some sport along
the way, killing a man in Amarillo and
another in Fort Worth.

Lazarus is a desperate character and a
skilled gunman and the Territory is well rid
of him. Good riddance, we say.

"They got his name wrong." Jacob tapped the
newspaper.

"That's neither here nor there and you know it,"
Shamus said angrily. "You can't match Lazarus in a
gunfight, Jacob. Let him go. He'll eventually meet
the fate he so richly deserves."

"The colonel is right, Jake," Samuel agreed. "He'll
die with his face in the sawdust."

"He killed Dromore vaqueros," Jacob stated. "Do
we just walk away from that?"

"In this case, yes." Shamus shifted in his chair.
"We've expanded our range to twice its size, so we
won this mountain war as the newspaper calls it. Let's
enjoy the spoils of victory, Jacob, and let others take
care of Lazarus."

"That's not my way, Colonel," Jacob answered
back. "And there was a time it wasn't Dromore's way."

"Are you suggesting I'm afraid of this man?"
Shamus said, his anger flaring again.

"You should be," Jacob said. "I know I am."

"And that's why you want to go after him." Samuel
shook his head. "It doesn't make any sense, Jake."

Softly, in a toneless voice, Jacob said, "I'll find him, and I'll kill him. Or he'll kill me. That's how it's going to be."

Shamus and Samuel exchanged glances, and after a while the colonel spoke into the silence that followed. "Jacob, do what you need to do. You're a grown man and I can't keep you here." Shamus glared at his son under lowered eyebrows. "Do you have money?"

"Enough."

"How much?"

Jacob reached into his pocket, then glanced at the coins in his hand. "Sixty-two cents."

"You'll need more than that to get you to Galveston and back. Samuel, see that your brother is supplied with sufficient funds." Shamus looked Jacob over from head to foot. "And a change of clothing might not go amiss."

Jacob smiled. "The duds I'm wearing are just fine, Colonel." He rose from his chair and looked out the study window for a few moments, then turned back to his pa. "Colonel, will you make sure that Constance Baker gets the cabin we promised her?"

"Of course I will."

"Constance has taken a shine to Alice, the little gal who survived Kingston's massacre."

"Jacob, I know who she is," Shamus said.

"Well, anyway, Constance wants to raise her as her own. Have you any objection to that, Colonel?"

"None whatsoever. I'll make sure Constance and her children, including Alice, are provided for."

"She's a proud woman," Jacob said. "She won't accept charity."

"She'll be sewing for Lorena and the other women," Samuel put in. "I reckon they'll keep her busy."

"And Sarah," Jacob said. "Take care of Sarah."

"Sarah can take care of herself," Shamus said. "But she'll have a home at Dromore as long as she wants it."

Jacob turned to his oldest brother. "Sam, my spare saddle and my old Henry rifle are for young Shamus when he's old enough to use them."

"Jake, you'll need your saddle," Samuel argued.

"No, it's for your son. And the Henry."

"But—"

"Samuel, heed your brother. Let Jacob be." Shamus looked up at his tall son. "Jacob, come back to us."

Jacob nodded. "It may be a while, Pa."

"Then may the grace of God go with you," Shamus said, his heart heavy as an anvil.

Chapter Forty-two

Miles Lazarus dressed carefully in a new black tail-coat and pants, a white shirt with a winged collar, and a white bow tie. He considered himself in the dresser mirror and decided he was more than presentable. His mustache was trimmed, hair pomaded and combed, and a ring with a stone the color of a green apple glittered on the pinky finger of his left hand.

He'd forgone his usual gun belt and heavy revolver, but carried a .32 caliber Sharps pepperbox in a shoulder holster. He was gratified to see that it did not mar the slender English cut of his suit coat.

He heard a knock on the door and his hand immediately went inside his coat. "Who is it?"

"It's who it always is."

Lazarus smiled and opened the door. "Hi, Dolly. Right on time."

Diamond Dolly Edmond stepped into the hotel

room, her beautiful face unsmiling. "I need a drink, Miles."

"Of course." Lazarus chose a bottle from the top of the drink table. "Hennessy cognac?"

"That's fine, so long as there's at least three fingers of it."

Lazarus opened the table's glass doors, grabbed a couple of crystal snifters, and poured for himself and the woman. Dolly downed hers in a single gulp, and Lazarus smiled. "Fine cognac is not meant to be drunk like beer."

Dolly extended the glass. "Hit me again."

Lazarus poured for her again, and she took her glass and sat on the corner of the bed. "Miles, I'm a whore, and men can't insult a whore."

"The gentleman knew you were a lady of my acquaintance, yet he chose to insult you in front of witnesses," Lazarus said. "He besmirched my honor, and I must call him out for that."

"Don't kill him, Miles. Charles Beaufort is a fool."

"You're correct, Dolly, Beaufort is a fool, but my honor demands satisfaction. As for me killing him, well, he'll have the same kind of pistol in his hand as I do, so the rest is up to him."

Dolly waited until Lazarus lit a cigar and said, "Miles, you've changed since you got back from the New Mexico Territory. You're . . . how do I say it? You're harder, a . . . a finger constantly looking for a trigger."

"You mean I'm more of a killer?"

"Yes. Just that."

Lazarus nodded. "But I'm not. You're right about the territory, it did change me, made me accept what I am, not what I was. Maybe it was the mountains and the mesas and the endless plains, maybe they work some kind of magic on a man and let him see what he really is. It's like a morning mirror that tells only the harsh truth." He smiled. "Do you understand me?"

"Not a word of it." Dolly sipped her brandy, watching him. "I'd go with you . . . back to Egypt."

Lazarus felt his anger rise and his mouth curled into a contemptuous snarl. "You, Diamond Dolly would go to Egypt with me? What do you think you'd do there? Would you presume to take the place of the finest, most beautiful woman who ever lived? A low-class whore playing the great lady, the only woman I ever loved? You must be out of your mind. Diamond Dolly, you're not fit to lace the shoes of Lady Victoria Lytton, or to even stand in her shadow."

Tears sprang into the woman's eyes. "Miles, I won't try to replace her, I know I couldn't do that. But we could be happy, away from here, away from all the death and killing."

"No. Like me you'll always be what you are, Dolly, a whore, any man's woman if he has the money. To take you to Egypt would be to desecrate a sacred memory, twist it, distort it, so it would never be the same again." Lazarus threw his brandy into Dolly's face. "Stick to your brothels and never mention Egypt again."

For a few moments Dolly sat in silence, brandy trickling down her face, dripping off her chin. Rising to her feet, her black silk gown rustling, she stepped toward the door.

"Where do you think you're going?" Lazarus sneered.

Her back stiff, Dolly answered, "Away from here, Miles. Away from you and your cruelty."

"Stay right where you are, Dolly, or I'll put a bullet into you." Lazarus aimed the Sharps at the woman's back. "Until I tire of you, you're my woman, bought and paid for. And I'm not tired of you yet."

Dolly turned. "Very well, Miles, I'll stay with you. But I won't be around when you die. In spite of everything, I don't want to see that day."

"You're afraid of the Raggedy Man."

"Aren't you? He disturbs your sleep at night. You toss and turn and talk about green apples and—"

"I'm not afraid of the Raggedy Man. I'm afraid of no man who walks the earth."

Dolly wiped brandy off her face with a tiny lace handkerchief. "He's coming for you, Miles. Isn't that so?"

"I don't know. Maybe"

"Then we'll go somewhere, not Egypt. Old Mexico maybe or California."

Lazarus slipped his gun back into the holster. "If the Raggedy Man comes, I'll kill him."

"Maybe he'll be faster than you, Miles, or luckier. You don't know these things."

"Nobody alive is faster than me, Dolly, and luck doesn't enter into it."

The woman crossed the floor and threw her arms around Lazarus's neck. "Let's not wait to find out, Miles. We can leave Galveston and go anywhere."

Lazarus tilted up the woman's chin and kissed her lush mouth. "We're not going anywhere . . . except to the Raggedy Man's funeral."

Dolly looked up at him. "Who is he, Miles, and why does he trouble you so?"

Lazarus smiled. "He's a Raggedy Man, and that's all he is."

"He's coming, isn't he? You saw him in a dream."

Lazarus hesitated a moment, then said, "Yes, he's coming."

Lazarus removed his coat and laid it on the counter in front of the Aphrodite Club's hatcheck girl. "Is Mr. Beaufort here tonight?"

The girl smiled. "Yes, he is, sir. He's at his usual table, with a couple of guests."

"Splendid," Lazarus said.

The girl gathered up Lazarus's coat and Dolly's velvet cloak and disappeared in search of hangers.

Dolly and Lazarus stepped toward the doors of the main dining room and the maitre d'. "Please, Miles," Dolly whispered, "don't make a scene."

"Of course not," Lazarus said. "I will demand satisfaction from Mr. Beaufort, one gentlemen to another, and set the time and place for our duel."

"Over my honor," Dolly mumbled.

"How mistaken you are, my dear," Lazarus said. "My honor is at stake, not yours. As you said yourself, a whore forfeits all claim to honor."

"Miles, you're a cruel, coldhearted SOB."

Lazarus smiled. "It goes with the job."

The Aphrodite Club was ostensibly a luxury restaurant with a huge dance floor and twelve-piece orchestra. But it catered to other appetites, too. It was also a high-class brothel with twenty discreetly curtained booths on the second floor and an opium den in the basement. The establishment permitted gambling and several roulette wheels and faro tables were in place for the high rollers. Content with their cut from the proceeds, the city fathers turned a blind eye to the illegal activities. Besides, the girls were pretty, the food excellent, and the liquor and cigars top shelf, all of which they sampled freely.

Lazarus and Dolly were seated at a table close to the dance floor but at a comfortable distance from the orchestra. Lazarus ordered wine, then his eyes roamed over the crowded restaurant. "Charles Beaufort sits over there by the pillar."

Dolly nodded. "I see he has his whores lined up already"—she shook her head—"while his poor pregnant wife spends another lonely night at home. Shame on him."

"Who are the gentlemen with him?"

"The fat man is Conrad Cord, the banker. Sitting

across from him, pawing the blond girl is Sims Jackson. He owns half the commercial real estate in Galveston. The other one I don't know. One of Charlie's hangers-on, I suppose."

Lazarus summoned a waiter. "Two bottles of your best champagne for Mr. Beaufort's table, with my compliments."

The waiter bowed and left.

"Charlie looks half drunk already," Dolly said. "Do you think he'll know good champagne from bad?"

"No, he won't. But I do." Lazarus watched as the wine was delivered to Beaufort's table. Smiling, he raised a hand as Beaufort followed the waiter's nod and peered over at his table.

Recognition dawned on Beaufort's face. He rose and walked unsteadily to Lazarus's table, supported by a pretty brunette whose scarlet dress revealed a deep V of perspiring cleavage.

"Miles, how nice to see you again. And Dolly, your look positively divine tonight." He grinned and pulled the girl closer to him. "This is . . ." A puzzled expression creased the man's once handsome face that showed signs of years of debauchery. "Hey. What is your name?"

"Suzette," answered the girl, a smiling coquette not yet out of her teens.

"Yes, yes, you're Suzette." Beaufort turned away slightly and waved his free hand. "Meet Suzette everybody," he yelled.

The crowd roared, "*Bonsoir*, Suzette!" and dissolved into laughter.

Lazarus watched all this with the glowing, predatory eyes of a hunting raptor.

Charlie Beaufort was the ne'er-do-well son of an English nobleman who was paid a handsome allowance to stay far away from England. A drunk, a gambler, and an adulterer, he was a pale, simpering wastrel and Lazarus greatly looked forward to killing him.

"Come join us, you two," Beaufort said, grinning foolishly, his habitual expression. "The night is young, and, Dolly, good old Cordy is anxious to meet you."

Lazarus nodded. "Miss Edmond and I will dine, and then I will call on you."

Beaufort staggered back a step and Suzette caught him just in time. "Have it your own way, old chap. I look forward to it."

Dolly watched him weave his way back to his table. "Charlie's a harmless fool, Miles. Please don't challenge him tonight."

"He can refuse to appear on the field of honor. The choice is his."

"You know if he ran away, he'd never again be able to stand in the company of men."

"I know that, but maybe Charlie doesn't." Lazarus smiled. "Now, Dolly, shall we dine?"

Displaying all the patience of a carrion eater, Miles Lazarus waited until after the orchestra played a polka before he decided to approach Charlie Beaufort's table.

As he knew they would, the dancers had exhausted themselves, the polka's two/four time not for the faint of heart. The ladies' fans fluttered like swan wings as they cooled their flushed faces while the menfolk sprawled in their chairs and mopped their brows with huge white handkerchiefs.

"Excuse me, Dolly." Lazarus rose to his feet and crossed the dance floor. When he reached Beaufort's table he made a little bow and smiled.

"Ah, Miles, you've decided to join us." Beaufort looked past Lazarus. "Where is Dolly?"

"Good-looking woman. You're a lucky fellow, Lazarus." Conrad Cord waved to an empty chair. "Sit down, man, and have a drink with us."

"I'm afraid this is not a social occasion." Lazarus hardened his voice. "Mr. Beaufort, I have been informed by my lady that you called her, on several occasions and in the presence of men of quality, a common whore. Is this the case?"

Beaufort was surprised. "Miles, she is a whore." He waved a hand around the table. "All the women you see here are whores. You know that."

"Mr. Beaufort, in calling Miss Dolly Edmond a whore, you implied that I habitually consort with such a class of women and thus you dishonor me. Sir, I demand satisfaction."

Beaufort grinned. "Well, Miles, I apologize. Does that satisfy you?"

"Yes, I accept your apology, and in turn I apologize

for this intrusion. But the matter at hand remains and must still be resolved on the field of honor."

"By God, sir," Cord said. "Are you challenging Charlie to a duel?"

Suzette giggled and Sims Jackson squirmed in his chair, looking uncomfortable.

"Yes, I am. But the gentleman can avoid meeting me if he flees Galveston tonight and gives me his solemn promise never to return." Lazarus knew Beaufort was cornered. He'd carefully chosen the word *flees* because it implied cowardice. If Beaufort refused the duel he'd never again be able to show his face in Galveston society.

A silence had descended on the restaurant. People stared at Lazarus with shocked faces that softened into sympathy when they saw how poor Charlie Beaufort sweated.

Aware that he was under scrutiny and his manhood hung in the balance, Beaufort lurched to his feet, knocking over his full champagne glass. The wine stained the front of his pants like a gush of urine. His voice loud in the silence, he exclaimed, "You are impertinent."

"And you, sir," Lazarus said, "are a liar."

Beaufort looked like he'd been slapped. There was no stepping away from this. "I'll meet you anywhere and anytime you like."

"The choice of weapons is yours, sir, of course."

Conrad Cord got to his feet. "I will act as Mr. Beaufort's second, and, since you have a reputation as being skilled with the pistol, he chooses sabers."

Lazarus fought hard to suppress a smile. During his years at sea he'd learned to use the cutlass well, and between cutlass and saber there was little difference. "Behind the Tremont Hotel where the bridal path ends. At dawn."

"I'll be there." Beaufort was adamant.

"You have a second, Mr. Lazarus?" Cord asked.

"I will have one in attendance." Lazarus bowed. "Now, I will bid you good night, and look forward to meeting you again tomorrow."

Chapter Forty-three

The hooves of the carriage horse clanged on cobbles as Miles Lazarus and Dolly sat in silence. Finally she said, "Will you kill him?"

"It's sabers, remember. He has a chance."

"Just cut him, Miles, then it's over and no real harm done."

"We'll see."

Dolly glanced out the hansom's window. "Why are we here?"

"I have to get a second."

"In the Strand?"

Lazarus smiled. "A grog shop's as good a place as any." He knocked on the roof of the carriage with his silver-topped cane. "Stop here, driver."

Lazarus passed the driver a coin. "Take the lady to the Tremont Hotel." To Dolly he said, "I'll be along directly." He stepped out of the carriage.

Dolly looked as though she was about to say something, but the cab lurched into motion and she sat back in the seat.

Fog swirled around Lazarus as he walked a block, then stopped at a tavern with a faded, creaking sign outside showing a buxom woman with a fish's tail and the name THE MERMAID INN. It was a disreputable dive and many a lively sailor lad had met his end there, some from knuckledusters or the knife, others from the French pox that killed them more slowly.

Lazarus opened the door and stepped inside. A wall of smoke, shot through with odors of spilled beer, cheap perfume, and ancient vomit and urine permeated the place. He stopped at the crowded bar and asked the bartender, "Nate Perkins around?"

The bartender jerked a beefy thumb over his shoulder. "Back there somewhere." He looked at Lazarus and said in a broad English accent, "Mister, we don't get many toffs in here, so watch your step."

Lazarus nodded. "Oh dear, yes, I'll be sure to do that."

He used his cane to part the crowd, to the annoyance of the seamen, toughs, and whores who inhabited the place, and found Nate Perkins at a table, a dry glass in front of him.

"How you doing, Nate?" Lazarus said as he sat opposite the man.

Perkins knuckled his forehead. "Just fine, Cap'n, as ever was."

"I've got a job for you."

"And I'm willin' and able, Cap'n. That's what folks say about old Nate Perkins, he's willin' and able."

"Yes, I've heard that."

Perkins was a peg-legged wharf rat who did odd jobs around the docks and Lazarus had used him a couple of times to run errands. He was small, wizened, and ugly, and he smelled like a sewer. He'd been practicing the pirate's profession when a cannonball fired from a Portuguese steam frigate ran off with his leg and he'd later done some hard time in Yuma.

"Meet me behind the Tremont Hotel at first light tomorrow," Lazarus said. "Can you remember that?"

"I surely can, Cap'n." Perkins looked sly. "But I can't do no heavy lifting, on account of me leg that isn't there, ye understand."

"The only thing you'll have to lift is my cloak. And that's light enough."

"Then I'll be there, Cap'n. Why, says you, Nate Perkins is a willing and able man right enough, but says you, he doesn't have the price of a drink and that's a sorry state of affairs for an old sailorman."

Lazarus passed a silver dollar across the table. "That's enough for a drink or two, but it won't get you drunk. Tomorrow I'll give you five more of those when the job is done."

Perkins clutched up the coin, his thin fingers looking like talons. He knuckled his forehead again and leaned forward. "There's a man at the bar looking at you mean, Cap'n. You be careful."

Lazarus turned his head. "Where? I don't see him."

"Damn my lights, he's gone. He was there, and then he wasn't."

"What did he look like?" Lazarus asked, thinking Perkins had seen some local tough.

"Look like? Well, says I, he was a raggedy man wearing one o' them big Texas hats."

Lazarus rose quickly to his feet. "Be there tomorrow morning, Nate."

Before Perkins could answer, Lazarus stepped into the night and fog.

The night held a myriad of sounds, the creak of ships in the harbor, the distant cry of night birds, the jangle of pianos from the dives along the waterfront, and the roars of drunken men and the laughter of women who were paid to encourage them. The air smelled of tar, reeking bilges, and fish shoaling out in the bay.

Listening into the night, his eyes sweeping up and down the street, Lazarus heard the distant chime of spurs.

To his right. No, to his left.

He grimaced, unable to get a fix on where the sound was coming from. Sliding the Sharps pepper pot from the holster, its cold blue weight reassuring him, he called out. "Raggedy Man! I know you."

The chimes grew faint . . . more distant . . . then faded into silence.

"Damn you, Raggedy Man," Lazarus said quietly to himself.

The fog closed around him, clammy as a damp blanket, and he shivered.

Chapter Forty-four

"I'll go to the kitchen and see if I can rustle up some coffee." Dolly Edmond shrugged into her robe. "You've got time yet."

Miles Lazarus nodded, but said nothing.

"You cried out in your sleep again last night."

"Did I?"

"You were running from the Raggedy Man with a scar on his face."

"I don't run from any man."

"But you did. In your sleep."

"Get the coffee."

"Who is he, Miles?"

"Nobody. Just a man in a dream."

"I'll get the coffee."

"Yes, do that. It will be light soon."

After Dolly left, Lazarus dressed in pants, elastic-sided boots, and a frilled white shirt. He laid his cloak on the bed and worked his right wrist and fingers, making sure they were supple.

Although he'd been taught the savage way of the

cutlass, he'd never killed a man with a sword before. Today would be a first. He felt no elation, no excited anticipation of the kill, and that troubled him. He felt empty inside, barren, as though every organ of his body had vanished in the night.

He shook his head, angry with himself. After he'd delivered the death thrust he'd feel whole again. It would happen. He was sure of it.

When Dolly returned with a coffeepot on a tray and a couple of cups, she poured for both of them. "The chef and underchef were already there. They get up early to light the ovens and bake bread rolls for breakfast. You should have seen the mounds of eggs and bacon and kippers, that's a kind of smoked fish, and . . ."

Dolly babbled on and on, but Lazarus paid no heed to her. Looking out the window, he waited for the glow in the eastern sky that would herald the dawn. Impatiently, he drained his cup, laid it back on the tray, and stood up. "I'm going. When I get back we'll go to breakfast together. Swordplay gives a man an appetite."

"Miles, what about the law?"

Lazarus threw his cloak around his shoulders. "What about the law?"

"They might arrest you. Dueling is illegal in Galveston."

"The law will look the other way. It always does. Besides, it will be a fair fight."

"Then good luck, Miles," Dolly said. "I'll be waiting for you."

"You can come see the duel if you like."

"No. As I told you, I don't want to be around when you die."

"I won't die."

"Not this time."

"Old Nate Perkins, right on time, Cap'n, as I promised." Perkins knuckled his forehead. "Now, what is it you want me to be doin'?"

"I'm fighting a duel with another gentleman," Lazarus explained. "When the times comes, you will hold my cloak and make sure you let my opponent and his second get a whiff of your odiferous person."

"That I will, Cap'n. But, says I, I don't know what that word you used means. Od . . . odif . . ."

"It means you stink. Stomp around on that wooden leg of yours and let others get a whiff of you."

"That I will, cap'n. And welcome, says I." Perkins looked around him. "Now where is the other duelist?"

Lazarus was surprised. "You know that word, duelist?"

"Aye, Cap'n. See, my pa was a gentleman's gentleman in New Orleans and when I was a boy, afore I ran away to sea like, I seen duels played out. Seen men killed by the pistol a couple of times."

"You're a man of parts, aren't you, Perkins?"

"That I am, Cap'n. Seen a lot of things in my life."

Lazarus was only half listening. Through the gloom and mist he saw the lights of a cab bob along the bridle path. As it got closer, he heard the rattle of wheels and the steady tramp of a trotting horse. "It seems that our friends are here."

The carriage creaked to a halt and the door swung open. Conrad Cord got out first, carrying a long, rectangular leather case, and Beaufort stumbled after him, looking hungover and pale.

"Good morning, gentlemen," Lazarus said. "It promises to be a fine morning."

Cord nodded, but didn't answer. Then he caught sight of Nate Perkins. "Is that your second, Mr. Lazarus?" he asked, a flash of anger in his eyes.

"Yes, indeed. His name is Nate Perkins, pirate, jailbird, and now professional drunk."

"Do you hold us in such contempt, sir?" Cord looked askance.

Lazarus smiled. "It would seem so."

Cord swallowed his anger, his throat moving.

The glow to the east had expanded into a wide band of steel blue sky and the light had changed from violet to pearl gray. A wind from the bay stirred the tall pine where Lazarus and Cord stood and carried with it the musky smell of wooden ships at anchor.

After the cab drove away, Cord said, "Mr. Beaufort is willing to apologize again, and swears that he meant no affront to your honor. He will also make a public apology to Miss Edmond."

"And in return?" Lazarus raised an eyebrow.

"Call off this duel, Miles," Cord said in an urgent whisper. "This is insanity."

"Hey, Charlie," Lazarus called out. "Are you planning to skedaddle out of town like a frightened rabbit, as we agreed?"

Nauseated as he was from too much champagne and a measure of fear, Beaufort reached deep and found courage of a sort. "Choose your weapon, Lazarus."

Cord opened the leather case and presented the two sabers inside to Lazarus. "The choice is yours."

The dueling saber was nothing like the heavy-bladed cavalry weapon. It had a slender, Y-shaped blade and if badly handled it could snap like a matchstick.

Lazarus chose a sword and made a trial of some quick parries and thrusts, the steel blade flashing like quicksilver in the morning light. "A fast blade, Mr. Cord. And of excellent balance."

Cord ignored that, stepped to Beaufort, and offered him the case. As an aristocrat's son, Charlie had been taught fencing as one of the accomplishments a man of good breeding was expected to master. But, sick as he was, his movements looked clumsy and ill timed, with none of Lazarus's natural grace.

Cord laid the case aside and once again walked to Lazarus. "The man is too sick to defend himself. Accept his apology and be done."

"He knows my terms." Lazarus felt a twinge of triumph in his belly and it pleased him. Perhaps he was not as empty as he feared.

Cord sighed. "Then come to my mark and cross blades. The duel ends when first blood is shed."

His saber up and ready, Lazarus stepped to the

mark, a line Cord had drawn in the damp earth with his cane.

Beaufort moved more slowly, at a dragging pace, the tip of his blade trailing in the dirt beside him. He looked haggard, his face ashen, and his hands trembled from alcohol or fear.

Lazarus decided it was both.

But something happened that changed everything . . . and a man's death in the morning came quickly.

Chapter Forty-five

Charlie Beaufort stepped to the line and brought up his saber.

Conrad Cord held the blades, and crossed them a couple of inches below their tips. "Ready, gentlemen?"

Lazarus nodded, his face set and grim.

But Beaufort did something strange. He dropped his saber and took a couple of steps back. His right hand dropped fast to his pocket and he drew a small, Colt .38 revolver. "Lazarus, you SOB!" he yelled.

Raising the revolver to eye level, Beaufort fired.

And missed.

"Charlie, no!" Cord yelled, stepping in front of Beaufort just as the man fired again.

The bullet slammed into Cord's shoulder. His face stricken, he staggered back, blood seeping between the fingers that clutched at his wound.

Beaufort fired a third time.

Lazarus stood perfectly still, his sword still in his hand.

The bullet missed. Then another shot and another miss.

Beaufort screamed his frustration. His shaking hand had betrayed him. Aware that he had only one shot left, he charged at Lazarus, his face twisted into a mask of hate and anger.

Almost casually, Lazarus brought up his sword and rammed the blade into Beaufort's belly to the hilt just as Beaufort thumbed back the hammer of his Colt.

Shrieking in pain and terror, Beaufort staggered back, the hilt sticking out from his blood-splashed belly. For a couple of long seconds, he stood still, and stared down at the sword that had killed him. Looking at Lazarus, his face puzzled as though he wanted to ask a question, then he fell on his back and within moments all the life that had been in him had fled.

Lazarus looked down at Beaufort's second. "Cord, are you all right?"

"I need a doctor."

"I'm sure you do." Lazarus stepped closer to the wounded man. "What is Charlie's widow's name?"

"Marianne," Cord said through pain-gritted teeth. "Why do you want to know?"

"I'll send her a hundred red roses. After all, it's the right thing to do."

* * *

Lazarus flagged down a passing cab and helped Cord load Beaufort's body inside.

"Here," the cabbie asked, "is he a dead 'un?"

"Dead as he's ever going to be," Lazarus answered.

"He'll bleed all over my upholstery."

Lazarus reached into his pocket and gave the man a double-eagle. "Take Mr. Cord to the hospital and then deliver the body to his home. Mr. Cord will tell you where."

"Right, sir," the cabbie said. "For twenty dollars in gold, I'd drive the devil himself."

Cord stared at Lazarus, his pained eyes thoughtful. "Did you murder him, Lazarus?"

"No, it was self-defense."

"You could've knocked the gun from his hand with your sword."

"He didn't give me time to think about it, did he?"

"In my book, Charlie's death was cold-blooded murder. It's a pity, but the police will see it differently, I'm sure." Cord turned contemptuously away from Lazarus and said, "Drive on, cabbie."

Nate Perkins handed Lazarus his cloak. "Cap'n, the man with the big hat is back."

Without turning his head, Lazarus asked, "Where?"

"Behind you, Cap'n, under the oak tree."

Uncomfortably aware that he was unarmed, Lazarus

tossed his cloak around his shoulders and turned slowly.

The Raggedy Man stood under the tree relaxed and easy, his right shoulder against the trunk. He wore a belted Colt and fixed Lazarus with an unblinking gaze.

"What do you want from me?" Lazarus yelled.

The man made no answer, his stare unwavering.

The new aborning day had washed the night shadows from the park and the bright morning gave promise of the rising sun. Birds chattered in the hawthorn bushes and the wind riffed a rustling melody in the mimosa trees.

Angrily, Lazarus strode toward the man by the oak. The shabby man smiled, then shouldered himself off the trunk and walked away.

Unwilling to chase after a man with iron on his hip, Lazarus halted and was content to watch the Raggedy Man fade into the morning.

"You know that feller, Cap'n?" Perkins asked.

"He knows me," Lazarus said.

"Is that a good or a bad thing?"

Lazarus looked thoughtful. "He could've killed me, but didn't."

"Then it's a good thing, says I."

"Maybe."

Lazarus handed Perkins some coins. "Now, get out of my sight."

"Wait, Cap'n. If that feller is bothering you, I could

lay for him and stick a knife in his ribs real easy, like.
I know some right lively lads who would help."

Lazarus shook his head. "If the time comes when
he bothers me too much, I'll kill him myself."

"All right, Cap'n. But if you want the job done, you
only have to ask."

Chapter Forty-six

"Are you sure you can't tell me where he was headed?" the tall man questioned. The Tremont Hotel desk clerk was suspicious. "Are you the law?"

"Do I look like the law? I told you, I'm a friend of Mr. Lazarus."

The clerk looked at the man and frowned, as though someone held a dead fish under his nose. "Mr. Lazarus knows some strange people."

"Yes, and I'm one of them."

"The police were here earlier," the clerk said. "You heard that Mr. Lazarus killed a man in a duel this morning."

"It was self-defense, I was told."

"That's how the police see it. That's why Mr. Lazarus is out celebrating tonight."

"And I wish to join him. Raise a glass or two with him, you understand."

The clerk was not impressed with the tall man at

the desk. The suit he wore was a size too large for him, indicating that he'd bought it at one of the used clothing stores along the Strand. And under the coat was a collarless shirt, much frayed, no doubt another rag store buy.

The ten-dollar bill the man pushed across the desk changed the clerk's attitude for the better. "He's at the Aphrodite Club with his friend Miss Dolly Edmond," he said, palming the bill. "Do you know how to get there?"

"Take a cab I guess."

"That would be as good a way as any."

"Evening dress is required for gentlemen at this club," the manager said, looking the tall men up and down, from his scuffed boots to the bowler hat perched precariously on his large head. "I'm afraid it's the rule."

"I'll only be here a few minutes. I want to congratulate Mr. Lazarus on winning his duel this morning."

The manager, small, plump, and officious, bowed a beautifully dressed couple inside, then said, "I'm afraid that's impossible, sir."

The tall man held up a double-eagle between his fingertips. "Will this make it possible?"

Samuel, usually parsimonious with Dromore money, had been more than generous when he financed the tall man's trip south.

The manager's pudgy hand moved like a striking

rattlesnake and the coin vanished. "You may enter, sir, but only for a few minutes." He shook his finger at the tall man. "Please don't overstay your welcome."

"I'll be quick. Very quick."

The tall man had never seen the like. The Aphrodite Club glittered like the night sky, the diamonds of the rich Galveston belles and pampered courtesans reflecting the light of the crystal chandeliers hangng from the ceiling. The languid air was heavy with the scent of French perfume, champagne, broiling chops, and money—new and old.

No one paid the tall, shabby man in the oversized suit the slightest heed as he stood just inside the door and looked around him like a country hick at his first cotillion. But he was not an overawed rube taking in the sights. He scanned the merrymaking crowd in search of Miles Lazarus.

And found him.

Lazarus, handsome, relaxed, and smiling nodded at acquaintances or raised the glass of golden bubbly in his hand. Beside him a beautiful woman dressed in black affected the regal air of a queen, but there was hardness in her eyes and around her mouth that pegged her as something much less.

The orchestra struck up a waltz and the tall man had to wend his way through whirling couples to reach Lazarus's table. He stood there for long moments before Lazarus deigned to acknowledge his presence.

Finally Lazarus looked up at him. "Yes?"

"You know who I am and why I'm here."

Lazarus smiled. "You're the Raggedy Man." He looked over the man's shabby suit. "And you're well named."

"I'm here to present the bill you owe for our men you killed at Dromore."

After a single horrified glance at the tall man, the woman suddenly jumped to her feet. "It has come, Miles. I told you I wouldn't be around to see it."

"Stay right where you are, Dolly." Lazarus rose to his feet. "I'll have this tramp thrown out."

But the woman walked away, her dress rustling, then she ran for the door, her face buried in her hands.

"It seems you've upset my woman," Lazarus said. "But I'm not a green apple you can pluck from a monastery tree. Now leave, or I'll kill you."

The orchestra faltered to a stop, the musicians distracted by the crowd that had gathered around Lazarus's table. The situation was just too, too exquisite to miss.

Lazarus looked around and waved over a waiter. "Throw this piece of trash out of here."

That did it for the tall man. His patience snapped and his hard, bony fist shot out, landing with a sickening smack on Lazarus's mouth.

Lazarus slammed onto his back, a trickle of blood scarlet on his chin. He lay there for a moment, stunned by the ferocity of the Raggedy Man's attack. Then he went for his gun.

By the time the Sharps cleared its shoulder holster, the tall man, drawing from his waistband, had pumped two bullets into Lazarus's chest.

Lazarus opened his eyes wide in shocked surprise. "You were faster. You were faster than me."

"Lazarus," the tall man said, "you weren't even close."

A well-dressed restaurant patron with his arm in a sling appeared at the tall man's elbow. "My name is Conrad Cord and I saw it all. You shot in self-defense and I'll swear that's the truth of it in any court in the land."

The tall man nodded his thanks and Lazarus said to him, "I shouldn't be lying here dying like a dog."

"You should've thought of that when you attacked Dromore."

Painfully, Lazarus reached into his coat pocket and took out the Shabti figure, glowing with the color of a green apple. "Bury her with me. Let me go to my grave like a pharaoh."

The tall man took the Shabti, stared at it for a moment, then threw it across the dance floor. The figure spun across the polished parquet and slammed into the raised orchestra dais.

With his last, gasping breath, Lazarus said, "I took you for a hard, unforgiving man."

Luther Ironside looked him in the eye. "You were right."

Turn the page for an exciting excerpt . . .

SMOKE'S BROTHER LUKE:
THE JENSEN LEGEND CONTINUES . . .

It's the last days of the Civil War. With Richmond
under siege, Confederate soldier Luke Jensen is
assigned the task of smuggling gold out of the city
before the Yankees get their hands on it.
He is ambushed and robbed by four deserters,
shot in the back, and left for dead. Taken in by a
Georgia farmer and his beautiful daughter,
Luke is nursed back to health. Though crippled,
he hopes to reunite with his long-lost brother
Smoke, but a growing romance keeps him
on the farm. Fate takes a tragic turn when ruthless
carpetbaggers arrive and—in a storm of bullets
and bloodshed—Luke is forced to strike out on
his own . . . searching for a new life and hunting
down the baddest of the bad . . . to become the
greatest bounty hunter who ever lived.

LUKE JENSEN, BOUNTY HUNTER

The explosive new series by
William W. Johnstone and J. A. Johnstone,
authors of *The Family Jensen* and
Matt Jensen, the Last Mountain Man

Available in July
wherever Kensington Books are sold.

Prologue

A rifle bullet smacked off the top of the log and sprayed splinters toward Luke Smith's face. He dropped his head quickly so the brim of his battered black hat protected his eyes. A splinter stung his cheek close to his neatly trimmed black mustache.

Luke looked into the sightless, staring eyes of the dead man who lay next to him. "Those amigos of yours are getting closer with their shots, José. Too bad for you that you're not alive to watch them kill me. Reckon you probably would've enjoyed that."

José Cardona didn't say anything. A bullet hole from one of Luke's Remingtons lay in the middle of his forehead, surrounded by powder burns. Most of the back of his head was gone where the slug had exploded out.

More shots rang out from the cabin about a hundred yards away, next to the little creek at the bottom of the slope. The sturdy log structure had been built for defense, with thick walls and numerous loopholes where rifle barrels could be stuck out and fired.

Luke had no idea who had built the cabin. Probably some old fur trapper or prospector. Those mountains in New Mexico Territory had seen their fair share of both.

Currently, it was being used as a hideout for the Solomon Burke gang. Luke had been on the trail of Burke and his bunch for several weeks. There was a $1,500 bounty on Burke's head and lesser amounts posted on the half-dozen owl hoots who rode with him. If Luke was able to bring in all of them, it would be a mighty nice payoff for him.

Unfortunately, it didn't look like things were going to work out that way. Luke had tracked the gang to the cabin and had been crouched in the timber up on the hill overlooking the creek, trying to figure out his next move, when someone tackled him from behind, knocking him out into the open. They rolled down the hill together, locked in a desperate struggle, even as the man screeched a warning to the others at the top of his lungs.

The big log, which had also rolled about twenty feet down the hill when it toppled sometime in the past, brought the two men to an abrupt halt as they slammed into it. Luke barely had time to recognize the bandito as Cardona from drawings he had seen on wanted posters when he realized the man was about to bring a knife almost as big as a machete down on his head and split his skull wide open.

Without having to think about what he was doing, Luke palmed out one of his Remingtons, eared back the hammer as he jammed the muzzle against Cardona's forehead, and pulled the trigger.

The point-blank shot blew Cardona away from him, and the dead outlaw flopped onto the ground behind the log. Luke rolled over and started to get up, when a bullet had whipped past his ear. Instinct made him drop belly down behind the log. A second later, more rifles opened up from the cabin and a volley of high-powered slugs smashed into the fallen tree. If it hadn't been there to give him cover, Luke would have been shot to pieces.

As it was, he was pinned down on the slope. The trees above him were too far away. If he stood up and made a dash for them, Burke and the others in the cabin would riddle him with rifle fire. Trying to crawl up there would make him an even easier target. The grass was too short to conceal him.

He was stuck, with a dead man for company and only a matter of time until some of those varmints slipped out of the cabin and circled around to catch him in a crossfire. Luke's craggy face was grim, in spite of the ghost of a smile lurking around his mouth.

In plenty of tight spots during the years he'd spent as a bounty hunter, he had always pulled through somehow. But he had known his luck was bound to run out someday.

After all, he had already cheated certain death once. A man didn't get too many breaks like that.

From time to time, he rose up long enough to throw a couple of shots at the cabin, but not really expecting to do any damage—too long range for a handgun. His nature wouldn't let him die without a fight, though. He could put up a better one, if his Winchester wasn't still in the saddle boot strapped to his horse, a good hundred feet upslope. Might as well have been a hundred miles.

"Blast it, José, I must be getting old, to let a clumsy galoot like you sneak up on me," Luke said, keeping his eyes on the cabin.

Cardona had been a big burly man, built along the lines of a black bear. Like all the other men in Solomon Burke's gang, he'd had a reputation for ruthlessness and cruelty. He had killed seven men that Luke knew of during various bank and train robberies, and was probably responsible for more deaths in addition to those. But he wouldn't be killing anybody else.

Luke took some small comfort from that. He tracked down outlaws mostly for the bounties posted on them, and he wasn't going to lie about it to himself or anybody else. It pleased him to know, because of him, men such as Cardona were no longer around to spread suffering and death across the frontier.

More bullets pounded into the log. One tore all the way through it and struck a rock lying on the slope, causing the bullet to whine off in a ricochet and bringing a thoughtful frown to Luke's face. He realized the log had been lying there long enough to be half-rotten in places. . He holstered the Remington he was still holding and drew a heavy-bladed knife from its sheath on his left hip. Attacking the log with the blade, he hacked and dug at the soft wood.

It didn't take him long to break through and see what he'd been hoping to see. The log was partially hollow. Luke began enlarging the opening he had made and soon realized the hollow part ran all the way to one end of the log. He could see sunlight shining through it.

It took fifteen minutes of hard work to carve out a big enough hole for him to fit his head and shoulders through. By the time he was finished, sweat was dripping down his face.

He sheathed his knife and looked over at Cardona. "*Adiós*, José. If I see you again, I reckon it'll probably be in hell."

Luke wormed his way through the opening into the hollow log. Down below in the cabin, the outlaws hadn't been able to see what he was doing. He could only hope none of them had snuck around to where they could observe him. If they had, he was as good as dead.

He began shifting his weight back and forth as much as he could in those close confines. He felt insects crawling on him. His nerves twanged, taut as bowstrings. The log began to rock back and forth slightly. Bunching his muscles, he threw himself hard against the wood surrounding him. Over the pounding of his heart, he heard a faint grating sound as the log shifted.

Suddenly, it was rolling.

He let out a startled yell, even though rolling the log down the hill was exactly what he'd been trying to do. Up and down switched places rapidly.

With nothing between the log and the cabin to stop it, the crazy, bouncing, spinning, dizzying ride lasted only a few seconds.

The log crashed into the side of the cabin with a loud cracking sound just as he had counted on. Luke bulled his way out of the broken trunk, pulling both Remingtons from their cross-draw holsters as he did so.

He was on his feet when one of the outlaws appeared in the doorway, unwisely rushing out to see what had happened.

Luke shot him in the chest with the left-hand Remington. The slug drove the owl hoot back, making him fall. His body tangled with the feet of the man behind him. Luke blasted that hombre with the right-hand gun, then pressed himself against the cabin wall and waited. The men inside couldn't bring their guns to bear on him from those loopholes, and the log walls were too thick to shoot through. If anybody tried to rush out through the door, he was in position to gun them down. And, if the door was the only way out, he had them bottled up.

Of course, he couldn't go anywhere, either. But a stalemate was better than being stuck behind that log and his enemies having all the advantage.

As the echoes of the shots rolled away through the mountain valleys, a charged silence settled over the area. Luke thought he heard harsh breathing coming from inside the cabin.

After a few tense minutes, a man called out. "Who are you, mister?"

"Name's Luke Smith." He wasn't giving anything away by replying. They already knew where he was.

"I've heard of you. You're a bounty hunter!"

"Am I talking to Solomon Burke?"

"That's right."

"Who are the two boys I killed in there?"

Burke didn't answer for a moment. "How do you know they're dead?" he finally asked.

"Wasn't time for anything fancy. They're dead, all right."

Again Burke hesitated before saying, "Phil Gaylord and Oscar Montrose."

"José Cardona's dead up on the hillside. I blew his brains out. That's nearly half your bunch gone over the divide, Burke. Why don't you throw your guns out and surrender before I have to kill the rest of you?"

That brought a hoot of derisive laughter from inside.

"Mighty big talk, Smith. You step away from that wall and you'll be full of lead in a hurry. How in blazes are you gonna kill anybody else?"

"I've got my ways." Luke looked along the wall next to him. One of the loopholes, empty now, was within reach.

"We've got food, water, and plenty of ammunition. What do you have?"

"Got a cigar."

"Well, go ahead and smoke it, then," Burke told him. "It'll be the last one you ever do."

Luke kept his left-hand gun trained on the doorway. He pouched the right-hand iron and reached under his coat, bringing out a thin, black cigar. He bit off the end, spit it out, and clamped the cylinder of tobacco between his teeth. Fishing a lucifer from his pocket, he snapped it to life with his thumbnail. He held the flame to the end of the cigar and puffed until it was burning good. "Smell that?"

"Whoo-eee!" Burke mocked. "Smells like you set a wet dog on fire."

"It tastes good, though," Luke said. "I've got something else."

"What might that be?" Burke asked.

Luke took another cylinder from under his coat. Longer and thicker than the cigar, it was wrapped tightly in dark red paper. A short length of fuse dangled from one end. Luke puffed on the cigar until the end was glowing bright red, then held the fuse to it.

"This," he said around the cigar as the fuse began to sputter and spit sparks. He leaned over and shoved the cylinder through the empty loophole. It clattered on the puncheon floor inside the cabin.

One of the other men howled a curse and yelled, "Look out! That's dynamite!"

Luke drew his second gun and swung away from the wall as he extended the revolvers and squared himself up. As the outlaws tumbled through the door, trying to get away before the dynamite exploded, he started firing.

They shot back, of course, even as Luke's lead tore through them and knocked them off their feet. He felt the impact as a bullet struck him, then another.

But he stayed upright and the Remingtons in his hands continued to roar.

Solomon Burke, a fox-faced, red-haired man, went down with his guts shot to pieces. Dour, sallow Lane Hutton stumbled and fell as blood from his bullet-torn throat cascaded down the front of his shirt. Young Billy Wells died with half his jaw shot away. Paco Hernandez stayed on his feet the longest and got a final shot off even as he collapsed with blood welling from two holes in his chest.

That last bullet rocked Luke. He swayed and spit out the cigar, but didn't fall. His vision was foggy, because he'd been shot three times or because clouds of powder smoke were swirling around him, he couldn't tell. The Remingtons seemed to weigh a thousand pounds apiece, but he didn't let them droop until he was certain all the outlaws were dead.

Then he couldn't hold the guns up anymore. They slipped from his blood-slick fingers and thudded to the ground at his feet.

I might not live to collect the bounty on these men, but at least they won't hurt anybody else, he thought as he stumbled through the cabin door. The single room inside was dim and shadowy.

The cylinder he had shoved through the loophole lay on the floor near a table. The fuse had burned out harmlessly. The blasting cap on the end was just clay and the "dynamite" was nothing more than a piece of wood with red paper wrapped around it. Luke had used it a number of times before. Outlaws tended to panic when they thought they were about to be blown to kingdom come.

Ignoring the fake dynamite, he stumbled across the room. Sitting on the table was the thing he had hoped to find inside.

It took him a couple of tries before he was able to snag the neck of the whiskey bottle and lift it to his mouth. Some of the liquor spilled over his chin and throat, but he got enough of the fiery stuff down his throat to brace himself.

He leaned on the rough-hewn table and tried to take stock of his injuries. He'd been hit low on his left side. There was a lot of blood. A bullet had torn a furrow along his left forearm, too, and blood ran down and dripped from his fingers. The bullet hole high on his chest was starting to make his right arm and shoulder go numb.

He needed to stop the bleeding before he did anything else. With little time before his hands quit working, he pulled the bandanna from around his neck and used his teeth to start a rip in it. He tore it in half and managed to pour some whiskey on the pieces. He pulled up his shirt, felt around until he found the hole in his side, and shoved one wadded up piece of the whiskey-soaked bandanna into the hole.

But that was just where the bullet had gone in. Wincing in pain, he located the exit wound and pushed the other piece of bandanna into it.

That left the hole in his chest. All the gun-thunder had deafened him for a few moments, but his hearing was starting to come back. He listened intently as he breathed, but didn't hear any whistling or sucking sounds. The slug hadn't pierced his lung, he decided. That was good.

The bullet hadn't come out, either. It was still in there somewhere. Not good, he thought. Fumbling, he pulled his knife from its sheath and used the blade to cut a piece from his shirttail. Lucky he didn't slice off a finger or two in the process. He up-ended the bottle and poured whiskey right over the wound, then bit back a scream as he crammed the piece of cloth into the hole.

That was all he could do. His muscles refused to work the way he wanted them to. He had to lie down. He took an unsteady step toward one of the bunks built against the side walls. The world suddenly spun crazily around him. The floor seemed to tilt under his feet. His balance deserted him, and he crashed down on the puncheons, sending fresh jolts of pain stabbing through him.

He felt consciousness slipping away from him and knew if he passed out, he probably wouldn't wake up again. He tried to hold on, but a black tide swept over him.

That black surge didn't just wash him away from his primitive surroundings. To his already fevered mind, it seemed to lift him and carry him back, back, a bit of human flotsam swept along by a raging torrent, to an earlier time and a different place. The darkness surrounding him was shot through with red flashes, like artillery shells bursting in the night.

Chapter One

The bombardment sounded like the worst thunder-storm in the history of the world, but unlike a thunderstorm, it went on and on and on. For long days, that devil Ulysses S. Grant and his Yankee army had squatted outside Richmond, pounding away at the capital city of the Confederacy with their big guns. Half the buildings in town had been reduced to rubble, and untold numbers of Richmond's citizens were dead, killed in the endless barrages.

And still the guns continued to roar.

Rangy, rawboned Luke Jensen felt the floor shake under his feet as shells fell not far from the building where he stood. It had been one of Richmond's genteel mansions, not far from the capital itself, but recently it had been taken over by the government. One particular part of the government, in fact: the Confederate treasury.

Luke was one of eight men summoned tonight for

reasons unknown to them. They were waiting in what had been the parlor before the comfortable, over-stuffed furniture was shoved aside and replaced by desks and tables.

In the light of a couple smoky lamps, he glanced around at the other men. Some of them he knew, and some he didn't. The faces of all bore the same weary, haggard look, the expression of men who had been at war for too long and suffered too many defeats despite their best efforts.

Luke knew that look all too well. He saw it in the mirror every time he got a chance to shave, which wasn't very often these days.

For nearly four long years, he had worn Confederate gray—ever since the day he had walked away from the hardscrabble farm tucked into the Ozark Mountains of southwestern Missouri and enlisted. Behind him he'd left his father Emmett and his little brother Kirby, along with his mother and sister.

It had been hard for Luke to leave his family, but felt it was the right thing to do. Fighting for the Confederacy didn't mean a man held with slavery, although he figured that was what all those ignorant Yankees believed. Luke didn't believe at all in the notion of one man owning another.

At the same time he didn't think it was right for a bunch of Northern politicians in By-God Washington City to be telling Southern folks what they could and couldn't do, especially when it came to secession. The states had joined together voluntarily, back when they'd won their freedom from England. If some of them wanted to say "thanks, but so long" and go their own way, it seemed to Luke they had every right to do so.

Even so, if they'd just kept on wrangling about it in the halls of Congress, Luke, like a lot of other Southerners, would have pretty much ignored it and gone on about his business. But Abraham Lincoln had to go and send the army marching into Virginia, and the battle along the creek called Bull Run was the last straw as far as Luke was concerned. He'd been raised to avoid trouble if he could, but when a Jensen saw something wrong going on, he couldn't just sit back and do nothing.

So he'd been a soldier for four years, fighting against the Northern aggressors, slogging along as an infantryman for a while before his natural talents for tracking, shooting, and fighting got noticed and he was made a scout and a sharpshooter.

He knew three of the men waiting in the parlor with him were the same sort. Remy Duquesne, Dale Cardwell, and Edgar Millgard were good men, and if he was being sent on some sort of mission with them, Luke was fine with that.

The other four had introduced themselves as Keith Stratton, Wiley Potter, Josh Richards, and Ted Casey. Luke hadn't formed an opinion about them based only on their names. He didn't blame them for being close-mouthed, though. He was the same way himself.

Remy fired up a cigar and said in his soft Cajun

accent, "Anybody got an idea why they brought us here tonight?"

"Not a clue," Wiley Potter said.

"The treasury department has its office here now," Dale Cardwell pointed out. He smiled. "Maybe they're finally going to pay us all those back wages we haven't seen in months."

That comment drew grim chuckles from several of the men.

Remy said, "I wouldn't count on that, my frien'."

Luke didn't think it was very likely, either. The Confederacy was in bad shape. Financially, militarily, morale-wise . . . everything was cratering, and there didn't seem to be anything anybody could do to stop it. They would fight to the end, of course—there was no question about that—but that end seemed to be getting more and more inevitable.

The front door opened, and footsteps sounded in the foyer. Several gray-clad troopers appeared in the arched entrance to the former parlor. They carried rifles with bayonets fixed to the barrels.

A pair of officers followed the soldiers into the room. Luke and the other men snapped to attention. He recognized one of the officers as a high-ranking general. The other man was the colonel who commanded the regiment in which Luke, Remy, Dale, and Edgar served.

The two men in civilian clothes who came into the room behind the general and the colonel were the real surprise. Luke caught his breath as he recognized the President of the Confederacy, Jefferson

Davis, and the Secretary of the Treasury, George Trenholm.

"At ease," the general said.

Luke and the others relaxed, but not much. It was hard to be at ease with the president in the room.

Jefferson Davis gave them a sad, tired smile and said, "Thank you for coming here tonight, gentlemen," as if they'd had a choice in the matter. "I know you'd probably rather be with your comrades in arms, facing the enemy."

Stratton and Potter grimaced slightly and exchanged a quick glance, as if that was the last thing they wanted to be doing.

"I've summoned you because I have a special job for you," Davis went on. "Secretary Trenholm will tell you about it."

Luke had wondered if they were going to be given a special assignment, but he hadn't expected it would come from the president himself. It had to be something of extreme importance. He waited eagerly to hear what the treasury secretary was going to say.

"As you know, Richmond is under siege by the Yankees," the man began rather pompously as he clasped his hands behind his back.

Luke preferred Confederate politicians to Yankees, but they all had a tendency to be windbags, as far as he was concerned.

"Although I hate to say it, it appears that our efforts to defend the city ultimately will prove to be unsuccessful," the secretary continued.

"Are you saying that Richmond's going to fall, sir?" Potter asked.

Trenholm nodded. "I'm afraid so."

"But that doesn't necessarily mean the Confederacy is about to fall as well," Davis put in. "Our glorious nation will persevere. The Yankees may overrun Richmond, but we will establish a new capital elsewhere." He smiled at the treasury secretary. "I'm sorry, I didn't mean to interrupt."

"That's quite all right, Mr. President. No one in this room has more right to speak than you." Trenholm cleared his throat and went on. "Of course, no government can continue to function without funds, so to that end, acting on the orders of President Davis, I have assembled a shipment of gold bullion that is to be spirited out of the city and taken to Georgia to await the arrival of our government. This is most of what we have left in our coffers, gentlemen. I'm not exaggerating when I say the very survival of the Confederacy itself depends on the secure transport of this gold."

Luke wasn't surprised by what he had just heard. For the past few days, rumors had been going around the city that the treasury was going to be cleaned out and the money taken elsewhere so the Yankees wouldn't get their grubby paws on it.

The secretary nodded toward Luke's commanding officer. "Colonel Lancaster will be in charge of the gold's safety."

"You're taking the whole regiment to Georgia, sir?" Dale asked.

The colonel shook his head. "Not at all, Corporal. That would only draw the Yankees' attention to what we're doing." Lancaster paused. "We're entrusting the safety of the bullion—and the future of the Confederacy—to a smaller detail. Eight men, to be exact." He looked around the room. "The eight of you who are gathered here."